SPECIAL MESSAGE TO READERS

THE ULVERSCROFT FOUNDATION
(registered UK charity number 264873)
was established in 1972 to provide funds for research, diagnosis and treatment of eye diseases. Examples of major projects funded by the Ulverscroft Foundation are:-

- The Children's Eye Unit at Moorfields Eye Hospital, London
- The Ulverscroft Children's Eye Unit at Great Ormond Street Hospital for Sick Children
- Funding research into eye diseases and treatment at the Department of Ophthalmology, University of Leicester
- The Ulverscroft Vision Research Group, Institute of Child Health
- Twin operating theatres at the Western Ophthalmic Hospital, London
- The Chair of Ophthalmology at the Royal Australian College of Ophthalmologists

You can help further the work of the Foundation by making a donation or leaving a legacy. Every contribution is gratefully received. If you would like to help support the Foundation or require further information, please contact:

THE ULVERSCROFT FOUNDATION
**The Green, Bradgate Road, Anstey
Leicester LE7 7FU, England
Tel: (0116) 236 4325**

website: www.foundation.

Fenella J. Miller was born on the Isle of Man. Her father was a Yorkshireman and her mother the daughter of a Rajah. She has worked as a nanny, cleaner, field worker, hotelier, chef, secondary and primary teacher, and is now a full-time writer. She has had over twenty-five Regency romantic adventures published, among other stories. Fenella lives in a pretty riverside village in Essex with her husband and ancient Border Collie. She has two adult children and two grandchildren.

BARBARA'S WAR
THE MIDDLE YEARS

It is 1939 and Hitler is beginning his rampage through Europe. As Britain sends its men to war, Barbara Sinclair is torn between a promise of marriage to her childhood friend, whom she does not love, and her passion for a fighter pilot, whom she barely knows. Her choice leads her down an unexpected path, and as she leaves home to start a new life as a married woman, she discovers she is pregnant — but which of the two men is the father? Can she hide the secret from her new husband that the baby might not be his? Then, as the bombing raids begin, disaster strikes . . .

FENELLA J. MILLER

BARBARA'S WAR
THE MIDDLE YEARS

Complete and Unabridged

ULVERSCROFT
Leicester

First published in Great Britain in 2014

First Large Print Edition
published 2016

The moral right of the author has been asserted

A catalogue record for this book is available
from the British Library.

ISBN 978–1–4448–2690–6

Published by
F. A. Thorpe (Publishing)
Anstey, Leicestershire

Set by Words & Graphics Ltd.
Anstey, Leicestershire
Printed and bound in Great Britain by
T. J. International Ltd., Padstow, Cornwall

This book is printed on acid-free paper

Dedication

My thanks to
Rachel Bevan, Fay Cunningham,
Kim Sheffield, Thorunn Bacon
& Susan Rhodes

1

Mountnessing, Essex, December 1939

It seemed odd to be sitting in the glow of the little electric lights on a Christmas tree with no presents. Barbara had suggested they take it down now Boxing Day was over, but her grandparents wouldn't hear of it. The tradition was to have the tree up until Twelfth Night, so until then it would remain, taking up a third of the space in the study.

The study door opened and Barbara turned to greet her grandfather. 'Are the boys still outside? It's knee-deep in snow out there. I don't want them to get cold.' His grey hair was liberally sprinkled with snow, but his faded blue eyes were bright and his cheeks glowed.

'Remember, Babs, I'm a medical man. Your brothers are safe with me.'

'Is John with them, Edward?' Grandma smiled at him.

He nodded and poured himself a mug of tea. 'I must say I've really taken to your young man, Barbara. It's a great shame we can't have a small celebration to mark your engagement.'

John had persuaded her to make their engagement official last week. Her mouth curved. He was a lovely man, and she was finding she quite enjoyed being kissed by him. He had hinted he would like to take things further and come to her bedroom, but so far she'd managed to put him off.

'Why don't we have that bottle of champagne we've been saving, Elspeth? John will be leaving first thing tomorrow morning. God knows when Barbara will see him again.'

'What a good idea, Edward. I'll go along and speak to Mrs Brown. I'm sure she can make us a special meal to go with it. Perhaps fricassee with the remainder of the capon?' She hurried off to speak to the cook.

Grandpa groaned and buried his face in his hands. 'I am heartily sick of leftover chicken. I'd be happy with boiled eggs, if we had any.'

'I promise you it won't taste anything like chicken. By the time everything else is added it will be delicious, and it's usually served with rice. That will make a pleasant change, won't it?'

'If you say so, my dear. It's strange, but I could eat leftover Christmas pudding, mince pies and cake until the cows come home — it's just the wretched chicken that seems to go on and on.'

Laughing at his curmudgeonly attitude, she

collected the empty mugs and headed for the door. 'We should be counting our blessings, Grandpa. Next year we will probably be having spam fritters for Christmas.'

John burst into the kitchen, chivvying her two small brothers in front of him. 'It's arctic out there, sweetheart. I think we're all going to need a hot water bottle up our jumpers in order to thaw out.'

David, his fair hair plastered to his head by melting snow, grinned happily. 'Your mare's had her supper and is being shut up for the night. The chickens didn't get up at all today — they stayed in the barn.'

Tom shoved his younger brother. 'Don't blame them. It's my turn to feed the puppies and yours to empty the dirt tray.' Amiably squabbling, they ran to the large wicker basket at the far end of the kitchen. They were greeted by Lavender, the large cat who was the puppies' surrogate mother, purring like a sewing machine.

Leaving them happily playing, Barbara wandered through to the breakfast room, which doubled as the dining room at night. John followed her. 'I hear we're having champagne tonight. What's that in aid of?' He slid his arms around her waist and pulled her gently until she was resting against his chest. The buttons and buckle of his RAF jacket pressed uncomfortably into her back.

'Grandma and Grandpa want to have a special meal to celebrate our engagement and to wish you good luck for your trip to Canada.'

'You don't sound too keen on the idea, Babs. Not having second thoughts, are you?'

She was glad he couldn't see her face. 'Of course not. It's just Canada is so far away. Crossing the Atlantic with all the U-boats about, in this horrible weather, is going to be dangerous.'

He turned her until she was facing him. With his thumbs he brushed away her tears. 'I'll be all right, darling. It's a damned nuisance having to train on the other side of the world. I don't want you to be sad; remember what I told you? Go out and enjoy yourself whilst I'm away. Good God, you're not even nineteen yet; I don't expect you to stay in with the old folk just because I'm not here.'

'I don't suppose I'll get asked out anywhere, but if you're sure you don't mind, I won't say no if it's somewhere I want to go.' She stretched out and pulled his head down so she could press her lips against his. They were cold; in fact his face was icy, the bristles standing to attention on his upper lip. She flinched as they rasped across her cheeks. Immediately he raised his head, his eyes dark.

'Sorry, I haven't shaved today. I'll go and do it now; Mrs Brown said the boiler's just been stoked and the water's hot.'

'Don't use it all; the boys will need a bath shortly. If we're going to have a small celebration they'll need to change first; in fact I think we should all dress up tonight.' She smiled, her initial reservations about a party gone. 'I'll make the breakfast room look pretty, use the candles and things we had on Christmas Day.'

Tom appeared, a wriggling puppy in his arms. 'We having a party? Good show — can we have balloons and crackers too?'

'What's this about a party? Is it someone's birthday?' David peered round the kitchen door with the second puppy perched precariously on his chest, its little pink tongue busy cleaning strawberry jam from his chin.

'Grandma and Grandpa think it would be a good idea to have a little family do to celebrate our engagement. I'm going to sort out the table. Why don't you two finish playing with the puppies and then come in and help me?'

'Righty ho — as long as we don't have chicken again,' David said as he elbowed his brother out of the way in order to be first there.

By the time the breakfast room was

prepared and the boys' bath had been supervised, there was barely enough time for Barbara to have a quick wash and change. She flicked through the long row of frocks hanging in her enormous closet. Should she select one of the smart dresses her grandma had chosen, or wear something she was more comfortable in? Perhaps the russet velvet with the cream lace collar and elbow-length sleeves would be dressy, but not over the top.

She snatched the frock from the hanger and dropped it over her petticoat. As this was a special occasion she'd worn her new silk stockings, her Christmas present from John. The others were going down already and she still had to find her shoes, and check her lipstick wasn't smudged and her hair was tidy. At least now that they were using the rear of the house, they no longer had to creep about with torches. The blackout made it impossible to have any lights on in the main hall because of the central glass rotunda.

'You look splendid, my dear. That colour suits your complexion.'

'Thank you, Grandpa. This is one I've not worn before. Is John down?'

Her grandmother answered. 'He has gone with the boys to fill up the litter tray, Barbara. I don't suppose he'll be very long.'

'I'm not comfortable having any sort of

celebration at the moment; John's leaving tomorrow and I don't know when I'll see him again.' She swallowed a lump in her throat. 'Grandpa, do you think we should be drinking champagne?'

'This is going to be a brute of a war. We've got to enjoy ourselves whilst we can.' He squeezed her shoulder. 'Remember, Barbara, celebrating your engagement tonight is a way of sending your young man away happy. It doesn't mean you'll actually marry him — a lot can happen before that day comes.'

He was right. Both her grandparents understood why she'd accepted John's proposal when she wasn't in love with him. This didn't make it any easier; she loved him, but not in an exciting way — more as a brother. She was being selfish and immature; his parents wouldn't be seeing their only child before he set sail for Canada, and here she was moping about drinking a glass of champagne in his honour.

'I'm sorry to be a wet blanket, Grandpa. I'm being silly. From now on I'll take every day as it comes and thank God we're warm and safe here and not freezing in France like our brave soldiers.'

John arrived with her half-brothers, his face pink from the cold; he really was an attractive young man. She was a lucky girl to have him as her fiancé. 'I hope you all washed your hands,' she said.

All three waved them in the air and John put his arm around her waist and pulled her close. His hip was hard against hers, his arm firm and protective. She relaxed into his embrace and smiled at him. Her heart almost jumped out of her chest at the scorching look he gave her.

David pushed past, making rude noises. 'Yuck! They've gone all soppy, Grandma. It's putting me off my supper.'

Grandma directed the boys to the far side of the table. 'Over there, young men, and be careful not to tip over the candles. Edward, we shall sit opposite them and, Barbara and John, you sit at either end as you are the guests of honour tonight.'

A large tureen of leek and potato soup steamed appetisingly in the centre of the table next to the freshly baked rolls. John grinned and held out his bowl. 'This is my favourite food. I wonder if Canadians eat soup.'

'From what I hear, dear boy,' said Grandpa, 'they serve steaks the size of dinner plates. No danger of you doing without — with rationing starting soon we'll be the ones on short commons.'

The champagne was drunk, the meal consumed and by the end of the evening

Barbara was beginning to enjoy herself. She was unused to alcohol and normally avoided it, but tonight was a special occasion and she hadn't the heart to refuse.

'Shall we go into the study?' Grandma suggested. 'I believe there are some chocolates left; I'm sure the boys wouldn't say no to them.'

'And a small glass of brandy to go with the last of the coffee, my dear, will make a perfect ending to a delightful evening.' Grandpa pulled out her chair and she smiled lovingly at him. It hardly seemed possible her grandparents were now happy together, the misery of the past eighteen years finally put behind them. Losing their only son so tragically in a motorbike accident, and not knowing about her existence, had caused a rift which her arrival a few months ago had remedied.

The abuse Barbara had suffered at the hands of her deranged mother was going to take a little longer to forget, but tonight, surrounded by the people she loved best, she truly believed it might be possible to put the past behind her.

At ten o'clock she decided her brothers should go to bed. 'Come along, boys, it's past your bedtime. Say good night to everyone.'

Their storm of protest was ignored and

John grabbed David and tossed him over his shoulder, squealing and laughing. 'Right, I've got this one. Can you manage Tom?'

'Babs,' Tom asked, 'I would like you to read a bit more of *Treasure Island* tonight — it's so much better listening to it than reading it myself.'

By the time she'd read the chapter the children were asleep. Quietly she put the book on the bedside table and stood up, surprised to find John had remained in the room. 'I'm not going down again; I'm really tired. Can you say good night to Grandpa and Grandma for me please?'

'Of course. I shan't be long myself. Don't forget I have to catch the eleven o'clock train tomorrow. I want to spend every last moment with you — we don't know when we'll meet again.'

He moved closer and she tilted her head expectantly. For some reason the thought of kissing him was sending the blood fizzing around her body. Her hands encircled his neck and she pressed herself against him, loving the feel of his body against her soft curves.

His lips were hard on hers; they tasted of brandy and champagne. 'Would you like me to bring you a brandy and cup of cocoa when I come up?'

'That would be lovely, but put the brandy in the cocoa as I don't really like it on its own. I can't promise I'll still be awake. I'm really tired, so you'd better not be too long.'

'You go ahead, I'll join you soon.'

How kind he was. He was the most loving man, and she wished she loved him as much as he loved her. Pushing these thoughts to the back of her mind, she began to get ready for bed, hanging up her dress and carefully folding her underwear onto a chair. She had only been wearing her camiknickers and petticoat for a few hours so there was no need to put them in the laundry.

She had two new novels to read, Christmas presents from Grandpa, both by Georgette Heyer: *The Devil's Cub* and *Regency Buck*. This was an author unknown to her, but a good romance was exactly what she needed right now. She would curl up in bed and start reading one of them and hope she hadn't fallen asleep before John returned with her drink. She was glad she'd bought some flannelette nighties; the ones Grandma had bought were pretty, but not warm enough in this freezing weather.

Her grandparents walked past twenty minutes later and she wondered why John hadn't arrived with her cocoa. She was about to call out and ask Grandma, but they

11

sounded so engrossed in their conversation she didn't want to interrupt them. Maybe John had forgotten and gone straight to his bedroom — he was sleeping at the far end of the corridor so she should have heard him go past.

She yawned, her jaw cracking, and put the book down on the side table. Reaching behind her, she switched off the bedside light and wriggled under the blankets. The remains of the fire flickered with a comforting red glow, softening the edges of the furniture and making the room look different somehow.

She was on the verge of sleep when the door opened softly and John slipped in. 'Sorry, darling, I thought it better to wait until the old folk had gone to bed before I came in here. I know we're engaged but I don't think they would approve.' She pushed herself up on the bed and waited for him to make his way across the shadowy room.

'I was just going to sleep; I thought you'd forgotten all about me.' He dropped down beside her on the bed, the rich aroma of brandy and chocolate wafting towards her. 'Golly, that smells a bit strong.'

He chuckled and his warm breath tickled her cheek. 'Doctor Sinclair put it in. I just made the cocoa and grabbed the last few chocolates from the box. Here you are

— which do you want first?'

'Both — can you drop the chocolates on my lap and hand me the mug, please?'

'Budge up, sweetheart, there's plenty of room for both of us on here.'

Her drink was sweet and heady, the sweets rich and velvety in her mouth. 'These will probably be the last ones we get until the end of the war. How am I going to live without chocolate?'

'I promise I'll bring you back as much as I can carry when I return from Canada. It's hard to believe there's a war on when we're snuggled up in here with so many luxuries.' He slurped his drink and she nudged him sharply with her elbow.

'I don't want any of your bad habits here, thank you. You sound like one of the boys.' She relaxed against his shoulder and he put his arm around her. 'Do you think you'll pass all the exams on navigation and things? I'd no idea learning to be a pilot was harder than being at school.'

'That's why so many bods didn't get through the preliminary training. As I'm going into Bomber Command, I'll have a navigator; I won't have to plot my own route. Fighter pilots have to learn it all though.'

At his mention of fighter pilots an image of Alex Everton flashed through her head. She wondered what he was doing tonight; he hadn't come home for Christmas as he'd volunteered to remain on duty so the married chaps could spend time with their families. She drained her mug and choked, spraying him with a mouthful of liquid.

'Bloody hell! What a waste — are you okay? What happened — did it go down the wrong way?' He wiped his face on the corner of a sheet and his teeth gleamed white in the semi-darkness.

'No, there was neat brandy at the bottom of the mug.' She giggled and bit into the last chocolate. 'Are you going to finish yours?'

'Not half! You've had more than enough for one night. I think you're a bit tiddly.'

He was probably right, she did feel rather light-headed and silly. 'It's a good thing you took off your jacket. If you take off your shirt I can rinse the cocoa out and it should be dry by tomorrow morning.' She expected him to argue but he pulled off his tie and unbuttoned his shirt immediately.

'Right you are. Dammit! It's gone right through so I'd better take my vest off as well.'

Before she could protest he was stripped to the waist. She scrambled out of bed and was about to pick up his shirt from the floor when she froze. She'd never seen a man half-naked — she couldn't take her eyes away.

14

Something compelled her to move closer and the shirt fell unnoticed to the floor. The firelight silhouetted his broad shoulders in a golden glow, making him look like something from a Greek myth. Her breath caught in her throat and she swayed towards him.

'Are you sure, darling? Because once we start to make love I won't be able to stop.'

She should say no, this was all wrong; but he was so beautiful, so handsome, so desirable that she wanted him to show her what physical love was like.

The experience was rather disappointing — the kissing and stroking beforehand far more exciting than actually doing it. It hadn't hurt much, which was a relief, but John had certainly enjoyed it far more than she had. She was relieved when he slipped away almost immediately afterwards. Blast! He'd left his shirt behind. She eased her way past a nasty wet patch on the sheet and snatched it up. She would have a bath and wash his shirt at the same time. She smelled a bit odd — a fishy sort of smell; not very pleasant.

The cocoa stain came out easily and she hung the shirt over the towel rail to dry. There were only a couple of inches in the bottom of the huge bath, but enough for a good wash. The nightie she'd been wearing was dumped in the laundry box and she pulled on a fresh one. She stared at her reflection in the mirror. Shouldn't she look different? Wasn't sleeping with someone supposed to show up on your face? She could remember . . . she shuddered and pushed the thought aside. What had happened in Hastings must be forgotten.

She rubbed the steam away with her sleeve to have a closer look. No, she just looked tired and rather sad — and definitely older than she had when she'd arrived at the Grove in September. Not surprising really, when so much had happened. She'd better get back to bed; John was leaving in a few hours and she had promised to spend time with him. Her mare, Silver Star, needed to be exercised even though the weather was dreadful.

The alarm was set for seven o'clock; this would give her two hours before breakfast. Joe started work then, so with luck he'd already have tacked up, which would save a bit of time. She hadn't expected to sleep after such a momentous event, but didn't stir until the alarm woke her.

After pulling on her jods she added an extra woolly over her blouse; even with a few embers glowing in the grate, the room was freezing. Her boots and riding mac were kept in the boot room, so she padded downstairs in her slippers. Her brothers, normally early risers, were not banging about in their attic bedroom, so they must still be asleep.

The cook-housekeeper, Mrs Brown, was busy raking out the Aga. 'Good morning, miss. Joe's getting your mare ready for you. I reckon you won't be able to do a lot; there's been a bit more snow overnight.'

She knelt down to fuss the two puppies, who were wriggling and yapping around her feet. 'Thank you, Mrs Brown. I hoped he would be out there before me. I don't think I've time for a cup of tea — I must be back by the time John comes down.'

Outside it was barely light, but the visibility was good enough to walk and trot around the lanes. Joe led Silver from her box. 'Morning, miss. She's that eager to go; she really missed her exercise yesterday.'

'I'm not going to canter; the going's too hard.' She patted the gleaming dappled neck of her horse and gathered the reins before turning for Joe to give her a leg up. 'If the boys or Mr Thorogood ask, can you tell them I'll be back for breakfast?'

The fields were silent — not even the single chirp of a bird; the snow deadened the usual sounds of the countryside. She stood in her stirrups and looked over the hedge to see if any livestock had been turned out, but the fields were as quiet and empty as the lane.

'Come along, Silver. We can trot down here; it's not too hard.'

Without deliberately intending to, she arrived at the Evertons' farm to be greeted by Mr Everton, who was tossing hay into a trailer attached to his tractor. 'I wondered if you'd come over our way, Barbara. Have you got time to stop for a cuppa?'

'Sorry, I've got to get back to have breakfast with John — he's off to Canada today.'

'He seems like a good lad. It's a shame our Alex wasn't here to meet him on Christmas Day. I can't tell you how much we all enjoyed ourselves at the Grove. The boys haven't stopped talking about it.'

'As soon as the weather improves they can cycle over and spend the day with Tom and David. Give my love to Mrs Everton. I'll get Grandma to telephone and make the arrangements.'

She'd wanted to ask after Alex, but she could hardly do that now the Evertons knew she was engaged to John. What a muddle things were — she had slept with one man whilst having feelings for another. Did this make her a bad person? Good girls didn't do things like that; they waited until their wedding day. If she hadn't had so much to drink last night she was sure she wouldn't have done it either. No point in worrying — she would think of it as a going-away present for John. But she was jolly sure she wasn't going to repeat the experience any time soon.

David was waiting in the stable yard. 'Hello, have you had your breakfast yet?'

'No, Grandpa told us to come out and make sure you came in immediately.'

'Is something wrong?' She dropped from the saddle and tossed the reins to Joe. Not stopping to scrape her boots, she ran behind her brother with a sinking feeling in the pit of her stomach. The fact that he hadn't answered her query must mean something dreadful had taken place in her absence. She burst into the kitchen to find her grandparents and Tom happily munching toast.

'There you are, my dear. I'm afraid we have some disappointing news for you. John had a phone call just after you left; it appears his group of trainee pilot officers are leaving earlier than expected. I had to drive him to Shenfield to catch the train.'

Barbara grabbed the edge of the table to steady herself. 'That's a shame, but we said our goodbyes last night. How did he take it? Was he very upset to have missed me?'

'Seemed remarkably chipper for a man abandoning his new fiancée for God knows

19

how long.' Grandpa waved his toast in the air. 'Come and sit down. Mrs Brown made porridge for us and there's a boiled egg for you.'

'I'll just hang up my things and wash my hands and I'll be right there. David, don't wait for me, you must be starving.' She retreated to the boot room, glad to have a few moments to herself. If she was honest, she was relieved she didn't have to see John face to face after what they'd done last night. Even if she hadn't changed outwardly, he was bound to have behaved differently and that would have been embarrassing. This was a secret she intended to keep — no one apart from John would ever know they had been lovers.

2

Later that day Barbara answered the telephone. 'Hello, Barbara Sinclair speaking.'

A plummy voice replied, 'It's Amanda, Amanda Hope-Grainger. How are you? I hope you had a good Christmas?'

'Hello, Amanda, yes, it was wonderful. Did you?'

'Yes thank you. Harriet and I are going to a New Year's party at a friend's house — would you like to come with us? We will have to stay overnight of course, but we'll drive back the next day.'

'That sounds absolutely lovely. I should love to come. I'm surprised you have any petrol for jaunts; Grandpa said it's going to be rationed soon.'

'Which is why we're going. We might as well use up what we've got on something super. Can you be ready at midday on the 31st?'

'Yes, that's no problem. I'll have time to exercise my mare before I need to get ready. Is it going to be terribly grand? I've got a couple of evening gowns I've not had the opportunity to wear yet.'

'Most of the chaps will be in uniform, but we girls dress up to the nines. Toodle pip — look forward to seeing you soon.'

As Barbara put the phone down her grandmother came into the study. 'Who was that, my dear? You look very pleased about something. Have you heard from John?'

'No, it was Amanda sending her good wishes. She's invited me to go with her and Harriet to a New Year's party somewhere outside London, a place called Radcliffe Hall. I said I would go. I hope that's all right?'

'Of course it is, Barbara. A party is exactly what you need to take your mind off everything.' She hesitated and then continued, 'Are things different between you and John? I noticed you were quite affectionate when he was here.'

'No, I've not fallen in love with him, if that's what you mean. We're a bit closer but I still hope he meets someone else and we can break the engagement.'

'In that case, I should leave your engagement ring on your dressing table and go and enjoy yourself. After all, nobody there will know you are engaged to John.'

'Grandma, I can't believe you've just said that.' She grinned and tried to look flirtatious. 'Is this the kind of thing you want me to do?'

'Good God! What's going on here?'

Grandpa raised an eyebrow and Barbara laughed.

'I'm going to a party on New Year's Eve with Amanda and Harriet, and Grandma has told me to enjoy myself.'

'Excellent idea — mind you don't have too much to drink, my dear. Alcohol can make fools of us all.'

She ducked her head and hoped her cheeks were not as red as she feared. 'I've never been to a grand party before. I'm going to take both my evening gowns and decide which one to wear on the night. Do you know Mr and Mrs Williams, Grandma?'

'I don't believe I do, but I'm sure if Amanda and Harriet know them they are perfectly acceptable. You'll come to no harm with those two girls. I've known them since they were babies. Excellent pedigree — '

'You make them sound like prize heifers, Grandma. I don't care who their parents are as long as they are nice.'

A letter arrived from John apologising for his abrupt departure and saying he was posting the note whilst waiting to board a ship. He promised to write to Barbara as soon as he was settled. She put his letter in her jewellery box alongside the engagement ring. She supposed she ought to wear this around her neck on the chain he'd bought her, but now he was about to leave for Canada she didn't feel the need to pretend. When he came back, if he was still in love with her, then she would honour the engagement — but she sincerely hoped he'd meet a beautiful Canadian girl and fall in love with her instead.

There had been no further fall of snow and she prayed this would remain the case until after the party. She hadn't spoken to either girl since the night she'd met them at the village social, so was a bit worried about spending two days in the company of strangers. She mentioned this to her grand-mother.

'You have nothing to worry about, my dear. Both are sweet girls; they'll look after you. I believe Amanda has joined one of the services and is waiting for her call-up papers. I can't tell you how relieved your grandfather and I are that you won't be leaving home. Once the war gets going there will be plenty to do in the WVS — it won't just be rolling bandages and knitting balaclavas.'

'I'm starting the first-aid course next week — I want to be able to do something practical. Do you think they'll want to evacuate children from around here when the bombing starts?' She couldn't bear it if her brothers were sent away for the duration.

'Good heavens, I should think not. It's perfectly safe here, and we've got that horrible Anderson shelter as well as the cellars.'

If that was the case, what use would her first-aid training be? She would have no injured civilians to minister to. 'As long as they don't start dropping bombs on London whilst I'm there. It might spoil the party. As New Year's Eve is a Sunday, what do I do about church? The vicar said last week the eight o'clock communion service is cancelled because of the snow and if I go to matins I won't be back in time.'

'Never mind, I'm sure missing one Sunday won't matter. I should have liked to see your friends and wave you goodbye, but it can't be helped.'

David and Tom clattered into the kitchen, closely followed by Ned and Jim Everton. 'I say, Babs, did you know the duck pond is frozen solid?' David said gleefully. 'Can we slide on it?'

'I should think it will be all right, as the water is only a couple of feet deep even in the middle. What do you think, Grandma?'

'Actually, boys, I believe we have four pairs of skates somewhere in the attic. Would you like to come with me and look for them?'

The suggestion was received with noisy

delight and the four boys vanished, leaving her alone with the puppies. Mrs Brown had gone to see her sister in Shenfield and Joe was busy in the yard. Grandpa had been called out to some sort of emergency in the village — no doubt another difficult delivery.

The soup was made for lunch, the bread freshly baked before the housekeeper had gone out. All Barbara had to do was lay the table in the breakfast room for three — the boys would eat in the kitchen as usual. She might as well take the carpet sweeper and tidy the study. The room smelled of pine and cigars; the enormous Christmas tree dominated the far end of the room and she wished it could be taken down. Much as she liked twinkling lights and paper chains, without the pile of presents underneath it looked sad and lonely.

Should she have accepted the invitation for Sunday night? Surely going out so soon after John had left might seem a bit flighty?

Lunch was enjoyed by all, and afterwards her brothers and their friends retreated to the playroom to enact another battle with the lead soldiers. They would stay up there until teatime and didn't need supervising. Her grandparents had gone out to see friends for afternoon tea, which left her at a loose end. Mrs Brown would be back to cook and serve

dinner and the children could have sandwiches and scones for tea. The Everton boys
were spending the night and then her two
would go back with them in the morning.
David and Tom were barely recognisable as
the two pale, subdued little boys she'd lived
with at Crabapple Cottage a few months ago.
Although there was little family resemblance,
that made no difference to the way she felt
about them. Thank God her grandparents
had welcomed them into their home — whatever happened in the future, all three of them
were together and both financially and
emotionally secure.

★   ★   ★

New Year's Eve eventually arrived and
Barbara was up early to exercise her mare
before she left. When she got back everyone
was waiting for her in the kitchen.

'It's a rotten show that you'll miss the
church parade this morning, Babs, just so you
can go to a party,' Tom said, grinning at her
across the table.

'I know, it's a hard life. I hope you two
behave yourselves whilst I'm away.'

'Course we will. Grandpa and Grandma
are taking us out to lunch tomorrow and then
to the pictures. We won't miss you at all.'

27

David didn't look quite as certain as his older brother but managed a wobbly smile. 'Golly, that's exciting. Is the Charlie Chaplin film still on?'

Her grandfather nodded. 'I should say so. Perfect for an afternoon out. Don't worry about us, my dear. Stay an extra night if you're invited. I shouldn't think there'll be any petrol for gallivanting about the country-side in future.'

'Grandpa says there won't be any chocolate or sweets or anything decent to eat once rationing starts,' Tom said sadly. 'But I'm looking forward to seeing the Spitfires fighting the Germans — that should be spiffing.'

Barbara was about to reprimand him, but Grandpa shook his head slightly. Instead she changed the subject. 'Have you been given any work to prepare for when you start, boys?'

'No, but I bet we'll get loads next week.' Tom dug his younger brother in the ribs with his elbow and David responded by hitting him on the hand with his spoon. By the time order had been restored she was feeling less fraught.

When the family left for church she hurried upstairs to have a bath and complete her packing. She'd already put in her carefully rolled underwear and her precious silk stockings. She was going to wear slacks and socks with her smart burgundy twinset to travel in — far warmer and more practical than a skirt in this weather.

Her hair might still be damp when Amanda and Harriet arrived but it couldn't be helped. It had been much easier to manage when she'd kept it short, but being able to put it up made her feel more grown up. There wasn't really time to wallow in the enormous claw-footed bath, but it seemed a waste of the measly five inches of hot water if she got out too soon. The geezer hissed and groaned and reluctantly spewed out the required amount of water. Every time she used this antiquated heater she expected it to explode.

After wrapping her hair in a warm towel she dried herself thoroughly. The scent of the lily-of-the-valley talcum powder the boys had given her for Christmas filled the bathroom. She scrubbed the mirror to see her reflection. No nasty spots, thank goodness. Still enveloped in a towel she hurried into her bedroom, horrified to see she only had half an hour to get ready.

She looked at the contents of her case, not sure if she'd packed too much or too little. She had two pairs of peach silk French knickers and her new camiknickers, plus a brassiere which matched the French knickers. There was her negligee set — another Christmas present from her grandparents — and her slippers. She decided to put in a spare pair of slacks and a blouse and cardigan — she didn't know how long she might be staying. All she had to do was roll her two evening dresses in tissue paper and place them carefully on top of everything else. Her make-up and toiletries were already tucked into each corner along with her evening slippers.

One of her gowns was in a similar shade of peach silk to her underwear; this was cut on the bias and swirled romantically around her ankles. The back was rather low, but fortunately the front didn't show too much bosom. The other one was more sophisticated: the revealing décolletage, the shoestring straps and figure-hugging bodice left little to the imagination. This was in a darker shade, more russet than peach, and it suited her beautifully. However, she wasn't sure she had the nerve to wear it. She would wait and see what the other girls had before deciding.

She was in the kitchen when a car pulled up. 'I'm going now, Mrs Brown. Happy New Year to you and Joe if I don't see you tomorrow.' Her case and handbag were waiting by the boot room door; she snatched up her coat and rammed her arms in the sleeves and was ready to go.

She had been expecting something a bit sporty, but Amanda was driving an impressive navy-blue Humber. The journey would be jolly comfortable in this.

'Take your case in the back with you, Barbara; there's plenty of room. I hope you haven't had any lunch, as I intend to stop somewhere Daddy recommended — it's just a few miles from Shenfield.' Amanda didn't get out and neither did Harriet.

'I haven't eaten since breakfast as I was far too excited.' Barbara wished she hadn't sounded so unsophisticated; if she was going to fit in with these two and their racy friends she would have to try and pretend she was as worldly as they were. 'I wasn't sure my grandfather would allow me to come; he's a bit overprotective especially since . . . well, you know what.'

She tossed her bags across the leather seat and scrambled in behind them. She scarcely had time to sit down before Amanda took off down the drive, scattering gravel and compacted snow in all directions.

Harriet turned round and grinned. 'Don't mind about her. This is the first and last time she's going to be allowed to use the family car, so she's making the most of it.'

'As long as we get there in one piece, I don't care how fast we go. Exactly where is Radcliffe Hall, Amanda?'

'It's not far from Hornchurch, and it isn't nearly as grand as it sounds. I was at school with Clarissa Williams — her parents are very bohemian, and Radcliffe Hall is a bit run-down nowadays. I think Mr Williams won it in a card game when he was at Oxford. They throw the most amazing parties where anything goes — if you know what I mean.'

Barbara's stomach lurched. She knew exactly what Amanda meant — too much to drink, loud music and couples vanishing upstairs whenever they felt like it. Grandma had told her about an event like this and warned her not to accept an invitation to this sort of thing under any circumstances. How could someone as knowledgeable as her grandmother not have known Radcliffe Hall was a den of iniquity?

'I say, are you all right, Barbara? You're not going to be sick, are you?' Harriet asked anxiously.

'Of course not. I was just wondering if I'd brought the wrong clothes for tonight. I rather thought it was going to be very formal and have packed two evening gowns; perhaps

I should have brought a cocktail dress instead.'

Amanda laughed. 'Don't worry about it, old thing. You can't be too glamorous at a do like this — there will be plenty of handsome young RAF officers to impress.'

This time Barbara was forced to dive into her handbag, as if looking for a handkerchief, to hide her dismay. When she'd been told the party was at Hornchurch she hadn't registered the name as the base at which Alex was based. The very last person she wanted to see at a party where 'anything goes' was this fiery-haired, very attractive Spitfire pilot. She prayed he would still be on duty and not able to put in an appearance.

The girls had several 'gin and its' with their lunch but Barbara had a cup of tea, much to the amusement of her companions. 'I think you must be the first person to ask for a cup of tea in a pub,' Harriet said, smiling.

'I don't care; I don't drink a great deal and never at lunchtime. I can get a bit queasy in the back of the car, so you should be grateful I stuck to tea.'

'A wise head on young shoulders — as Mummy often says, but unfortunately never about me.' Amanda giggled and reached for her glass.

Barbara hoped it wasn't too far to Radcliffe

Hall, as both girls were definitely tiddly. She dreaded to think what would happen if they had to make an emergency stop of any sort. She swallowed a mouthful of steak and kidney pie with difficulty, no longer hungry.

'If you don't mind, I'm going to have a bit of a walk round whilst you finish your drinks and your lunch. Don't hurry on my account; I'm just not very hungry at the moment.'

The girls exchanged glances and both tossed back the remains of their drinks and stood up. 'Lunch is on me, Barbara, so Harriet can keep you company whilst I pay the bill.'

After the fug of the dining room, the courtyard of the Rose and Crown seemed icy. 'I'd forgotten how cold it is. Do you think Amanda would mind if we got straight into the car?'

'Absolutely not. Barbara, we promise we'll try not to abandon you when we get to Radcliffe Hall. Ma thought an outing would do you good.' Harriet bundled Barbara into the car and slammed the door, then jumped in the passenger seat. 'God knows how long Mandy will be. She's probably gone to spend a penny.'

'I wish you hadn't mentioned that. I should have gone as well.'

'Too late, old thing, she's coming now.

Anyway, if we don't get held up by a convoy of soldiers or a flock of sheep, we should be there in no time.'

Surprisingly, Amanda drove with more caution when she was squiffy and Barbara was able to relax, no longer worried about an imminent crash. She gazed out of the window, enjoying the panorama of snow-covered fields and occasional houses. 'Is this the main road to London? If it is, I wonder why it's so quiet today.'

Harriet answered as Amanda was crouched over the steering wheel, concentrating furiously. 'Not many people have any petrol — there's a war on, you know!'

'I suppose the snow doesn't help either,' Barbara said. 'Good heavens, whatever's going on ahead? There's an army lorry and the soldiers are standing in the hedge.'

'Can't you guess? It's a call of nature — even soldiers have to pee.'

Barbara hastily averted her eyes, but Amanda honked the horn and the men cheered. How embarrassing! These two were not only older than Barbara, but far more experienced and sophisticated. She smiled. If she was going to enjoy this excursion she'd better try and be a bit more like them; she didn't want to be treated like a child at an adult event.

'We're almost there, Barbara. You see that big house over there? That's Radcliffe Hall,' Amanda said.

'I can't tell you how pleased I am. I'm desperate. Seeing all those soldiers relieving themselves just made it worse.'

Amanda ground the gears and spun the wheel, and the car shot through a dilapidated gate. The drive was full of potholes which even the snow couldn't disguise. They bumped and lurched their way to the front of the house and the car pulled up beside two other vehicles. Neither of these had any snow on the roof, so they must have been recent arrivals.

'Come on, girls. Let's get inside; it's perishing out here.' Amanda switched off the engine but didn't remove the key from the dashboard. 'Grab your bags, Barbara. They don't have any staff here; we have to look after ourselves.'

The building was bigger than the Grove. How did the family manage to run such a large establishment without any help? Barbara crunched behind the girls to the front door, expecting it to open at any moment and their host or hostess to come out and greet them. Instead Harriet turned the handle and put her shoulder to the door. With some difficulty she pushed it open.

'I'm not sure about this, Harriet. I don't

36

even know Clarissa Williams. Won't she think it a bit odd to find a complete stranger wandering about the house?'

'Not a bit of it. It's freedom hall here. I just told you, we all muck in and do whatever needs doing.'

'I can hear a racket going on in the billiard room — they must be in there,' Amanda said. 'Chuck your bags at the foot of the stairs; Clarissa will sort out where we're sleeping later on.'

Whatever Amanda suggested, Barbara wasn't going to leave her precious handbag unattended in this vast, freezing cold entrance hall. She was jolly glad she'd had the forethought to put on warm clothes — she hated to think how cold she was going to be in her evening dress later on.

She followed her new friends towards the rear of the house; it got no warmer, but was certainly a lot louder. The place had a miserable air, neglected and grubby, and she wished she'd not accepted the invitation and was back in her nice warm home.

When Harriet pushed open the door everything changed. Light and music, laughter and the smell of applewood logs gushed into the corridor. Amanda hung back and took her arm.

'I know this place seems pretty dismal.

They can't afford to keep all the rooms up to scratch, so you just have to ignore the in-between bits.'

Inside the noisy billiard room were about a dozen people of all ages. Enormous swags of holly and ivy tied with bright red ribbon hung from the high ceiling. Everywhere Barbara looked there was something Christmassy. Even the blue haze of cigarette smoke failed to dampen her excitement.

'I love it! What a clever idea. I must do the same next year. It's . . . ' Before she had time to complete her sentence she was surrounded by several of the guests. A very tall young man in army uniform pumped her hand vigorously.

'You must be Barbara Sinclair. I'm so glad you've come. There's always a shortage of beautiful young women at parties.' He transferred his grip to her waist and moved her into the circle of smiling people. 'Everybody, let me introduce the newest recruit to Radcliffe Hall entertainment. This is Barbara Sinclair from Ingatestone.'

A ragged cheer and a round of applause greeted his announcement and Barbara found herself handed round like a parcel. She was kissed and patted by a variety of young and old, male and female, but she was so overwhelmed by her welcome she instantly forgot their names. She'd no idea who the young man was — no doubt a relative of the owners — but she was surprised neither Mr nor Mrs Williams had done the introductions.

Someone placed a mug of hot, sweet tea into one hand whilst another shoved a plate with a sandwich into the other. She retreated to the comparative peace of a window seat and sat down, not sure what to do with her drink and food; she really wasn't hungry.

A friendly voice spoke from the far end of the window seat. Startled, she slopped her tea and almost dropped the sandwich.

'Good afternoon, Miss Sinclair. I'm Neil Partridge, another distant relation of Clarissa's.'

'Hello. Please call me Barbara. Is it always as lively as this?'

'Usually much worse — we're saving ourselves for tonight. I should drink your tea and eat your sandwich before someone else snaffles it.'

Barbara sat and took a sip from the mug. Whilst doing so she surreptitiously glanced in the man's direction to see what he looked like. Her tea spilt for the second time when she saw his blue uniform. 'Are you at the base nearby, by any chance?'

'Indeed I am, fair maiden. I've got a twenty-four hour pass and intend to make the most of it. I hope you're impressed by these.' He tapped the gold wings sewn above his left jacket pocket. 'I just got them, you know. Didn't think I'd get them after the prang I had last week.'

'I assume you're a fighter pilot. Do you fly Spitfires or Hurricanes?'

'Spitfires — nothing like them. I'm a lucky bloke to be with Squadron 54.'

She was tempted to ask him about Alex but thought better of it. He leaned across and helped himself to her sandwich. 'As you don't seem to be eating these, I'll help you out. It's every man for himself here. Probably won't be any more grub until tonight.'

'Cheek! I'm an honoured guest and I don't expect to have my lunch stolen by a rookie pilot.' She grinned. He really was rather nice. 'Actually I've already had my lunch, so you're welcome to eat it all.'

He laughed and munched his sandwich with obvious relish. She finished the tea. Neil was an easy man to sit with; he didn't attempt to flirt or make unwanted suggestions, merely pointed at various members of the party and told her amusing anecdotes about each. She had no idea where Amanda and Harriet had gone; so much for their promise to keep an eye on her.

Eventually Mrs Williams drifted across in a

cloud of lavender chiffon — a very glamorous outfit, but quite unsuitable for the weather. 'My dear, I'm so sorry not to have spoken to you sooner. We're in a bit of a pickle in the catering department. Amanda seems to think you're a dab hand in the kitchen.' She smiled hopefully.

'I don't know about that, Mrs Williams, but I'm certainly very happy to give it a go.'

'Thank you so much, Barbara. I'll take you to the kitchen. I'm afraid it's a bit primitive, not at all what you're used to I expect, but you look a resourceful young lady. I'm sure you'll manage.'

The trek to the rear of the building was as unpleasant as her arrival in the billiard room, but far worse was to follow. The kitchen was freezing cold and she wasn't expected to just help, but to organise supper for one hundred guests from a miscellany of anonymous boxes, tins and fresh vegetables.

Mrs Williams waved a languid hand and vanished, leaving her alone with an ancient gentleman who looked as though he might be a gardener from his weather-beaten appearance, and two equally bewildered girls about her own age.

'Thank God. Are you the chef?' the taller, more buxom girl asked.

'No, Mrs Williams just asked if I'd help.'

41

She looked helplessly at the mountain of stuff piled haphazardly all over the room. 'Surely we aren't expected to turn this into food for everybody?'

'Oh God! I scarcely know one end of a spoon from the other. I'm Gillian, by the way, and this Mary.'

'I'm Barbara. I'm sorry, I know this is the first time I've been to one of these events, but I'm not going to spend the next few hours in here. What we need are another half a dozen helpers.' She started opening boxes and peering inside. 'Golly, there's all sorts in here. Butter, cheese, tins of salmon — in fact I think this would make a perfectly splendid buffet supper, but not without more people in here to make it happen.'

The other two were looking at her in admiration. She was surprised at herself; maybe having been almost murdered, and sleeping with John, had toughened her up. 'Right, I'm going back to the billiard room to rustle up some troops. Can you start sorting out all this? Put cooked food over there on the dresser, uncooked leave on the table, and anything that can be made into cakes, pastry and so on by the cooker.' She snorted with laughter. 'Not that you could call that contraption a cooker — it looks like something out of the dark ages.'

3

Barbara marched to the billiard room, determined to drag some of the occupants back to the kitchen. She flung the door open and it crashed satisfactorily against the wall. The stunned silence was more than she expected — she'd just wanted to get their attention.

'I've been asked to organise the party food and I need volunteers. Gillian and Mary are already in the kitchen; we need at least another half a dozen or tonight will be a disaster.' Her heart was hammering, her hands clammy. She was glad she was leaning against the door jamb.

Neil, the RAF chap she'd been talking to earlier, sprung to attention and saluted smartly. 'Pilot Officer Partridge at your service.'

Immediately two more RAF officers did the same and two girls joined them. Amanda and Harriet showed no sign of stepping forward to offer their help. That made eight of them; it should be enough if they got on with it.

'Thank you. I think that those who are

helping prepare the food should be exempt from the washing-up tomorrow.' A general chorus of agreement echoed around the room. 'There seems to be plenty of food, but most of it's still at the ingredients stage.' She led her willing band down the icy passageways to the kitchen.

Mary and Gillian greeted their arrival with delight. 'We've sorted everything out, Barbara, but have no idea what to do with it,' Mary said, pointing at the various piles around the room.

'Bloody hell, it's arctic in here. No danger of the food going off, I suppose,' Neil said, blowing on his hands.

'There you are, always a bright side,' said Barbara. 'Now, I think the only way we're going to get anything done is for anyone who knows how to cook a particular dish to do that, regardless of whether it's actually party food. Mary, do you have anything you know how to make?'

'I'm a dab hand at bread and butter pudding, and I know there are two stale loaves, a bag of sultanas, sugar, eggs and milk. I can probably find nutmeg if I look hard enough. Is that any good?'

'Excellent — I like it better cold. You do that. What about you, Gillian?'

In no time at all the makeshift cooks were

busy at their allotted tasks. Barbara was making fairy cakes and meat pasties, the other two girls were making a vast pot of vegetable soup, and the men were doing whatever they were told. Neil had managed to get the antiquated range working, which was a relief.

'I suppose there are soup bowls and things somewhere?' Barbara asked Mary.

'I've no idea — I've never been here before. I think they get the newbies to do all the work whilst the old hands enjoy themselves.'

Neil, who was up to his elbows in warm suds, nodded vigourously. 'Very true. It's a rite of passage we all have to go through. Next time you come, someone else will do all the hard work and you can swan about enjoying yourself.'

'There's enough bread to make lots of sandwiches. We've got cheese, ham and egg, but I don't think we should make those until later on,' Barbara said as she got her third lot of fairy cakes from the oven. 'I hope we're not expected to put all this out as well as make it.'

One of the other girls explained that those who made the food were exempt from any further domestic duties. 'Do you know which room you're staying in, Barbara? If you don't, you'd better find Clarissa and put your stuff on a bed or you might find yourself homeless tonight.'

'I thought I'd be sharing with Amanda and Harriet, but they seem to be busy elsewhere.'

An RAF chap laughed. 'Those two popsies come for the booze and the blokes — can't remember ever seeing them do anything useful.'

'I haven't got time to go and look for a room right now; I've got to keep an eye on my cakes and then I have to ice them. Thank you for the suggestion, but I'll take my chances.'

A little after seven Barbara declared the buffet supper complete. 'This looks absolutely super; thank you everyone. We've got over thirty mugs for the soup and plenty of plates for the savoury stuff. People can eat the cakes and bread and butter pudding with their fingers.'

The three men had done all the washing up and the kitchen was cleaner than when they'd started. The sandwiches were made, crusts removed, and were waiting under a damp cloth on various large plates. Barbara had discovered a selection of stands which were perfect for the cakes and pudding. The meat pasties and sausage rolls were neatly arrayed on napkin-covered trays — not a particularly glamorous buffet, but more than enough to go around.

The group parted, promising to meet up at nine o'clock when the party really started. The remaining guests had blown up balloons and put them in a net in the ceiling of the ballroom. These would be let down at midnight. The drink was in the breakfast room and the food would be put out in the dining room at eleven o'clock. All Barbara had to do was find the elusive Clarissa Williams and discover where she was going to be sleeping.

The entrance hall had been filled with trestle tables pushed up against each wall. A large square piece of cardboard with a letter printed on it had been stuck behind each section. A tall, willowy blonde was pushing drawing pins into the panelling to hold the notices as Barbara arrived.

'Do you need any help with that? We've finished in the kitchen and I'm at a loose end until I find Clarissa and see where I'm sleeping tonight.'

The girl turned and smiled. 'You must be Barbara. I'm Clarissa. I've been waiting for you. I'm finished here now — I expect you're wondering what's going on.' She waved at the tables and the notices. 'These are for coats; everyone knows what to do. You put your coat on the table that corresponds to the first letter of your name; that way people can find their belongings when they go home.'

'What a brilliant idea. Do they use their first name or their second?'

'Doesn't really matter, as long as they know which one they've used. Now, I've saved you the best room and you don't have to share. It's next to a bathroom and tucked away in a corner so you won't get disturbed by unwelcome visitors in the night.'

'I shall push a chair under the doorknob anyway, just to be sure. Thank you for thinking of me — Mary thought I might find myself sleeping on the floor somewhere.'

'After what you've done for us in the kitchen? I should think not. Grab your case and I'll take you up.'

When Clarissa had said the room was tucked away she hadn't been exaggerating. Barbara was worried she might have difficulty relocating the room when she wanted to go to bed. Although the room was half the size of her bedroom at home, it had a double bed, a fine mahogany wardrobe and dressing table, plus a comfy armchair, hexagonal side table and reading lamp. More than enough for a one-night stay.

She looked at her watch and saw she had barely an hour to get ready. She'd heard a couple of people walk past and go into the bathroom but was fairly sure the room was empty now. Both evening dresses had travelled remarkably well, no doubt because of the years of packing she'd had to do for boarding school. She laid out her underwear on the bed, arranged her make-up on the dressing table and quickly stripped off and slipped on her robe. She shivered and regretted bringing this flimsy negligee set and not the serviceable flannelette dressing gown she normally wore.

With her toilet bag and bath towel she ventured outside into the corridor, and was delighted the bathroom was not only empty but reasonably warm, having being used by others before her. It would have been nice to have a long soak in the bath, but there wasn't time and there probably wouldn't be enough hot water anyway, with so many people in the house.

She filled the sink and had a quick strip wash, surprised that Radcliffe Hall, for all its dilapidation, was able to supply such a remote bathroom with sufficient warm water to wash. Satisfied she'd removed the lingering smell of the kitchen, she unlocked the door and nipped back to her bedroom.

If she wore the less daring frock, she would need the camiknickers. These were a brassiere and knickers in one and the only way you could have a pee was by unbuttoning fiddly hooks underneath. The other gown had built-in support for the bosom, was fully lined so didn't need a petticoat, and only required a pair of French knickers and a suspender belt. Decision made, she sat down at the dressing table and carefully applied lipstick and powder — she was tempted to add rouge, but would probably get so hot dancing her face would be bright red anyway.

Whoever was sharing this quiet corner of the house had already gone down; she'd better hurry as she didn't want to be the last to arrive in the ballroom. Being a resident must give her a certain status, and she needed all the help available if she was to hold her own amongst the glittering throng.

She stepped into her dress and carefully pulled up the metal zipper at the side, making sure she didn't catch the delicate material in the teeth. The close-fitting bodice seemed safe enough, but she prayed her bosom would remain encased in the silk even when she danced. The speckled mirror only showed her top half, but she was satisfied with that. She hoped she didn't trip over the long skirt and make a fool of herself, as she'd never worn anything quite like this. If she was honest, everything about tonight was a first.

With just a torch and handkerchief in her beaded evening bag, she was ready to go. She gathered up the floating hem of her gown just in case she trod on it on the stairs, and feeling rather like a debutante in one of Georgette Heyer's Regency romances, headed for the sound of laughter and tinkling glasses filtering up from the party.

★　★　★

'Alex, are you coming to this bash or are you just going to sit there and mope all night?' Bob Davis slapped him rather too hard on the back, slopping his beer on to the bar.

'Not really in the mood for celebrating. It's going to be a pretty bloody New Year for everyone, especially those poor sods stuck in France up to their necks in snow.'

'Exactly why we need to go out and enjoy ourselves. Once this war gets going we won't have a minute to ourselves, and parties will be a thing of the past.'

'I haven't got any petrol, so I'd have to cadge a lift with you.'

His friend beamed. 'Good show! Get that pint down you; we're leaving right away.'

Outside it was pitch black and colder than it had been earlier. Like the others, Alex waited a few moments for his eyes to adjust to the darkness and then followed to the car. His night vision was legendary in Squadron 54 and he rarely needed his torch. The racket his friends were making as they scrambled into the vehicle was enough to find them with his eyes closed.

'Shut up, you three. I bet there are people trying to sleep in the cottages next door.' As usual they ignored him and he climbed in the back seat next to Pete; the car roared off, pinning him to the seat with the G-force. 'For God's sake, Bob, take it easy. You're not flying a Spitfire now, and I'd like to see in the New Year in one piece.'

The trouble with fighter pilots was they were so used to speed in the air they preferred to travel the same way on the ground. He closed his eyes and let their banter wash over him. He frowned at the thought of the man who'd been at the Grove over Christmas, an Acting Pilot Officer, John something. His mother had said this bloke was good-looking and in love with Barbara.

Mum was almost certain Barbara had been wearing an engagement ring, so he'd missed his chance there. He'd thought she might be the one for him, as from the first moment he'd met her, when she called in at the farm to order hay and bedding for her horse, there'd been a connection. It wasn't just her stunning green eyes, pretty face, or her perfect figure that had attracted him. She was sweet, innocent and vulnerable, and this made him want to protect her. It was rotten luck this John bloke had got in first — if she was engaged to him she was off-limits. You didn't mess with another bloke's fiancée — especially not a fellow RAF pilot.

The drive from Hornchurch to wherever they were going was over as the car lurched to a halt. The four of them climbed out and Pete shone the tiny beam of his torch up at the massive building. Alex didn't have to ask if they were at the right place: even though not a chink of light came through the blackouts, the noise from inside meant the party was in full swing.

'Bob, are you sure the hostess won't mind me gate-crashing?'

'Not a bit of it, old boy. Open invitation to all the officers at the base. Blimey, it's parky out here. Let's get inside and join in the fun. Sounds like they got started without us.'

'I sincerely hope you know where the front door is. We could be wandering about out here all night,' Pete chimed in.

'Follow me; I've been here before.' Sure enough, Bob guided them through the other parked cars, into the pillared portico and up the steps. He didn't bother to knock but pushed open the door. 'Last man in close it behind you, then we can go through the curtain without alerting the Jerries.'

The noise was deafening; it sounded like they had a full dance band, which was going flat out with one of the lively American numbers. Alex stripped off his heavy great-coat and cap. He was about to chuck it on the nearest pile of coats when he saw the cards on the wall. 'Shall we put all our stuff together? That will make it easier to find later — as I am your flight commander they can go under E.'

A couple of pretty girls appeared in the hall. Bob immediately enquired where the drink was and they escorted him down the passageway. 'I've already had two pints. I'll get something later on,' Alex called to his departing friends. The music was lifting his spirits. He was glad he'd come. Nothing like a party to cheer a chap up.

The double doors at the far end of the corridor were where the action was. He pushed his way through a group of inebriated brown jobs and arrived at what was obviously the ballroom. Sure enough, a live dance band was belting out a tune and the floor was full of swirling couples. The few blokes in evening dress stood out amongst a crowd of brown and blue servicemen. The women, in contrast, were dressed to the nines. He felt as if he'd been transported to another world — a world of fast cars, fast women and unlimited trust funds. He was an alien amongst this lot and he wished he'd not agreed to come, but stayed in the warm fug of the public bar at the Horse and Groom.

★　★　★

Barbara was aware people were staring at her — had her dress caught in the cheeks of her bottom? Should she nip into the downstairs cloakroom and check, or was she being silly? Then two young men in RAF uniform whistled loudly as she walked past. Heavens, that had never happened before. This dress must be just the ticket.

She felt like someone else, a film star or someone famous, and her face relaxed and her smile became genuine. Several guests greeted her by name but she had no idea who they were. Where were Amanda and Harriet? She really didn't want to drift about the ballroom on her own for much longer. There were several predatory young men prowling about, just waiting to pounce if she showed the slightest inclination to stop and talk to them.

'Blimey, Barbara, you scrub up well. Didn't recognise you in that glamorous outfit.' Neil grinned and offered his arm; she took it gratefully.

'Thank you, I feel quite different in this evening gown. I can't tell you how glad I am to see you, Neil. I'm not comfortable being the centre of attention. Could you pretend to be my escort, please? No one would dare approach me if I'm with you.' She smiled. 'How tall are you, exactly?'

'Six feet and four inches, and built like a barn door. I was determined to be a fighter pilot, but it took a lot to convince the powers that be a bloke as big as me could actually fit in a fighter.'

'They probably thought you would be better flying a bomber — mind you, I don't suppose the cockpit of a Blenheim is much bigger.'

'No idea, and no intention of finding out. As a matter of fact it's a tight squeeze in my Spitfire, but as long as I can get in and out at speed, nobody seems particularly bothered. Now, shall we dance?'

The band was playing a quickstep and she was fairly sure she could do that without disgracing herself. 'I'd love to, but I warn you I've never danced with a man before.'

He chuckled and winked at her. He really

was a nice man, but he didn't have the same effect on her as Alex did, and even John made her heart beat a little faster. There was no time to dwell on this as he grabbed her hand and swept her onto the dance floor. For a man of his size he was remarkably light on his feet, and when she missed a step he just lifted her so her feet dangled.

For the first time in ages she forgot about the past and just enjoyed the dance. When the music stopped she was breathless, but had enjoyed every moment. 'Golly, that was a lot quicker than I expected.'

'That's why it's called a quickstep, my dear.' Neil touched her bare arm. 'There's a bloke from my unit coming over — do you want me to get rid of him?'

She was about to say yes when something prompted her to turn. Striding towards her, his eyes blazing, was Alex Everton. He was the most handsome man in the room — his russet hair and startling green eyes turned several female heads.

'Barbara, I couldn't believe it when I saw you. You look spectacular — even more beautiful than usual.'

'Thank you. It's amazing what an expensive frock will do.' Her tongue seemed too big for her mouth, her throat was dry and her heart was trying to jump out of her chest.

'Are you feeling okay? I'll take you somewhere quieter and cooler where you can sit down.' He gently put his arm around her waist and guided her through the milling people and into the corridor.

She should step away from him, tell him she was officially engaged to John, say she was with Neil, but the words refused to come. Being with Alex felt so right, and spending an evening in his company couldn't do any harm.

'I'm fine, but I would like to talk to you if we can find somewhere quiet and warmer than here. I know where the billiard room is. That might be all right.' He didn't remove his arm and she didn't protest.

'I wasn't going to come tonight; in fact was rather taking a dim view of the whole procedure, when I saw you talking to Neil.' His tone changed. 'Friend of yours, is he?'

He had no right to question her behaviour and her irritation gave her the strength to pull away from him. 'It's none of your business, Alex, and I really don't know why I agreed to come out here with you.' She faced him and this was a big mistake. When he looked at her like that she couldn't think straight.

'We both know why you're here. I've never met anyone like you. I've been thinking of you every day. I don't care about that John bloke; you belong with me. I'm crazy about you.'

He moved closer. His warm breath tickled her cheek. Then his mouth covered hers and she couldn't prevent herself responding. She was crushed against his jacket, the roughness of the material harsh against the bare skin of her shoulders. She didn't care; she wanted every inch of her body hard against his, wanted the kiss to lead to something more intimate.

'Bloody hell, Everton, you didn't waste much time. No chance for us lesser mortals once you're in action.' The man laughed and staggered off towards the billiard room clutching a brimming glass.

Thoroughly embarrassed, and sharply reminded of Alex's reputation as a ladykiller, she pushed him away, no longer enthralled by his kisses. 'This is quite ridiculous. I shouldn't have let you do that.' Now was the time to tell him about her engagement, but she did so want to dance with him just once before she ruined the evening for both of them.

He grinned and recaptured her hand. 'I didn't give you much choice, so don't worry about it. Didn't anybody tell you there's a war on? You've got to be kind to the boys in blue.'

'Being kind is what's got me into this pickle. I'm engaged to one RAF officer and in love with another.' She hadn't meant to say that, hadn't even known it herself until she spoke the words out loud.

'That's why we have to talk, Babs. It's bloody freezing out here. Let's find somewhere warmer.'

'From the racket, there must be a secondary party going on in the billiard room, so that's no use. There won't be anybody in the dining room at the moment as supper isn't going to be put out until eleven o'clock.'

She shivered and immediately he removed his jacket and draped it around her shoulders. 'One extreme to the other in here — you must be frozen in that dress.'

His jacket was heavy and scratchy, but the warmth was welcome. 'In here. I shouldn't think there's a fire, but I'm fine like this. Will you be okay?'

'I spend most of my days skidding about the skies in sub-zero temperatures — positively balmy in here for a tough bloke like me.'

His lopsided grin made her stomach somersault. If he wasn't so attractive he would be far easier to resist. She giggled and he raised an eyebrow.

'Something I said?'

'Nothing I can tell you — your head is quite big enough already, Flight Lieutenant Everton.'

Fortunately she was correct about the dining room being empty, but she was wrong about there being no fire. She was pleased someone had already put out the tablecloths, crockery and cutlery ready for the buffet. 'I was roped in to organise the catering for tonight. I'm afraid it's not canapés and party food, but a peculiar mix of the things my helpers knew how to make.'

'Don't suppose anybody will even notice; by the time it's served they'll all be pie-eyed.' He carried two mismatched dining-room chairs across to the fireplace, carefully dusted one off with a clean handkerchief, and nodded for her to sit down. 'Go on, Babs, you'd better tell me. I can see you're pleased as punch with your catering efforts.'

She carefully smoothed the silk under her bottom and sat. She didn't really need his jacket, but she liked the smell and the thought that he'd been wearing it. 'I made the fairy cakes and meat pasties, someone else made soup, and there are tons of sandwiches and lashings of bread and butter pudding. I'm pretty sure one of the blokes found pickled onions, and I think there's quite a bit of cold meat and cheese as well.'

By the time she'd finished her list he was laughing. 'That's the most unusual party supper I've ever come across. I'm sure it'll be the talk of the mess tomorrow.'

'I think it's a bit of a cheek expecting guests to prepare the food anyway — so Mr and Mrs Williams will just have to lump it. They're jolly lucky to have anything. Do you know, they don't even supply alcohol, they expect their guests to bring it? All they do is open Radcliffe Hall. I bet all the food was donated as well. Nobody would buy such a strange mix of things.'

He spun his chair and straddled it, then leant on his folded arms. His intense stare gave her goosebumps. 'This John bloke, the one you're engaged to . . . ' He swallowed and his eyes glittered.

'I don't want to talk about him anymore, if you don't mind. I shouldn't have said what I did earlier. It doesn't matter what we feel for each other, I've given my word to John.'

'That's bullshit, and you know it. Are you telling me you'd marry a man you don't love? That's a recipe for disaster and it isn't fair on either of you.'

'There's no need to use such bad language, and I could hardly break the engagement after he'd saved my life. I only agreed to marry him because he loves me and I wanted him to be happy.' He looked at her as if she were talking rubbish. 'Surely a pilot is going to take more care if he's got something special to live for? If I broke his heart then he's more likely to make a mistake, isn't he?

'And what about me? Don't you care if I go for a Burton?'

'You don't really love me, you just want something you can't have. You've got a dreadful reputation for breaking hearts.'

He stood up so violently his chair crashed to the floor. 'Don't you dare tell me how I feel! I've been in love with you since you arrived on your bicycle and I found you talking to the dog.'

She was on her feet too, scarcely able to believe what he was saying. How could she have got him so wrong? What a mess she'd made of everything. 'I'm sorry. It's such a shock to hear you say you love me. What are we going to do?'

'You've got to write and break off your engagement. Will your grandparents kick up a stink?'

A rush of happiness pushed away her doubts. 'Actually, they already know how I feel about John and wouldn't be at all surprised to hear that you and I have feelings for each other.' She held out her left hand, showing him her ringless finger. 'I'm not even wearing my ring; it's on my dressing table at home.'

His expression changed. 'Did you come here to hook up with some posh bloke? To have a good time somewhere nobody knows you?'

How could he accuse her of behaving like that? She stiffened and glared at him. 'It's none of your business, Alex Everton, what I do. I was actually having a delightful time with Neil before you barged in.'

His smile was brittle and he shrugged as if he didn't care either way. 'Fair enough. Forget what I said. You're not the girl I thought you were. You go ahead and enjoy yourself, but I warn you, I'm not interested in second-hand goods.'

She turned away and bile flooded her throat. Sleeping with John might have made *him* happy but it had ruined *her* life. Alex obviously had old-fashioned views when it came to selecting a partner, however he behaved himself. She'd never liked a man with double standards. In fact, if she was honest with herself, she might be head over heels in love with him, but she didn't really like him very much. Why couldn't she be in love with John instead?

He hadn't stormed off, but was putting the

chairs back where he'd got them from. She would slip away and find Neil and forget what had happened. She'd accused Alex of imagining he was in love with her because she was off-limits — was she doing the same? Were her feelings just infatuation coupled with lust?

As she quietly pulled open the door he spoke from close behind her. 'Christ, I'm such a berk. I'm sorry; I've no excuse for accusing you of behaving like a goodtime girl. Can you forgive me? It's just the thought of you being with anyone else drives me crazy.'

4

Barbara bit her lip and ignored his apology. Getting involved with Alex would be wrong on every level. She did the mature thing, straightened her shoulders and stalked away down the icy corridor. She'd left his jacket on the chair and her teeth were chattering by the time she rejoined the party in the ballroom.

He hadn't pursued her or tried to change her mind, and she wasn't sure she would have had the strength of mind to reject him a second time if he had. There were more than one hundred people in the ballroom; it was stifling and blue with cigarette smoke. What she needed was a stiff drink to calm her nerves and give her the courage to ignore Alex for the rest of the evening, but she didn't want to brave the corridor in order to get one.

Several hopeful young men in uniform asked her to dance but she refused politely; she wanted to find Neil and ask him if he would get her something. She scanned the room hoping to see his head above the other couples, but he wasn't visible. Then she was grabbed from behind and dragged onto the floor.

'Right you are, darling. I've been looking for you everywhere. You're the prettiest girl here tonight — '

'Excuse me, but I don't wish to dance, and certainly not with someone as rude as you.'

The man, who was attempting to swing her about in a jitterbug, ignored her comment. He was in evening dress, fairly tall with mousy brown hair and insipid blue eyes but a determined expression. If he carried on like this he was going to rip her dress, or even worse, cause it to slide down and expose her bosom.

'You heard the lady, she doesn't want to dance with you.' Alex had the man's shoulder and was squeezing hard.

'Bugger off, she's mine. I got here first.'

Barbara refused to be argued over. She wrenched herself from the obnoxious man's grip and stepped back. 'I have no wish to dance with anyone. If you two neanderthals want to fight, then do it over someone else. Good night.'

She picked up her skirts and hurried away. Her cheeks were wet by the time she reached the vestibule and she ran up the stairs, determined to find sanctuary in her room. She should never have worn this frock. It made her look like something she wasn't.

The sound of feet pounding behind her increased her speed. It didn't matter which of the men was pursuing her; she didn't want to speak to either of them. She skidded around the corner expecting to see her bedroom door on the left, but in her hurry to escape she'd taken a wrong turn. Her torch was somewhere downstairs and the feeble glow of the single lightbulb didn't make it any easier. Should she hide in one of the bedrooms for a while and allow whoever this was to return to the party?

The corridor was too cold; in her flimsy gown she would freeze. Unpleasant memories of being trapped on the balcony in the snow came flooding back. She had to find somewhere warm. The first door she tried was locked; the second was a bathroom. She didn't have time to try a third as Alex arrived at her side.

'Here, little idiot, put my jacket on again. Do you have a death wish or something?' His light-hearted comment released the tension between them.

'I don't like you, Flight Lieutenant Everton, but as I'm so cold I'll borrow your jacket until I can find my room.'

'Fair enough. Have you any idea where your room is, exactly?'

'If you hadn't been chasing me I wouldn't have got lost.'

His face changed from friendly to frightening. 'I didn't chase you. I'm not that stupid. That bastard must be up here somewhere. I'm going to kick him down the stairs and then — '

'You'll do no such thing. There's been far too much violence in my life and it doesn't solve anything. Just take me downstairs and then I'm sure I'll be able to find my way.'

'If that's what you want, but the man's a creep and if I don't punch him tonight someone else will do it next time.'

This time he didn't attempt to put his arm around her but walked beside her, keeping up a steady stream of light-hearted conversation. He seemed to have an unerring sense of direction as they were soon at the main staircase. She was about to say good night when Clarissa saw her.

'Brilliant. I've been looking for you everywhere, Barbara. The cooks and bottle-washers get to eat first, before the ravening hordes are set loose on the buffet. Pa also has a large drink for you to say thank you.' She nodded to Alex. 'You can come too. I'm Clarissa Williams, by the way.'

'Alex Everton, and thank you for your kind offer. Like all RAF bods, I'm always hungry.'

Clarissa grabbed his hand and shook it vigorously. 'The famous Alex Everton — I heard you threatened to beat up that vile Cyril Worley. I wish you had. He always gate-crashes parties because no one would dream of inviting him.'

'Believe me, Miss Williams, I'd be glad to but I've promised Babs I'll leave him alone.'

The three of them walked briskly along the passageway to the dining room, which was ablaze with candlelight and the central table groaning with food. Everything looked delicious and smelt even better. Barbara's stomach rumbled loudly, much to the amusement of the others. 'I'm so sorry, but I realise I've not had very much since very early this morning.'

Her willing helpers were already eating, as were half a dozen other guests. Mary waved when she saw Barbara. 'Isn't this terrific? I've already had soup in a mug and a meat pasty and I've started on the sandwiches.'

Finally Barbara was able to relax and begin to enjoy herself, but she didn't think she'd ever get used to being at an overcrowded party. There was somebody missing. 'Clarissa, why isn't Neil here? I couldn't see him in the ballroom, either, a while ago.'

'Oh, he didn't feel well. Thinks he's getting a bug of some sort. So he left just after you went away with your gorgeous pilot.'

'What a pity. I thought he was rather nice. By the way, Alex is a friend. His parents have a farm nearby and his younger brothers play with my brothers.'

Clarissa looked sceptical. 'Are you sure he knows that? I'd say he was hopelessly in love with you.'

Not wishing to continue this conversation, Barbara walked across to the food. Alex was there before her and returned with two steaming china mugs. 'I've got some soup. Can you grab a couple of plates and pile a bit of everything on? This is the craziest buffet I've ever seen, but I reckon it'll be the tastiest.'

When the plates were full Barbara followed him to a small table in the far corner where he was waiting. 'Did you want me to put the bread and butter pudding and cakes on the same plate as the savoury stuff?'

He grinned. 'Wouldn't have minded if you had. It all goes down the same way, doesn't it?'

Several people wandered across and spoke to them. Alex appeared to know, at least by sight, all the boys in blue and he was happy to introduce her to them. 'I was wondering why there're no women in uniform here,' Barbara said. 'Don't you have them on your base?'

'Not at the moment, no, but the powers that be are busy converting a building to accommodate them. Once this lot gets going, we're going to need all the help we can get.'

'Why did all those men come over? Was it because of me? Do they think I'm your girlfriend?'

'Too right they do. Every bloke needs a beautiful young woman on his arm. It will do my kudos no end of good.'

She pursed her lips and tried to look disapproving. 'You have a dreadful reputation in that department already, Flight Lieutenant. I hardly think you need to show me off to improve your status on the base.'

His smile vanished and he stretched out to cover her hand with his. 'Would you believe me if I told you I've not been out with a girl since I met you last September?'

She had been going to laugh and shake her head but just in time realised he was serious. Her throat constricted and she couldn't swallow her mouthful of pasty. He'd been faithful to her even though they weren't going out — and what had she done?

'Here, spit it out in this.' Alex handed her his handkerchief and gratefully she did as he suggested.

'I'm sorry — '

'Don't be, I shouldn't have told you that. It's not your fault I'm carrying a torch for you. I'll get over it. I'll be too bloody busy fighting the Germans to worry about anything else.'

She pushed her half-eaten food away and wanted something to wash away the taste. Without thinking she drank her large glass of wine in one gulp. She coughed and for a horrible moment thought her supper was going to make an unwanted reappearance.

Instead of being sympathetic, he laughed. 'Serves you right. What a waste of a decent white wine.'

'And it would serve you right if I'd been sick all over your uniform. I don't usually drink alcohol; I thought it was water.' Her head was spinning a bit and she felt rather peculiar, but the sensation wasn't unpleasant. 'Could you see if you can find me something non-alcoholic please?'

He stood up and picked up the plates. 'I'll take these back to the kitchen and find you some water. Can I interest you in a piece of bread and butter pudding or a couple of fairy cakes?'

'No thank you, delightful as that sounds, I think I'd better not eat anything else.' She watched him stroll across the room with easy grace and couldn't help noticing the other girls were doing the same. He really was the most attractive man. His eyes were the same green as hers, but his hair was the colour of autumn leaves whereas hers was a very ordinary brown.

Clarissa clapped her hands. 'If everybody has finished, could I ask you to return your used crockery and cutlery to the kitchen before you go? Ma is going to open the doors in a minute and we'll be crushed in the stampede.'

Barbara helped Clarissa gather up the debris and followed the others to the kitchen. Alex was on his way back with her water, but he waved her past and then dropped in behind her. 'The band are going to have a break; it will be quieter in the ballroom now. I'd really like to dance with you before you go up.'

Once she'd disposed of the plates she'd been carrying she eagerly gulped down the glass of water he held. She was about to put it with the other crockery in the sink when he stopped her. 'No, keep it. I could do with a beer and I bet they've run out of glasses.'

She handed it to him. 'If the band is having an interval, how are we going to dance?'

'Someone's bound to have the job of putting on records. There, that sounds promising.' The sweet sound of 'Moonlight

Serenade' by Glenn Miller echoed down the corridor. Even the pandemonium of the guests rushing to the dining room couldn't quite drown out the melody.

The ballroom wasn't empty by any means, but was no longer heaving with people. There was plenty of room to dance. Maybe it wouldn't hurt to stay a little bit longer. After all, Grandpa had told her to enjoy herself, and there was no harm in a dance or two, was there?

Alex chucked his jacket onto a chair. 'Thank God it isn't anything fast. I've eaten too much to risk bouncing about,' she said. He held out his hand and she took it. As long as he made no further comment about being in love with her, or made any attempt to kiss her, she should be able to maintain her distance.

His palm was rough against the bare skin of her back — she rather liked it. He led her smoothly around the dance floor, making the occasional comment about the other couples. When the record finished another waltz was put on and away they went again. People began to drift back from the dining room and the band was reassembling on the dais at the far end.

'I could do with a drink. I hope I didn't break the glass when I threw my jacket down.

It will be midnight soon; you'll need something to toast in the New Year.'

'Something non-alcoholic if possible. Shall I come with you?'

'No, stay in the warm. Isn't that one of your friends over there? You could go and talk to her whilst I'm gone.'

Barbara glanced over and saw Harriet talking to an army officer. 'I will — I want to know where she and Amanda have been all evening. They gave me their word they would keep an eye on me but they haven't done a very good job. Also, I must know what time they're leaving in the morning, I don't want to miss my lift home.'

Alex removed the glass from the pocket of his jacket, gave her the thumbs up, then followed a stream of like-minded guests into the passageway. Harriet left her companion and rushed over to embrace her. 'I'm so sorry not to have been with you. It's a bit complicated. Do you mind if I leave the explanation until we're driving home?'

'Of course not. I've been absolutely fine. I couldn't believe it when Alex Everton turned up — so much easier to dance with someone I already know.'

'I hear you were press-ganged into organising the catering. Everyone's saying it's the best food they've ever had here. Usually all we get are a few sandwiches and sausage rolls.'

'People were very generous with their donations; I expect that was because of leftover Christmas goodies. I know we've got tons of things in the larder — Grandma drastically over-ordered. I think those who could afford it went a bit mad this year. Rationing starts soon, doesn't it?' She frowned as she recognised the nasal whine of Cyril Worley behind her. 'I hope that objectionable man isn't coming in this direction. Alex threatened to knock him down a little while ago.'

'I'm afraid he is. His father is a bigwig in the Cabinet and has got him a post at the War Office; that's why he hasn't been called up.'

The band struck up an opening chord and launched into a lively rendering of 'This Can't be Love'. Harriet's companion gestured towards the dance floor but her friend shook her head. 'I can't leave Barbara alone at the moment. Her boyfriend will be back in a minute and then we can dance.'

'The divine Miss Sinclair and the equally beautiful Miss Chilvers. Would one of you ladies be kind enough to dance with me?'

'Absolutely not, Mr Worley. Go and bother someone else.' Harriet waved a dismissive hand and turned her back on him.

'Then I shall dance with Miss Sinclair.'

His clammy hand slithered across Barbara's shoulder and she stepped back. 'I don't want to dance with you either. Please go away before my boyfriend comes back.' She hoped this would be enough to deter him because the last thing she wanted was a repeat performance from Alex. He could get cashiered for fighting with the son of a Cabinet minister.

Worley leered at her and she realised he was very drunk. In her limited experience inebriated men tended to behave badly when provoked. She had to get rid of him before Alex came back or there was bound to be a scene.

'I won't take no for an answer. I'm quite determined to dance with the most beautiful woman in the room.' He lurched towards her for a second time and she quickly moved aside. To her astonishment he fell flat on his face, unconscious. An army officer immediately grabbed Worley's feet and Alex gripped the drunk under the shoulders. They staggered out of the ballroom to a spontaneous round of applause.

'I hope he won't freeze to death if they throw him outside,' Barbara said anxiously.

'He'll sober up quick enough in the cold. He's got a car; no doubt he'll take himself

78

home if he can't get back in.'

Less than ten minutes later Alex and the soldier returned, laughing and slapping each other on the back. 'Mission accomplished, Babs. We dumped him in his car and bolted the door when we came back in.' He collected the drinks he'd come back with and drew her to one side of the ballroom. 'Are you okay?'

'I am now you've removed Mr Worley.' She sniffed the glass suspiciously. 'What is this?'

'No idea, but Clarissa assured me it's perfectly harmless. There's going to be champagne at midnight, so we've got to hang on to our glasses. You won't say no to that, will you? It will probably be the last time anyone drinks it until the war's over.'

After two more dances someone turned on the radio so they could hear the chimes of Big Ben. Clarissa and her mother rushed round with champagne, someone stood ready to release the balloons, and the countdown to New Year 1940 began.

When the final chime rang out the room erupted. The balloons tumbled and everyone started kissing their neighbour. Barbara moved into the protection of Alex's arms; she couldn't bear the thought of being mauled by complete strangers. Several balloons bounced on their heads and Alex kicked them away. 'Happy New Year, Barbara, although I don't think it's going to be.' He sounded so fed up she tilted her head, stood on tiptoes, and kissed him. She should have realised how he would react but when his arms pulled her hard against his chest and his mouth crushed hers she was unprepared.

The noise from the other guests seemed to fade away; they could have been alone. Heat raced around her body and for the first time she welcomed his mouth. Her lips parted and he deepened the kiss. Then someone barged into them and Alex had to release her. She couldn't speak. Her heart was pounding. Things had changed between them.

'Come on, you two, canoodling's over. We're going to sing 'Auld Lang Syne',' a girl in a scarlet chiffon gown announced loudly. Barbara had never sung this before and was taken aback when Alex grabbed her left hand and the girl took the right, forcing her to cross her arms. There were too many people for one circle so another formed outside the one she was in.

'Alex, what's going on? I don't know any songs.'

'I don't think very many of us know all the words. It's a New Year's tradition. Just enjoy it, darling.'

No sooner had the raucous singing of an incomprehensible song finished, than some wag suggested a conger all over the house. Now this Barbara did know — the girls at her school had done it once. Alex pushed her into position behind the girl in the scarlet dress and he gripped her waist from behind.

The ensuing chaos was hilarious and she enjoyed every moment. When eventually her part of the line returned to the ballroom the band was already playing a slow number. Alex didn't need to ask permission. She turned into his arms willingly and spent a magical hour drifting about the dance floor being held by the man she was madly in love with. What a perfect way to start the New Year.

Eventually the band played the last number and the packed ballroom whistled and clapped. 'Come on, sweetheart, I'll take you back to your room. I'll pick up my coat on the way then you can wear it and I can keep my jacket on.'

The entrance hall was already bustling with like-minded guests collecting their belongings from the tables. 'I hope I can find my way this time. I don't want to be wandering about like a lost soul all night.'

With his coat over her shoulder she was lovely and warm, but it kept slipping off her shoulders. 'Let me do up some of the buttons. You'll break your neck if you tread on this.' His hands were hot and his touch sent shockwaves up her arms.

'I'm pretty sure it's down here, Alex. I must have turned right instead of left last time. Yes, this is it. Thank you for bringing me up.' She pushed open the door and he followed her in. 'Give me a minute and I'll take this off.'

'We need to talk, darling, before I go. What are we going to do about us?' He looked strangely uncertain as he spoke. 'I'm assuming that after tonight there is an *us*?'

She flopped down on the bed, still enveloped in his coat, and he sat on the dressing table stool. 'Of course there is, but it's not going to be as easy as all that. I can write to John and break off the engagement, but your parents are not going to be very impressed with either of us. As far as they know my engagement to John was a genuine one and I'm now being unfaithful to him.'

'They'll have to get used to it. It's nothing to do with them.'

'That's all very well for you to say, but they're my neighbours, and our brothers are best friends. I'm very fond of your parents and I don't want to upset them if we can avoid it.' He yawned loudly and smiled. Her heart flipped. He was irresistible when he looked at her like that.

'Okay, what do you suggest? I'm bloody well not going to pretend when I come home.

I love you and I'm not ashamed of that. Why can't we just tell them the truth about John?'

'How silly of me, of course that's what we'll do. But I don't want to tell anyone until I'm sure John knows — I've also got to write to his parents. Mr and Mrs Thorogood have been like family to me over the years.'

'Right, I'll not say anything to my parents until I get leave again. God knows how long it will take for a letter to reach Canada, but I don't expect the poor sod will reply. I know I wouldn't if you did the same thing to me.'

Hearing what she was about to do put so plainly punctured her happiness like a pin stabbed in one of the balloons. She scrabbled to undo the buttons of his coat and shrugged it off, then stood up and handed it to him. 'I'm sorry, I can't do this to John. I made him a promise. I won't break off the engagement until he comes back from Canada and I can tell him face to face. We mustn't see each other. Promise you won't say anything to anyone.' She blinked back tears, swallowed hard and continued. 'I really love you — I want to be with you for the rest of my life, so waiting a few months won't hurt either of us.'

'You're right, but it's going to be hard. I'm not going to come home until we can be together.' He reached out and brushed her cheek with the back of his hand, then without another word he flung his greatcoat over his shoulders and walked out of her life — but only temporarily, she hoped.

★   ★   ★

Alex closed the door quietly behind him and moved a few feet away before turning his face into the wall. He wanted to bang his head, smash his fist into the panelling — do something, anything, to stop the pain of possibly losing Barbara. He brushed his hand across his wet cheeks and pushed himself straight. She was right, of course she was, but it didn't make it any easier. God knew when Thorogood would return. He wasn't sure he could keep away from her until then.

Once the Huns attacked he might be killed; the life expectancy of a fighter pilot wasn't long. Already two of his squadron had died in stupid training exercises. He shoved his arms into his coat, rammed his cap on his head and ran down the stairs.

The hall tables were empty. Every coat had gone. His lift had gone without him. They must have thought, because his coat was missing, that he'd left with another bloke from the base. Bugger it! What the hell should he do now? He'd never find his way to the 'drome in the dark. He couldn't dither about down here; he'd have to go back to Barbara's room and kip on the floor in there. He could walk easily enough in the morning.

When he arrived on the top floor there was a light filtering from under the door of what was obviously a bathroom. Was Barbara in there, or was it someone else? He'd better not knock just in case he upset a complete stranger. A quiet tap on her door elicited no response; he opened the door and peered round. The room was empty, but she must have changed into her night things because her evening gown was draped over the dressing table mirror.

He left the door ajar and propped himself against the wall. It would be impolite to make himself comfortable before he'd spoken to her. He crossed his arms and his eyes flickered shut. He was proficient at sleeping on his feet.

★   ★   ★

There was no hot water, but that was hardly surprising at this time of night. Barbara washed her face and hands but decided against a strip wash. She cleaned her teeth and then shoved everything back in her toilet bag. The lino was so cold that even with slippers on she could feel it, and her flimsy

85

negligee set was no protection from the cold.

After switching off the bathroom light she scurried into her bedroom. There was no need to switch on the light as she knew where the bed was. She'd already positioned a wooden chair beside the door and it took only a moment to jam it under the doorknob. She was about to scramble into bed when she froze. There was somebody in the room with her — she could definitely hear breathing coming from the far side of the room. Should she scream? Could she find her way to the door and remove the barrier before she was pounced on?

She breathed slowly through her nose, hoping to steady her nerves. She sniffed again and her fear evaporated. The intruder was Alex and it sounded very much as if he was fast asleep. What on earth was he doing in here? 'Alex, wake up. You can't sleep standing up.'

'I can. In fact I was doing so quite happily until you woke me up.'

'I thought you were a rapist. Why didn't you knock on the bathroom door and tell me you were up here?' Her fear was now replaced by anger. 'I can't believe how stupid you are. I suppose your friends went without you and you didn't want to walk home in the dark.' Her comments were greeted by silence and she wondered if he'd gone to sleep again. Then he moved towards her and became entangled in the chair under the doorknob.

He crashed to the floor and his language made her ears burn. She drew her legs up on the bed while he thrashed around in the darkness. When he eventually recovered his breath and his temper she was laughing. 'What was I saying about stupid? Are you hurt or just making a fuss about nothing?'

'I'm okay, but the chair's had it. What in God's name was it doing there anyway?'

'I put it there to keep out unwanted visitors. It didn't really work, did it?'

The bed dipped as he joined her. 'Stable door comes to mind, sweetheart. Can I sleep on the floor? I'll go as soon as it's light. I can curl up in my greatcoat and you'll not even know I'm here.'

'You can sleep on top of the covers. If I scrunch up against the wall there'll be room for both of us.' She wriggled until she was sitting on the pillow and then slipped her legs under the blankets. She still couldn't see a thing; the blackouts also stopped moonlight from getting in.

'Are you sure? I've slept in worse places than this floor, and at least there's a rug of some sort on the boards.'

'It's so cold tonight I'll be grateful to have

you next to me.' He took off his shoes, jacket and tie and folded them up to make himself a pillow. If she kept her legs straight there would be plenty of room.

'Good night, darling. Thank you for letting me stay. I'll try not to snore too loudly.'

'I'm glad you're here. I'm going to be a lot warmer now.'

He settled down beside her and before she could say anything else, his breathing became regular. She relaxed and was drifting off to sleep when she remembered she'd forgotten to go when she'd been in the bathroom. Better not wait until she was desperate. Carefully she pushed back the covers and inched her way up the bed.

Alex was dead to the world, which was a good thing as she was going to have to climb over him in a very revealing nightdress. Even though she'd kept the robe on, neither of them left much to the imagination. He was lying with his back to her, his knees poking over the side of the bed. In order to get out she would have to straddle him. She prayed he wouldn't wake up.

She carefully placed one hand on either side of his head and then, with her weight on them, raised her bottom and lifted her left leg. As she was completing this delicate manoeuvre he decided to turn over. Her hands were swept out from under her and she landed on top of him.

His reaction was instinctive. He reached out to prevent her from falling and inadvertently clasped her naked bottom. The sensation of his hard, male hands on her most private area should have shocked her. Instead, a wave of exquisite pleasure made her forget her inhibitions and she pressed herself against him.

'Babs, don't do this to me. I want to make love to you and unless you move right now, that's what I'm going to do.'

She didn't answer with words, but put her arms round his neck and kissed him passionately.

5

Barbara rested her head against Alex's shoulder, loving the feeling of her bare skin against his. Making love with him had been wonderful — nothing like the lukewarm experience she'd had with John. She glowed all over and was rather hoping they would repeat the experience a third time before he had to dress.

'Darling, we have to talk before I go tomorrow. Do you have an alarm clock with you?'

'No, but I always wake early — years of having to get up and sort out Silver.'

He drew her closer so every inch of her hot, sticky naked body was touching his. Then he sighed, kissed the back of her neck tenderly and fell asleep. She still hadn't been to the bathroom but she wasn't going to move now she was so comfortable. Sleeping in his arms was going to be difficult as she was trapped facing forwards, his thighs underneath hers and her bottom resting in a very strange place.

She eventually dozed off, but slept fitfully, unable to relax completely whilst encircled by a naked man. When she wriggled free she wasn't sure what the time was, but she just had to go before she burst. She could hardly leave the room in her birthday suit but had no idea where her nightie had ended up and it was too dark to see.

'Are you looking for this, sweetheart?'

He must be holding out her negligee but she couldn't see him. 'I need to go to the bathroom right now. I'm going to put your coat on as I've just tripped over it.' Hastily she dragged it on and began to feel her way to the door. A searing pain shot through the sole of her left foot and she squealed.

'Sod it! Stand still, Babs. You've just trodden on the broken chair.' He was out of bed and groping for the light switch before she had time to answer. After the total darkness even the dim bulb made the room seem bright. 'Here, let me carry you. We don't want a puddle on the rug.'

After opening the door he picked her up and shouldered his way through. The corridor was quiet, the bathroom empty. 'I can manage, thank you. You'd better go and put something on; you can't lurk about in the corridor with no clothes on.'

His smile curled her toes. 'No point in getting dressed, I'll just have to take everything off again in a minute. I'll wait outside. Don't be long; it's bloody freezing.'

By the time she'd managed to extricate herself from his greatcoat she was almost too late. When she'd finished she looked down at her injured foot and was shocked to see blood all over the floor. After grabbing the sink to heave herself up, she hopped to the bath and stepped in.

'Alex, there's a lot of blood. I'm going to need a first-aid box and you can't go and get it like that.'

The door swung open and he came in fully clothed. 'Let me see. It might not be as bad as you think.'

She perched on the edge of the bath and he gently examined the injury. 'It's not deep; it won't need stitches. But we do need to stop the bleeding.'

'I've got a couple of clean hankies in my case. We could use those and you could tie them on with yours until we can get proper bandages.'

He turned on the tap and held her foot under the trickle of water. 'Stay where you are. I'm going to fetch what we need.'

'How on earth did you get dressed so quickly? Very impressive — apart from the fact your shirt is buttoned up all wrong.'

'Be grateful I'm decent. There's someone coming out to investigate the racket.' She clutched the coat closer and stared at him with horror. He was laughing as he went out; he had been teasing her.

But his words had been a warning. She wasn't going to be discovered dressed only in an RAF overcoat — her reputation would never recover. Ignoring his advice, she lifted her legs over the rim and hobbled into the corridor. She was almost at the door when he came out carrying the handkerchiefs.

'What the hell are you doing out here? Are you mad?' He dropped to his knees and quickly bound her injury, then tossed her over his shoulder like a sack of potatoes. He strode back into the bedroom, kicking the door shut noisily behind him. Someone was bound to come out after that.

'Put me down, Alex, and then go away whilst I get dressed.' All thought of resuming their lovemaking had gone. All she felt now was embarrassment and irritation.

He dumped her unceremoniously on the bed. 'It's a bit late to be shy, sweetheart, don't you think? I've seen everything and you're my girl now.'

There was something about his expression and the glint of possession in his eyes that made her lose her temper and do something extraordinary. With slow deliberation she removed his coat and tossed it into his face.

'Now you have everything, Alex. You can go. No doubt you can get breakfast at the base when you get back.'

She looked straight at him, her gaze unwavering, her shoulders back and his cheeks flushed. 'What happened last night was a mistake. I'd had too much to drink; you took advantage of the situation.' For a moment she thought he was going to argue, but then he looked away and without another word slung his coat over his arm and vanished.

Her shoulders slumped and she shivered. Her knees went weak and she flopped onto the bed. Her head felt heavy, her neck too slender to support it, but her eyes remained dry. She wasn't sorry she'd stood naked in front of him; she was proud she'd had the courage. She'd grown up today and from now on would try and behave like an adult. However hard it was, the right thing to do was keep him at a distance at least until she'd broken off her engagement with John. However much she loved Alex, it didn't feel right being with him at the moment.

Her foot throbbed a bit, but the makeshift bandage appeared to be working as no further blood had seeped through. She was dressed in her warm slacks and two jumpers in less than five minutes. It had been painful squeezing her foot into her brogue, but she'd persisted. She looked at the rumpled bed and felt ashamed. She had behaved so badly — betrayed John's trust and effectively lied to Alex. A decent girl wouldn't have slept with one man without being married, and she had slept with two in less than a week.

The sheets could go downstairs into the laundry room; it was doubtful anybody would ever know from which guestroom they came. She stripped the bed and carefully folded the blankets. Only then did she look at her watch. Only six o'clock — no one would be downstairs yet.

She carefully collected the broken pieces of chair and put them inside the sheets. If she tipped them onto a fire the evidence would be gone before anyone got up. Next she limped into the bathroom and, using one of her own towels, carefully cleaned away the evidence of her cut. She rolled the dirty towel and stuffed it in the corner of her case. She was ready and just hoped Alex had already gone.

In the cold light of day all their declarations of undying love seemed tawdry and a pathetic excuse for behaving badly. She was going to forget last night ever happened and try and get on with her life. It took far longer going down this morning than it had taken to come up last night.

The front door was unbolted. She carefully pushed the bars back. With luck, nobody would ever know Alex had stayed the night with her. She remembered the way to the kitchen and shivered as she went in; it was as cold as it had been yesterday.

Everywhere she looked the surfaces and tables were piled high with leftover food and dirty crockery. If she could get the range going it would be warmer and she could boil some water and start washing up. The splintered wood from the chair made perfect kindling and soon a welcome warmth filled the room.

When Mrs Williams and Clarissa came into the kitchen several hours later Barbara had almost finished clearing up. 'Good heavens, you shouldn't have been doing this on your own. How absolutely splendid!' Her hostess rushed forward and flung her arms around her. 'What an absolutely lovely girl you are. First you organise the supper and now you've washed everything up.'

Clarissa, more observant than her mother, pointed to Barbara's foot. 'What have you done? Have you sprained your ankle?'

'No, I just caught it on something sharp in the bedroom. It's fine, really. Now, I've put some meat pasties in the oven and the kettle's boiling, so we can have breakfast.'

'You sit down at once, Barbara my dear. We'll do everything else. My goodness, our guests are going to be spoiled this morning. Normally they have to do the washing-up before they get anything to eat.'

Sitting around a freshly scrubbed kitchen table munching hot pasties and drinking sweet tea was very enjoyable and almost made Barbara forget why she'd been up so early. When the rest of the house party drifted into the kitchen they were equally appreciative of her efforts. Harriet and Amanda finally put in an appearance at eleven o'clock.

'You must come and see us again very soon, Barbara, and I promise next time you won't have to work for your keep.' Mrs Williams kissed her fondly and Clarissa followed suit.

'I should love to come and see you again, but I don't know when that will be as nobody will have any petrol very soon.'

They were the last to leave and in some ways she was sad to go. She turned to wave as she got into the car but both of them had gone inside, probably because it was so cold. The temperature had dropped several degrees and the gravel crunched under the wheels as Amanda roared away.

'I had a really good time; thank you so much for including me in your invitation. I do hope I can go back again. I really liked Clarissa and her mother. I don't think I actually saw Mr Williams — was he there last night?'

Harriet swung round in her seat. 'He doesn't socialise; he was in the library playing cards all night. I think that's how they survive — he's a very good poker player.'

'I see. So having a big party is just a way of getting his victims inside the house. Anyway, I don't really care about him. I thought it was a perfectly splendid do. By the way, Harriet, you were going to tell me what happened to you and Amanda last night.'

'I was being interviewed by someone from the Foreign Office. I'm going to join the Intelligence Service. Very hush-hush! I shouldn't really be telling you. Because I'm fluent in French and German I'm going to be very useful to them, but I'm not sure exactly how. My parents think I'm going to train as a nurse at St Thomas' Hospital; I'm leaving at the end of the month.'

'How very brave of you. Both of you are going to do something really important for the war effort, and all I'm doing is knitting balaclavas and doing a first-aid course.'

'God, Barbara, you're only eighteen. Plenty of time for you to do your bit once things get going. You've had a rough time lately; Ma told me about Hastings — '

'Please, I don't want to talk about it. I can't imagine how your mother knows; it's a very private matter. I'm happy now and I've got my half-brothers with me; we're doing our best to forget.' Barbara sat back on the seat and deliberately closed her eyes.

Who could possibly have spread this gossip around the county? Having a lunatic mother and an abused childhood wasn't something she wanted discussed by anyone, and particularly not by strangers. Tom and David were starting at Brentwood School in a couple of days; she would be upset if the gossip followed them.

The boys were going to be adopted by her grandparents; although they had no blood relationship to them they were her half-brothers and Mr Evans, her stepfather, had abandoned them without a second thought. They would be known as Thomas and David Sinclair from now on, and their financial and emotional future was secure.

She gazed aimlessly out of the window, not really seeing the countryside flashing past. Once the boys were settled and the adoptions finalised, she would persuade her grandparents to allow her to join one of the women's services, or maybe she could go and train to be a nurse in London. She had her school certificate, and she seemed to have a natural aptitude for first aid.

The car screeched to a halt at the front of the house, jolting Barbara forward. 'Thank you so much for the lift. I don't suppose I'll see you again before you join up, so the best of luck.'

'You too, Barbara. Take care of yourself,' Harriet called and they were gone.

She decided to go straight to the stable yard and see how Silver had coped without her. Mrs Brown's son Joe was brilliant, but he couldn't ride so her mare didn't get any exercise. If she wanted to keep the horse then she must forget about joining the forces or becoming a nurse.

Her original intention had been to join the Land Army; she'd even got as far as sending off her application just after she'd arrived at the Grove. Fortunately they'd told her they weren't recruiting and to apply again in the New Year. She would definitely reapply in the spring and hope to be billeted at home with her brothers and grandparents.

'Babs, you're back at last. Come and see — we've got the puppies out with us today. Grandma thought they might like some fresh air,' her younger brother, David, shouted gleefully.

She hid her smile — far more likely her

grandmother had wanted some peace and quiet. 'Have you behaved yourselves? Did you stay up and hear Big Ben strike midnight?'

Tom scrambled to his feet and rushed over to throw his arms around her as if she'd been away for weeks and not one night. 'Yes and yes — we didn't go to bed until after that and we didn't get up until two hours ago.'

The two puppies yapped and tried to hang on to her slacks. 'I expect you'll be ready for bed early tonight. I know I will. I got up at dawn to do the washing-up, so I didn't get more than a few hours' sleep myself.'

'Why did you have to do it? Didn't they have a housekeeper?' Tom asked.

'No, they might live in a big house but they're not very well off and don't have any staff. I don't sleep very well away from home anyway, so I thought I'd make myself useful.' She went into the stable yard and Silver whickered a greeting. 'Hello, lovely girl. I'm going in to change and then I'll come out for you.'

She returned to the courtyard outside the back door where her brothers were playing. 'I'm going in to see Grandma and Grandpa — are you coming in or staying out here for a bit longer?'

They each scooped up a wriggling puppy and followed her in. The housekeeper greeted her with a friendly smile. 'Good morning, miss. Happy New Year to you. I expect you'd like a nice cup of tea. I'm just taking a tray in to the study; I'll pop another cup on for you.'

'Thank you, Mrs Brown, and the same to you. I didn't see Joe outside. If he comes in, could you ask him to tack up for me in half an hour?'

'He's doing the boiler for Doctor Sinclair. He'll be up in a minute and I'll tell him.'

The puppies were returned to their box, where they curled up contentedly with Lavender. Barbara could hear the cat purring as she and the boys made their way to the room they now used as the sitting room.

'Did you have a good time, my dear?' Grandpa asked as she walked in.

'I did. It was great fun. I really liked Clarissa Williams and her mother.' She kissed him and then joined her grandmother on the sofa. Tom and David sat on the carpet in front of the fire and resumed the game of snakes and ladders they'd obviously abandoned earlier. 'I don't really like saying happy New Year, as I can't really see it being one.'

'I know what you mean, but we do wish you a happy New Year, because having you and the boys here makes it very happy.

Talking about children, have you seen the news today, Barbara?'

'No, Grandma; has something awful happened?'

'It depends how you look at it, but it would seem thousands of evacuees went home for Christmas and are refusing to leave.'

Her grandfather folded his paper. 'Damn stupid, if you ask me. I know there's not been any bombing since the war started last September, but it's only a matter of time. I hope the parents have the sense to send them away again before it gets nasty in London.'

Mrs Brown came in with the tea tray, but Barbara didn't stay long because she wanted to ride before it got dark. Dusk was falling when she returned to the stable yard and she was relieved to find Joe waiting for her. 'Happy New Year, Joe. She's not hot, so she can go straight in. Thank you; I expect I'll see you later.'

The boy, like his mother, was almost part of the family; he ate with Tom and David in the kitchen. She hadn't eaten since breakfast. At this rate she'd be like a stick. She hoped there would be plenty for supper — as long as it wasn't meat pasties or bread and butter pudding, she'd be happy.

★ ★ ★

Rationing was introduced, and the queues at the shops got longer and more acrimonious. Barbara had persuaded her grandfather to buy a dozen chickens and these were now her concern. Joe wanted them to get a pig but so far this idea was being firmly resisted. They had a birthday tea for Grandpa's sixty-eighth birthday on January 7th and all the decorations came down.

Her brothers settled into their new school and after the first couple of days were quite happy to catch the bus from the village with the other boys. In the third week of January Grandpa rushed into the kitchen, where Barbara was helping Mrs Brown prepare vegetables for soup.

'Here we are, my dear. We didn't even have to go to court. Tom and David are now officially part of the family. Imagine, I now have a granddaughter and two sons.'

'That's wonderful, Grandpa. I can't believe it's happened so quickly. Does that make them my uncles now?'

'Silly, isn't it? Elspeth doesn't know yet; she's at one of her WI meetings. God knows what they find to talk about every week. I think this calls for a celebration supper, Mrs Brown. Can you rustle up something a bit special?'

'I reckon I can; there's still a few tins of

luxury items left over from Christmas. I'll have a rummage through those. I'm that delighted it's all gone through. My Joe will be pleased as well.'

'When you've finished in here, Barbara, there are one or two things we need to discuss. Can you join me in the study? I have to be at the hospital this afternoon but I've got this morning more or less to myself.'

Mrs Brown removed the knife from Barbara's hand. 'You go off, lovie. I can manage on my own.'

The house was quiet without the boys, but at least they were no longer at boarding school and came home every night. The puppies were banished to an empty loose box during the day, where Joe could keep an eye on them. They came back inside when Barbara's brothers returned.

The study still had a whiff of Christmas tree and Grandma would be complaining about pine needles for months. 'Is there something wrong, Grandpa?'

'You tell me, my dear. Rumour has it that you spent New Year's Eve with Alex Everton. Is that true?'

'I'm afraid it is. I didn't know he was going to be there, but he was a friendly face and we sort of gravitated together.'

This wasn't really the truth, but she'd no

intention of telling him exactly what had happened between. 'You know I find it difficult being in a large group of people. I'm just not used to it. Amanda and Harriet abandoned me and so I was relieved when Alex turned up. And yes, I did kiss him at midnight — that way I didn't have to be mauled by complete strangers.'

'I thought it must be something like that. You have to be careful; there's always someone at any event who knows someone who lives around here. Nothing remains a secret for long.'

'What happened wasn't a secret — I didn't mention it because he was just my date for the night. Actually I spent more time in the kitchen than I did with him.' She sat down and he handed her the adoption papers. When she'd read them she smiled and gave them back. 'We must sort out the financial side of things. They are your legal heirs now — I have my trust fund; I don't want anything else.'

'Understood, my dear. I was hoping you would say something like that. You do realise the boys are no longer your responsibility? From now on Elspeth and I will take care of them. Of course, we won't make any decisions without consulting you.'

'This couldn't come at a better time,

Grandpa. I'm going to reapply for the Land Army. I know the Evertons are looking for help and if I go there, I can stay at home and still be able to exercise Silver.'

'Excellent decision, Barbara. We were worried you would want to join one of the services now you are a free agent. Being a Land Girl will be bloody hard work, but at least you'll be safe.' For a moment he looked sombre. 'Well, as safe as any civilian is going to be once the damned bombing starts. It's only a matter of time before the Luftwaffe come.'

'Hopefully there won't be many bombs here — we don't have anything the Germans might want to destroy. There are factories in Chelmsford, and the RAF base at Hornchurch, but nothing in Ingatestone.'

'Very true, but remember the train line runs directly to London and those bastards will use that to guide them. If they get caught by our fighters then they might well drop their load here and scarper.'

'Anyway, I'm not going to worry about it now. Life is complicated enough with coupons, gas masks and the blackout to cope with.'

'Don't send in your papers until after your birthday; we want to make this year special for you. I know it's not your coming of age, but nineteen is grown up nowadays. Some bod was telling me the other night that you have to be nineteen to be a pilot. So obviously the War Office thinks it's a significant age.'

'I don't suppose waiting until after 10th March will make a lot of difference. Tom's birthday is next month, the 25th, and David's is in May; maybe I'll wait until after that. It's hard to believe my baby brothers will be eleven and nine this year.'

He chuckled. 'Let's hope I'm still around to see them grow up. Don't look so worried, my dear; I'm extremely fit and intend to remain on this earth until I'm a hundred years old.'

She hugged him. 'I'm glad to hear it. I've only just got to know you, and I want you around to meet any children I might eventually have.'

★　★　★

Alex stared morosely into his pint. He had too much time to think about Barbara; the sooner this bloody show got off the ground the better. He was fed up to the back teeth with training flights, drills and practice patrols. Some bloody fool had tried to shoot him down last week; the waiting gunners around London were also getting bored.

108

Already three weeks into 1940 and the country was waiting for the real war to start.

The New Year had started spectacularly well, but somehow it had all gone wrong. The image of Babs, tall and proud, breathtakingly beautiful and stark naked, was forever imprinted on his mind. How could she have said she loved him, spent several glorious hours making love with him, and then told him to get lost? He'd agreed to wait until she could tell this John chap she was breaking off the engagement, so what had he done to put her off?

Pete slumped down beside him. 'Have you heard? Dave Ellis is with Squadron Leader Leathart, getting permission to marry. His Sally's up the spout. They got a bit carried away Christmas Eve.'

Alex sent his beer flying, soaking himself and his friend. 'Sod me! Sorry about that, Pete, I've got to go. I'm owed some leave; I'm going to see the CO and arrange for a couple of days off.'

He could find his way to his MG blindfold — they always drank at the same pub and he always parked in the same place. How could he have been so stupid? Barbara could very well be pregnant — she was such an innocent she might not even have realised this could happen the first time. His mouth curved. Or the second, or the third.

The man on the gate waved him through without looking up from his paper. You'd never know there was a war on, the way everybody was behaving. He shot into his rooms and threw what he needed into his bag, then headed for the officers' mess. He was bound to find the adjutant somewhere in there.

Less than half an hour later he had his slip and was on his way to Ingatestone. He'd better go and see his parents first, tell them what he was going to do and explain about Barbara's false engagement. Whilst he'd been talking to Leathart he'd broached the subject of marriage and had got a favourable response. His CO liked his blokes to be settled; it kept them focused on the job in hand.

As he drove carefully down the treacherous lanes he rehearsed what he was going to say when he got to the Grove. He would speak to Dr Sinclair first, do it properly, and then ask Barbara to marry him. He wanted her to know he wasn't asking her because he had to, but because he loved her. Then if she wasn't pregnant, they could keep the engagement quiet until she was able to speak to John when he got back from Canada.

Was he ready to get married and be a father? Twenty-two was the same age his father had got married, but he hadn't been about to fight a war. Being a farmer like his sister Valerie's husband, he had been in a reserved occupation. He would be happier being a husband, but the start of a war wasn't the best time to bring a baby into the world.

The collies barked as he crunched across the yard and he yelled at them to shut up. The back door was never locked and he edged his way in, being careful not to let even the smallest sliver of light escape.

'Mum, Dad, it's me. I've got a spot of leave.' He chucked his greatcoat and cap on a chair in the passage. The kitchen door was flung open and his entire family rushed out. He hadn't seen them for several weeks, as he had been on duty over the holiday season, and they were overjoyed to see him.

'Alex, why didn't you give us a ring and let us know you were coming? Our Valerie was here yesterday. She came to tell us that we're going to be grandparents in the summer.' His mother hugged him and he swung her round.

'That's terrific news. It's bloody cold out here; shall we go inside where we can talk?' His younger brothers scampered around him, patting him on the back and laughing. 'I've got some news for you as well, but I'm not sure you'll think it's particularly good.'

Once they were all sitting down, he told

them everything apart from him having slept with Barbara. 'So you see, she's not really breaking a real engagement.'

'John is such a lovely man; it will break his heart losing Barbara. He told me he's loved her since she was a young girl. I knew you had feelings for her and that's why you didn't come home at Christmas. At least their engagement hasn't been announced any-where, so there shouldn't be too much gossip.' His mum patted him on the hand and smiled, but he could see she wasn't exactly thrilled by his announcement.

It remained to be seen whether he could persuade Dr and Mrs Sinclair that Barbara should break off her engagement to John and become his fiancée instead. He could imagine the furore if he left his proposal until after she discovered she was pregnant — that was if she was, of course. A shotgun wedding was something neither family would appreciate.

With any luck they would be safely engaged before anyone knew. Then they could be married and no one around here would be any the wiser; as there was no accommoda-tion for married officers they would have to rent a cottage somewhere. Just knowing Barbara was waiting when he got a few hours free might make things easier when the fighting started.

6

'Aren't you going to eat your scrambled egg, Babs? I'm still hungry — can I have it?' Tom stared hopefully at her plate and she pushed it across to him.

'I'm not very hungry this morning. I'm quite happy with a piece of toast. Are you and David seeing the Everton boys this weekend?'

David slurped his tea and his brother nudged him. 'Don't know. I expect we will. There are still dozens of things upstairs we haven't played with yet.'

'I've got to go into Brentwood for the final session of my first-aid training; Grandpa is giving me a lift when he goes to the hospital. I should be back by lunchtime.'

She left the boys to finish their breakfast and hurried to the boot room. She just had time to put on her coat and boots when her grandfather shouted he was ready to leave. 'I'm not sure it's a good idea leaving the boys unsupervised,' she said. 'Mrs Brown hasn't got time to keep an eye on them as well as do her work. I wish Grandma hadn't gone to her meeting.'

'They'll be fine, Barbara. They're sensible

boys. They've promised to stay indoors and not go out and bother Joe.'

She had to be content with that. Although the boys were no longer her responsibility, she would always be their big sister. As she was following her grandfather into the yard, where his Austin Seven awaited them, the distinctive roar of an MG sports car approached.

Why had Alex broken his word and come here? She didn't want to see him; she was doing her best to put him out of her mind. She had behaved disgracefully, and the fact that they were in love didn't make it any better.

'Sounds like young Everton's coming to visit. Were you expecting him?'

'No, Grandpa. I can't think why he's here. He can't be bringing the boys over; there's no room in his little car.'

The noise of the engine faded. She couldn't very well leave; Alex would see her sitting in the car. As she dithered, he strode through the arch. He skidded to a halt on seeing her and her grandfather and poised on the doorstep.

'I have to go, Barbara,' said her grandpa. 'Do you want me to make your excuses?'

'If you don't mind, Grandpa, I suppose I'll have to stay and see what Alex wants.'

114

To her surprise Alex didn't approach her, but waited by the Austin. She couldn't hear what he was saying, but her grandfather glanced at her a couple of times and then nodded. The two men shook hands and then Alex stood aside and waited whilst the car drove away. What on earth was going on?

'Alex, why are you here? I thought we agreed we wouldn't see each other again.'

For some reason he looked nervous. He was crushing his cap against his chest and he seemed to lack his usual confidence. 'I'm sorry, Babs, but we need to talk. Are you going to invite me in or do we have to talk out here in the freezing cold?'

'You'd better come in; we can go in the study. But I warn you, the fire isn't lit, so it'll be jolly cold.' Not a very welcoming speech, but his being here was unnerving. The past three weeks had been difficult, but she had managed to get through them.

She marched inside, leaving him to follow. She wanted to be angry but she was worried he had bad news for her — maybe his squadron was being moved elsewhere. She ought to be pleased, as this would make her life so much easier, but the idea of him being posted the other side of the country was dreadful.

Being in the inhospitable study reminded

her of the afternoon when John had proposed. They had been at his parents' farm, in the little-used front room. He'd looked so miserable when he thought she had been going to refuse that she'd changed her mind and accepted his offer. With hindsight she realised this hadn't been fair to either of them; in fact it had been the action of a child trying to keep everybody happy.

She stood in front of the window with her back to Alex, gazing out over the snow-filled park. Soon the grass was going to be ploughed up and potatoes and wheat planted for the war effort. Grandpa was determined to help in any way he could, and every acre of arable land was going to be needed. Already the German submarines were attacking the convoys of merchant ships and making life difficult for the seamen.

'I've spoken to Doctor Sinclair and my parents; now all I have to do is speak to you.' Alex was right behind her and her stomach lurched. For some reason he'd decided to propose to her. God knew why — she couldn't be engaged to two people at the same time. 'Please, turn around so I can see you.'

Reluctantly she faced him. She raised her hand. 'Don't say anything else; I don't want to hear it. I don't care what my grandfather and your parents said, I'm remaining engaged to John until I can speak to him in person.'

'For Christ's sake, why are you being so bloody difficult? You love me and I love you and I want to marry you. It won't make any difference to John *when* you tell him. If it was me, I'd rather know now and get over it, than come back expecting my fiancée to fall into my arms and then be told it was all over.'

His anger helped her. 'Don't use that language in front of me. It might be suitable on the base but it isn't here.'

'I'm sorry, but I'm finding this so difficult.' He ran his fingers through his hair and for a moment he looked completely defeated.

This time she wasn't going to let her emotions rule her head. Feeling sorry for him wasn't a good enough reason to break John's heart.

'Look, I'm going to be blunt. Have you considered the possibility that you might be pregnant?'

Her eyes widened and her head swam. She tried to speak but the words wouldn't come, and a strange whirring noise filled her head and her world went black.

* * *

Alex caught her as she crumpled and carried her to the Chesterfield. He wasn't sure if he should prop her up and push her head between her knees or just raise her legs. As he was deciding, her eyes opened and she stared at him blankly.

'Sweetheart, you fainted. I'm so sorry; I didn't mean to scare you like that.'

She pushed herself upright and swung her legs to the floor, making room for him to sit down next to her. 'It's not your fault. I've been feeling a bit peculiar the past few days, but it just hadn't occurred to me I might be pregnant.' She closed her eyes and leant back as if unable to continue.

Her face was thinner, her complexion paler than usual, but this didn't mean anything really. He wanted to put his arms around her, tell her it was going to be okay, but he wasn't sure if his actions would be welcomed or rejected. 'Do you want me to fetch a glass of water? Something to be sick in?'

She smiled and opened her eyes. 'Please don't even suggest such a thing. I'm prone to vomiting when I'm upset, and I must admit that lately I've been feeling rather queasy.'

'Are you late?' This seemed rather a personal question but in the circumstances he had no choice.

'I've no idea. No, really, my monthlies are rarely on time. I can have as much as six weeks between periods. I always know the day before, so don't worry about it until I get the signs.'

'Bloody hell! Most girls would know as soon as they missed one — don't you remember the last one you had? It must have been before Christmas.'

She frowned. 'You're right, I certainly haven't had one since then.'

'More than five weeks — what's the longest you've ever been?'

'This is a ridiculous conversation, Alex.' She stood up, swayed a bit and sat down again. 'I still feel a bit dizzy. I shouldn't have got up so quickly. I've been off my food this week and feeling light-headed occasionally. I'm pretty sure those are symptoms of a pregnancy. I'm also sure that until I've missed at least two periods a doctor can't confirm it.'

'In that case, shall we get married right away? Don't look at me like that; I haven't gone down on one knee. I love you. I've never been in love before and doubt I will be again. I thought you felt the same way, otherwise you wouldn't have slept with me, would you?'

Her cheeks flushed at the reminder and he wished he hadn't mentioned it. She was unlike the other girls he'd been around with; making love with him must have been against all her principles. She was the sort of girl who would have preferred to wait until she was married, but he'd spoiled that for her.

Should he risk taking her hands? 'Darling, look at me. If you tell me you don't love me then I'll go. Of course, if you do turn out to be having my child we'll have to get married, you do realise that?'

She looked up and her voice was barely audible. 'I've been so miserable these past few weeks. I do love you and I will marry you. I'll write to John tonight and break off the engagement. I should never have agreed to marry him in the first place.'

He scooped her up and put her on his lap and she didn't complain. In fact she snuggled in with a sigh and rested her head against his shoulder. This was the best moment of his life, even better than the day he got his wings. He had everything he wanted and couldn't be happier. This wonderful girl was going to marry him and might even be having his baby.

★　★　★

Barbara hid her face in his jacket. He mustn't see her crying. She loved him so much and wanted to be his wife more than anything, but if he ever discovered he wasn't the first man she'd slept with he'd never forgive her. Her stomach clenched. If she was pregnant it could just as easily be John's child as his. She gulped and looked around frantically for something to use as a basin.

Alex reacted with commendable speed; he tipped her on to the sofa and snatched up the aspidistra pot. Without a second thought he emptied the plant on the carpet and returned not a moment too soon. Several unpleasant and disgusting minutes later he removed it and handed her his handkerchief.

'I suppose I'd better get used to that, sweetheart. I'll go and get rid of this and find a dustpan and brush to clear up the mess.'

'Soil is a lot better than sick.'

He grinned and headed for the door. 'You stay here, Babs; you still look a bit peaky. I'll get you some weak tea — I seem to remember when my mum was expecting, that was all she could keep down.'

This was all such a muddle. Whatever happened, whether she was pregnant or not, one thing she was sure of was that she loved Alex and wanted to spend the rest of her life with him. There was no point in panicking over the parentage of a baby she wasn't even sure she was having.

Although Alex had conker-coloured hair and green eyes, and John had fair hair and blue eyes, the fact that she had brown hair and green eyes should make things work out.

She didn't know a lot about genetics, but was fairly sure whatever hair colour a baby might have would fit in with what was expected.

Even if they couldn't get married right away, it wouldn't matter. Everyone knew she and Alex had been together on New Year's Eve and would just assume they had pre-empted their wedding night by a few weeks. If Alex hadn't come today and then she'd discovered she was pregnant, she would never have known if his proposal was because he loved her or because he had to marry her. What a wonderful man he was to have asked her today.

He returned with two mugs of tea, looking remarkably happy considering what he'd just been doing. 'I've brought a basin, just in case. Now, we have a lot to talk about before your grandparents get back. Do you think they will insist on a church wedding? I'd be quite happy with registry office and I think the waiting time is less.'

'They might think it's a bit odd if we don't get married in church — but I don't really mind as long as we do it as soon as possible. I've already got something really pretty to wear, and you have your uniform, so that's one problem solved.'

'If we stress the point that we don't want to use up precious rations, that we want to keep everything small, they should be okay with that. We could have a reception here. If we just have your family and mine as guests it should be easy enough to arrange at short notice.'

He made everything seem so simple, but the more she thought about it the more doubts she had. 'I'm not sure this is really sensible. We hardly know each other, do we? We've never actually been out on a date and yet we're talking about getting married and spending the rest of our lives together.' She sipped her tea, hoping it wouldn't make an unexpected and unwelcome return. 'Don't you think it would be better to wait and see if I'm actually pregnant before we do this?'

'No, I don't. We mightn't have been on any dates, but we've spent quite a lot of time together.' His eyes blazed. 'If we hadn't slept together I wouldn't be so certain you're the one for me. Also, I took advantage of you and as an officer and a gentleman, I insist you let me put things right.'

'You sound like something out of a Jane Austen novel. Things are different nowadays. I'm quite sure lots of girls go all the way and don't expect their partner to marry them.' His shocked expression made her laugh. 'So if it's fine for a man to do what he likes, why is it different for a girl?'

'Where did you get that claptrap from? I bet Amanda and Harriet have been filling your head with nonsense. As far as I'm concerned I wouldn't want to marry a girl like that. I know it's unfair, but that's how things are. A bloke wants to be the only man in his girl's life — I suppose things might change once this bloody war gets going, but at the moment there are two kinds of woman — one you have fun with, the other you marry.'

'After what we did the other night, I rather think I fall into the first category. Therefore — '

'I can see I'm going to have my work cut out keeping you in order when we're married, sweetheart. I'm not one of those men who think a woman is inferior, don't get me wrong, and we won't be able to fight this war without the help of you lot. But I'm old-fashioned, I suppose. I want to be your protector, your one and only lover. I promise I'll make you happy.'

She gave in. She'd done her best to dissuade him short of telling him her secret, so must accept and enjoy the moment. 'Then I won't say any more. I'll be a meek and subservient bride-to-be.'

'Fat chance of that. Now, we've got to sort out where we're going to be living once we're married. When I go back I'll try and find a cottage we can rent near the base. I won't be able to come home very often — but at the moment I get a few hours free most days.'

The thought of being stuck in a dingy rented cottage didn't fill her with joy. She would go out of her mind with boredom unless she had something to do.

'Good grief! There's something you don't know about me, Alex. I'm incredibly rich. I have a massive trust fund, so we don't have to move into a pokey little cottage; we can find somewhere decent to live. I'd be quite happy to take in evacuees, or have Land Girls or service women billeted with me. It would give me something useful to do whilst you're busy.'

'Bloody hell! I'm marrying an heiress — good show. I'll find something decent for us, but I think you can forget about evacuees; Hornchurch is too close to London.'

'I wonder if Mr and Mrs Williams would rent us their Dower House. I noticed it when I was there. They have stables as well, so I could bring Silver with me.'

'It's certainly a possibility, but if it's anything like Radcliffe Hall it'll be dilapidated and freezing cold.'

She wasn't going to be put off; the more she thought about it the more she believed this was the perfect answer. She would have Clarissa and Mrs Williams for company, and there would be plenty for her to do looking after her horse and helping in the garden.

'As soon as we've settled on a date, I'll ring Mrs Williams and ask her. We might have to do a bit of redecoration ourselves, but I'm sure we can manage. The attics here are full of unwanted furniture, curtains and so on. I bet your parents have got lots of things we could have as well.' She was warming to her theme. 'And the boys could come and stay with us in the holidays.'

He grabbed her hands and smiled at her in that particular way he had, the one that melted her insides. 'On second thoughts, I'd be happier if you were here, but it's too far to come if I've only got a couple of hours.'

'The way you drive, it doesn't take you more than five minutes even in the blackout. And if you don't have any petrol you can walk or borrow a bicycle. Anyway, I'm not going to stay here; I want to be closer, and it's only two miles to the base from Radcliffe Hall. I can ride over during the day; there's bound to be a paddock I can leave Silver in for a couple of hours. And don't forget I can cycle over, so I don't see any problem.'

'Right, I'll leave you to organise our accommodation and I'll go and see the vicar.

If he calls the banns this Sunday, we can be married by the middle of February. Are you quite sure about this, Babs?'

She had never been more certain of anything in her life. 'My only worry's that people will say we're too young to know our own minds. I'm so glad your parents understand about John.' Her eyes prickled. 'I've got to write to his parents as well; Uncle Bill and Auntie Irene will be almost as upset as John. I wish being happy ourselves wasn't going to make the people I love so miserable.'

He rubbed away her tears with his thumbs and kissed her gently. 'You were never going to marry him, so better to make things clear now than leave them all dangling, possibly for years.'

She hugged him and scrambled up from the sofa. 'My grandparents will be home for lunch. I want everything to be arranged by the time they get here. Do you have to see the vicar in person?'

'He's not famous for answering his phone, and I want to make sure he actually writes down the details. I need your date of birth and full name, as well as written permission from Doctor Sinclair, but I expect that can be given later.'

He left with the information he needed and she made the phone call to Radcliffe Hall.

Mrs Williams was delighted to rent the Dower House to them and promised to have the chimneys swept and start lighting fires in all the rooms so the house wouldn't be damp.

'Alex has two more days' leave, so we'll come tomorrow if that's all right, and bring as much of the furniture as we can manage. I expect there's someone in the village who has a van we can borrow for the day as long as we can put petrol in it.'

'It's all very exciting, Barbara. Clarissa said you and Alex were involved, but I didn't expect things to move so fast. You young people don't want to wait — but with Alex being a fighter pilot I suppose you don't know how much time he has. Oh dear — I really shouldn't have said that. I'm so sorry . . . '

'Please, Mrs Williams, you're quite right. The Germans could invade at any moment and nobody knows what's going to happen. We love each other, and under normal circumstances we would have waited for a year or so, but we don't know if we've got that long.'

'I think it's really romantic. Clarissa and I are going to love having you next door, and it will be wonderful to have a horse in the stables again.'

When she hung up Barbara was certain

128

she'd made the right decision. Now all she had to do was tell the boys and write to John and his parents. She wasn't looking forward to doing any of these. Tom and David were very fond of John and had been really excited when she'd got engaged to him.

Well, she couldn't tell them until they came back from school, so she'd better get on with her letters. Writing to Auntie Irene and Uncle Bill was going to be awful, as seeing the words on the page would make her feel like the worst kind of cheat; a heartless, cruel girl who didn't mind hurting other people.

It took her several attempts to get it right and when she finally did, her tears had made the ink run. She wasn't going to do it again; at least they would know how upset she'd been when she wrote it. She blotted the page, folded the paper and squashed it into the envelope. In the end she had found it easier to put more or less the same wording to John as she had to his parents.

She had explained why she had agreed to marry him in the first place and why this had been the wrong thing for both of them. Telling him she was marrying another man was much harder, but he had to know there was no chance for him to persuade her to change her mind. Thank God he was only training in Canada and not flying dangerous missions over Germany.

There were usually spare stamps in the desk but she couldn't find any. She would have to take John's letter to the post office, so she might as well leave posting the other one until tomorrow as well.

She glanced at her watch; Alex had been gone more than an hour and her grandparents were due back any moment. She'd better lay up in the breakfast room — as Alex was eating with them, Mrs Brown would expect the meal to be served in there and not in the kitchen.

'Alex Everton is staying for lunch, Mrs Brown, so I'll lay up for four.'

'I thought I heard his car earlier, but it sounded as if he was leaving not arriving.'

Barbara could hardly tell the housekeeper what was going on, not before the boys knew. 'He had a couple of errands to run for his mother, but he's definitely coming back. Then I'm going to see Mr and Mrs Everton. It seems ages since I was there.'

As she was putting out the cutlery and water glasses something else occurred to her. Joe Brown was employed to look after her horse; would Grandpa keep him on if Silver wasn't there? He could always come with them to Radcliffe Hall, but he was only fourteen and his mother probably wouldn't want him to leave home. Just another thing to worry about — and she hadn't even told her brothers yet. That was going to be nearly as difficult as writing the letters.

The distinctive, throaty roar of the MG approaching meant Alex was here. She abandoned the table and ran out into the yard to meet him.

For some reason he'd put the hood down and was wearing his flying goggles and scarf. He screeched to a halt, and with his usual gravel-spattering panache, vaulted over the door. He held out his arms and she threw herself in. His lips were cold and there were ice crystals in his hair, but she didn't care. When she was in his arms everything slotted into place; she was where she was meant to be.

'It's too bloody cold out here for this. You haven't got a coat on and you're wearing your slippers.'

'And you've been driving without the hood up. That's even sillier.'

'I'll tell you why when we get inside.' He kept his arm around her waist as they hurried indoors. Too late, she realised Mrs Brown could see them from the kitchen window. She didn't dare glance in that direction, as she didn't want to see the look of disapproval that was bound to be on the housekeeper's face.

'Shall we go into the study? Or can we go in the kitchen where it's warm?' he asked.

'Breakfast parlour — I'm in the middle of laying up and you can help me whilst you tell me what happened. There's a fire in there.'

He carefully hung his greatcoat on an empty peg before following her. 'Good, that's much better. I'm afraid I skidded the other night and a branch went through the hood. It's absolutely done for — no chance of repairing it, and I doubt I'll get a new one. I'll have to use it as it is, or try and buy another one. With the petrol rationing, I expect a lot of people will want to get rid of their car. At the moment pilots can still get petrol from the base.'

'As long as you weren't hurt, I don't much care about the car. You can ride a bicycle like everyone else if necessary. Now tell me what the vicar said.'

'It took me several attempts to make myself understood, but he got the gist in the end. I've booked the church for Valentine's Day — I thought that way I'd never forget our anniversary.' He grinned and she smiled back.

'That's just an excuse to only have to buy one bunch of flowers instead of two,' she said. 'I've spoken to Mrs Williams and everything's arranged; I said we'd go over tomorrow with as much furniture as we can. I've decided I'm going to bring Silver — there's no one here to ride her and I'll have plenty of time to take care of her myself.'

His smile slipped. He didn't look very impressed by her efficiency. 'You haven't thought this through, Barbara. How the hell are we going to move furniture and a horse when we don't have a van or a box?'

'I'm sure there's someone in the village who will be only too glad to help for an extra pound or two. I thought your father might take Silver in the trailer he uses for the cattle when they go to market. We could put all the bedding, hay and hard feed in with her. Come to think of it, don't you have an old lorry in your yard that we could use for the furniture?'

'I give up. You're quite determined to get everyone jumping about regardless of what they might have intended to do tomorrow.' He folded his arms across his chest and for a horrible moment she believed he was serious. Then he reached out and tumbled her into his arms and she forgot about table-laying, lorries and everything else.

'Well I never did! Whatever next!' Mrs Brown's startled exclamation brought Barbara back to the present with a jolt.

Her face was scarlet when she turned round. 'I'm sorry; this must be a shock to you. Alex and I are getting married on the 14th of February — we do have my grandparents' and his parents' approval. I'm afraid my engagement to John was never genuine on my side; I only agreed to it so he would go away happy. I never intended to marry him.'

Despite her explanation, the housekeeper remained stony-faced. 'It's none of my business, Miss Sinclair, I'm sure. I came in to tell you that Doctor and Mrs Sinclair have just arrived and I'll be serving lunch right away.' She stomped out, bristling with righteous indignation.

'Oh dear, she's very cross. I do hope she comes round as we're going to need her to organise the wedding breakfast.'

He dropped a light kiss on top of her head and chuckled. 'That's the least of your worries, my love. I don't think I mentioned that your grandfather gave his permission for me to ask you to marry me, but I didn't tell him we intended to do it immediately.'

'Golly! You could have told me that before. What if he refuses to sign the form?'

'He won't. I'll just drop him a hint that you could be pregnant.'

'You'd better not — at least only if you absolutely have to. Here they come — I feel really sick.' She swallowed hastily. 'I'm going to the cloakroom. You tell them. It's your idea anyway.' She rushed from the room and reached the cloakroom just in time.

When she finished retching she rinsed her mouth and wiped her face. Was this her nervous stomach, or could she actually be pregnant and experiencing morning sickness?

7

Strangely enough, Barbara's grandparents embraced the idea of an immediate wedding. 'How exciting. We can certainly have the wedding breakfast here,' her grandmother said.

'I think it might be a good idea to have an open invitation to the church,' her grandpa added. 'A marriage is just what the village needs to take their minds off what's coming. Elspeth, I think we should consider inviting friends as well.'

Barbara exchanged a worried glance with Alex. The last thing either of them wanted was a big wedding. 'We don't want to make a fuss, Grandpa. After all, I only got officially engaged to John a month ago.'

'Only immediate family know that, Barbara. As far as everyone else is concerned, this is a normal engagement and marriage. We would really like to give you a good send-off; we've not had one here before.' He was remembering about her parents and the fact that their marriage and her birth had been kept secret from them.

'You're right, Grandpa. If Alex doesn't

mind having a bigger do, then I'm happy for you to do whatever you want.'

'My mum and dad will be delighted if they can invite more than just my sister and her husband. I warn you, Mrs Sinclair, I have dozens of relatives all within driving distance.'

Seeing her grandmother so excited at the thought of organising a proper celebration made Barbara pleased that she and Alex had agreed. 'I've got a very pretty two-piece I can wear and all the accessories to go with it, so we don't have to worry about buying anything new.'

'I think we can do better than that, my dear. If you'll excuse us, gentlemen, Barbara and I have important things to do. Don't leave, Alex — you and Edward can start finding the furniture you want to take with you tomorrow.'

She led Barbara up the back stairs and into the bedroom she now shared with Grandpa. 'I have something in my dressing room that you might prefer to wear. It's entirely up to you, my dear, but the offer is there. Wait here whilst I get it.' She vanished into the enormous walk-in closet that was now designated a dressing room. Moments later she reappeared with what could only be a wedding dress over her arm. Barbara braced herself — if the dress fitted, she would wear it even if she hated it.

'What do you think, my dear? It's a trifle old-fashioned, but only worn once — one could say it is almost new.' Her grandmother smiled brightly and held up the gown. 'It's ivory satin, and I have the veil, gloves and shoes to match somewhere at the back of the cupboard.'

'I love it — it's absolutely beautiful.' She stepped forward to examine the gown more closely. It had a close-fitting bodice, and the skirt was floor-length and cut on the bias. The frock had a high neckline and long fitted sleeves, and a swirl of tiny pearls ran from the left shoulder around the dress and completely encircled the hem. 'I hope I can get into it; it looks really tiny.'

'No time like the present, my dear. I'll close the door so Alex won't see you in it. We are of similar build, I think, and almost the same height. I do believe this dress could have been made for you.'

Her grandma was right; it fitted perfectly. She gazed at herself in the long mirror. 'Are you quite sure you don't mind me wearing it? You've kept it all these years — '

'I always wanted a daughter and then, like a miracle, you came into our lives last September. I know I didn't make you as welcome as I should have done, but I want you to know that I love you dearly and you have made us both feel young again. Having your darling boys here as part of the family is unbelievably wonderful.'

Without a second thought, Barbara hugged her grandmother. 'I love you and Grandpa so much, and I don't know why I'm even thinking about leaving you so soon.'

'You've fallen in love with a handsome young man; of course you want to be with him. Nobody knows what's going to happen in the next few months. Now, let's see you in the whole ensemble.'

Even the shoes would work; they would need a little padding in the toes, but better too big than too small. There was an exquisite cream silk bouquet with tiny seed pearls sewn to the rose petals.

As she was removing the dress, Alex and Grandpa walked by on their way to the attics. 'Are you going to come up and help us find furniture for the Dower House?' asked the latter.

'Of course,' her grandma replied. 'Barbara, you get dressed and I'll put this away. I can probably discover things up there that Edward doesn't even know exist.' She called out, 'Have you any idea if there's any furniture at all in the house?'

'Mrs Williams said there are bits and

pieces, but whatever we take will make it more comfortable.'

An hour later there was a satisfactory collection of items. The three comfortable, if a bit tatty, armchairs were the best find. 'We have a table and four chairs, curtains and blackouts for half a dozen windows, book-cases, and a complete dinner service,' said Barbara. 'Thank you so much. It's like a treasure trove up here.'

'There's plenty of spare linen and bedding you can take as well.' Grandma had cobwebs in her immaculate grey chignon and Grandpa had a large hole in the knee of his tweed trousers, but neither of them were the least bit bothered.

'The boys will be home from school in a minute, I'm rather dreading telling them. They've had so much upheaval in their lives these past few months; I'm not sure how they'll react to my leaving.'

'They can come and see you whenever they want and I'm assuming you will come here frequently, my dear.' Grandpa sounded rather unsure about this.

'Of course I will; Alex isn't a free agent so when he's busy I can cycle over. Although I'm not sure I'd be able to negotiate the ice at the moment.'

'Remember, my dear, the Grove will always

be your home whether you're married or not.'

'Thank you, that's good to know. It's the first real home I've had. I think I can hear the boys downstairs, I better go and tell them my news before Mrs Brown does it for me.'

The puppies were yelping in excitement and Tom and David were larking about with them. She looked round expecting to see Alex behind her, but she was alone in the corridor. Better get it over with. Everyone else had understood, but would her brothers feel the same?

'Hello, boys. Did you have a good day at school? Have you got tons of homework?'

David scrambled up and rushed over to fling his arms around her. 'The lunch was absolutely beastly! It reminded me of the horrible stuff we had at boarding school. I hope there's something scrummy for tea.'

Mrs Brown sniffed audibly at the far end of the kitchen. This wasn't going to be easy, and especially not in front of a disapproving housekeeper. 'Are you going to change out of your uniform before supper?'

'No point, really. We can't go outside because it'll be dark soon and we don't get mucky indoors,' Tom answered.

'I've got something very important to explain to you. Why don't you sit down at the table and drink your milk whilst I tell you about it.' They did as Barbara suggested and Mrs Brown plonked a plate of home-made biscuits in front of them. She must think the boys were going to need cheering up, because biscuits were only for high days and holidays.

Barbara explained about John first and then told them she was engaged to Alex and they were going to get married on Valentine's Day. David was the first to break the silence.

'I don't want you to move away from here. You belong with us, not him.' His lip quivered and he hung his head.

'I'm not going very far, darling. You can come and stay with us one weekend and I'll come back the next time. You'll hardly know I'm not here, especially in term time.'

Tom squeezed his brother's shoulder. 'We're Sinclairs now. We belong here, and Babs isn't going a long way. I reckon we could cycle over in the summer. That would be an adventure, wouldn't it, David?'

'I think that's a splendid idea, Tom, and maybe Alex will let you go and look at the Spitfires on the base.'

This did the trick and David sat up and smiled. 'Do you think so? The other boys would be ever so jealous if we could get a souvenir to show them.'

'I think I could arrange for a photograph of

you both sitting in the cockpit,' Alex said from the door.

Both boys forgot about their reservations; the thought of being able to sit in a Spitfire more than made up for the loss of their big sister. Barbara left Alex with the boys and went in search of her grandparents.

They were in the library, sitting contentedly together on the Chesterfield as if waiting for her to come and speak to them. Grandpa gestured towards a comfortable chair on the far side of the apple-log fire.

'We were expecting you, my dear. There are a few things we need to talk about.' Her heart sunk. 'Don't look so worried. We haven't changed our minds about giving our permission.'

Barbara curled up in the chair. 'The boys are absolutely fine with everything. Alex has offered to let them sit in his Spitfire. Having me living here can't possibly compete with something as exciting as that.'

He chuckled and Grandma joined in. 'Children are resilient,' said the latter. 'I've told you that before, my dear. They are happy here and know you'll always love them and that they can see you whenever they want.'

'I told them that, Grandma, and they suggested they cycle over in the summer. It's probably too far for them, but I didn't want to put them off.'

Grandpa leaned forward. 'Did you and Alex sleep together on New Year's Eve?' Barbara was temporarily speechless. 'I heard you vomiting and Elspeth and I guessed you think that you might be pregnant.'

Barbara found her voice. 'I'm so sorry; you did warn me that alcohol makes you behave badly. Alex had the same idea and decided to propose to me before we actually knew. That way we aren't getting married because we have to, but because we love each other.'

'Would you have accepted his proposal if you hadn't slept together?'

She nodded. 'Definitely. I've been in love with him for ages, but thought it was hopeless because of John. I realise now I was very wrong to pretend I loved him just to keep him happy. Even if Alex and I hadn't got together, I was still going to write to John and break off the engagement.'

Her grandparents exchanged glances. 'Excellent, that's the answer we wanted,' said grandpa. 'As you know, we were never happy about you stringing that poor young man along, however noble your motives. Although we would both prefer to have kept you here much longer, in the circumstances I think you've made the right decision.'

'Do you mind if I go with Alex and speak to his parents? We'll be back in time for supper.'

'Good idea, Barbara. If you're going to move all that furniture, Mr Everton will need to help. How long has Alex got before he has to report to base?'

'Until Sunday. That gives us tomorrow and Saturday. I'm hoping everyone will come over to the Dower House and help us get organised.' She looked hopefully at her grandmother. 'Unless you have too much to do sending out invitations and organising everything for the wedding?'

'I'm going to ring Mrs Everton; I'll invite the family over for potluck supper tonight. Then we can sort out the details together and decide who is going to do what.'

The phone was in the library and Barbara was able to listen to the one-sided conversation. From what she was able to gather, Mr and Mrs Everton and Alex's younger brothers were happy to come.

'Mr Everton and the boys are just going to change and are then coming straight over. I think Tom and David had better run upstairs and take off their school uniforms.'

'I'd better try and make my peace with Mrs Brown. By the way, Grandpa, will you still keep Joe on if I take Silver with me?'

'Absolutely. He's a good lad, and very hard-working. In fact, he'll be far more use working in the garden growing vegetables than taking care of your little mare.'

Everything was working out so well. If the Evertons were also happy with their plans, they had nothing to worry about. Barbara went to find Alex and told him she'd written both letters and they could be posted first thing in morning.

★ ★ ★

Mr Everton was only too happy to lend them the van; he was also going to use the cattle truck to help transport their furniture. All four boys had volunteered to help, and the next morning even Mrs Brown joined in the excitement.

'I can't say I'm not a bit shocked, miss, but now I know what's what, so to speak, I understand. I've always had a soft spot for young Alex Everton myself. He'll make you an excellent husband once he settles down.'

'I'm glad you're not cross with us anymore. With Joe helping as well, we're going to get everything moved today. That means Alex and I have tomorrow to try and sort things out before he goes back to base. We still have two weeks before the wedding, so hopefully I can go over a couple of times on my own and do some cleaning and things.'

The front door had been opened today especially for the removal of the furniture; Grandpa had decided that bringing the things down the narrow back stairs would be too difficult. The shouting and banging from the upper landing meant more things were descending. Alex and his father staggered into view at either end of a chest of drawers. Barbara's brothers were carrying one of the larger drawers between them, and Alex's brothers had a smaller one each.

'I can't believe how much stuff we've got, Alex. Both the trailer and the van are almost full. I've no idea how you're going to get this in.'

'We'll manage somehow; this is the last thing. Your grandparents are waiting in the car for you and the boys. Dad will bring Ned and Jim, and Joe's coming in the van with me.'

With much puffing and swearing, the final item was shoved into the trailer and they were ready to leave. Even Barbara's grandmother had dressed in her oldest clothes, although she still managed to look stylish. 'It's going to be a bit of a squash in the back, boys, but it's not very far,' Barbara told her brothers.

'We don't mind, Babs. It's good fun

helping you and Alex. Do you think we might get a squizz at his Spitfire today?' Tom asked eagerly.

Her grandfather answered from the front as they pulled away, 'I doubt it, young man. You'll be too busy sorting out the house. However, I think I could probably drive past the base on the way home and you might be able to see some of the fighter planes then.'

'Smashing! Thanks, Grandpa. Me and David are going to keep an eye on the landmarks so we know the way when we cycle next summer.'

Driving with her grandparents took longer than when she'd travelled the same route with Amanda at the wheel. The car turned into the weed-infested drive of Radcliffe Hall twenty minutes later.

'It's about twelve miles from door to door, maybe a bit far for you two to cycle,' Grandpa said.

'It wouldn't take us more than an hour, especially when the road's dry,' Tom replied.

'Anyway, boys, we don't have to worry about it until next summer,' Barbara said. 'I tell you what — Alex and I will cycle over as soon as the weather improves, then we can see how long it takes us.' They were satisfied with her suggestion and piled out of the car, eager to see where she was going to be living.

There was a short path branching off from the main drive that led to the front of the Dower House. It would be quite a long walk up the garden path to the front door, so the furniture would probably have to be taken in through the back. Also, Barbara couldn't see where the van and the cattle truck could park in order to unload the furniture. Then Clarissa and her mother appeared at the front gate.

'There's a little lane that runs around to the back. Vehicles have to drive to the turning circle and then turn left,' Mrs Williams called out.

Barbara scrambled out of the car, followed by her brothers. 'Thanks, I'll get Tom and David to direct the traffic. Alex and his father aren't far behind.'

'We'll find it, Babs. You don't need to come,' Tom insisted, and she was happy to agree. She couldn't wait to see inside what was likely to be her home for the next year or so.

Clarissa was genuinely delighted to see her, but it was hard to tell with Mrs Williams as she was so vague. 'It's going to be lovely having you almost next door, Barbara,' said the former. 'Most of my friends have joined one of the services or gone off to train to be a nurse, but as I have a weak heart nobody will take me.'

That explained why she looked so pale and interesting. 'I'm sorry to hear that. I hope you haven't been doing anything too strenuous on our behalf.'

'No, Ma won't let me. I bet you're dying to have a look round. Come in and I'll show you where everything is.'

From the front door they stepped into a reasonable entrance hall. The tiles were a bit dingy and some were cracked, but they should clean up okay. Barbara turned to Mrs Williams. 'Was your husband happy with the rent we agreed on? I thought maybe we should be paying a bit more, as I'm going to be using the stable as well.'

'Oh no, he thinks your offer's more than generous. I can't tell you what a difference it will make to us, having a regular income. We tend to live precariously here, staggering from one financial disaster to another. I think I can hear your furniture arriving. I'll wait in the yard whilst you and Clarissa have a look round.'

The house was double-fronted with a substantial drawing room on the right of the front door and a dining room and study on the left. All three rooms were a bit damp and musty-smelling, but reasonably warm as there

150

were fires burning everywhere.

'I'm afraid there's very little furniture, and the kitchen's a disgrace, quite as bad as ours,' said Mrs Williams. 'I hope you can afford to have it modernised.'

Barbara was about to say she thought it the landlord's duty to do this, but instead she smiled and nodded. 'Fortunately I have a generous trust fund. I'm going to enjoy redecorating and updating this lovely old house. I hope I'll be living here for some time.'

'What if Alex and his squadron are relocated? Won't you want to go with him?'

'We'll worry about that when the time comes, but once this war really gets under way I expect Alex will be too busy to worry about me. I intend to make this my home and will probably stay here even if he's posted elsewhere. Anyway, we'll need somewhere to live when the war's over, and this is in an ideal position.'

'If you don't mind, Barbara, I won't come upstairs with you. I'll wait here and direct Alex and the others to the correct rooms.'

Upstairs there was a galleried landing with a pretty oriel window which faced south and overlooked the sadly neglected park. This would be ideal for sitting and reading. Barbara shivered as her breath condensed in a cloud in front of her face. They would need to light fires up here before they moved in. She was delighted to see a paddock which would be ideal for her mare.

There were four bedrooms of reasonable size but only one bathroom. When Barbara turned on the tap over the washbasin no water came out. Never mind, plenty of people managed without indoor plumbing. So far all the windows were intact, and there were no obvious signs of damp on the ceiling or walls.

Alex shouted up the stairs and she ran to the gallery and leaned over. 'I'm up here! I haven't decided which bedroom we're going to use. Can you come up and look?'

'Not now. Come down and tell us where to put everything. Clarissa and her mother have vanished and we've no idea which room is which.'

Two hours later the place was looking more like a home. Barbara's grandmother had amazed her by putting on an apron and tackling the kitchen. The incredibly ancient range was barely alight, but the sink and draining board were now spotless and the French dresser had been neatly dressed with waxed paper frills along each shelf.

'My dear, this kitchen is impossible. We must get someone in immediately to remove that old monstrosity, replace the dresser and sort out the plumbing.' She pointed to the dresser. 'It's perfectly clean and usable, but I'm sure it's riddled with woodworm.'

'It is rather dreadful, but I expect I'll manage if I have to. I shouldn't think it will be very easy to find a new cooker or a plumber.'

Joe backed into the room holding one end of a scrubbed pine table, with Ned and Jim staggering along with the other. Barbara rushed over and guided them to the centre of the room. 'There, this is absolutely perfect. All we need are the chairs and we can sit down and have a cup of tea.' She laughed. 'That's if we can get the kettle to boil. That range doesn't seem to be working too well.'

Eventually the vehicles were unloaded, the laden picnic box brought into the kitchen, and everybody was sitting around the table enjoying a welcome lunch. Somehow the recalcitrant range had been persuaded to not only heat up a kettle, but also to warm the pasties and the soup.

'That was splendid, Elspeth — exactly what we needed on a cold day after such hard work. I'm afraid I've got to get back; I have a surgery this afternoon. Are you coming with me, my dear, or staying here to help put up curtains and things?'

'I shall come with you. There's still a lot to

do if we're going to make the wedding really special.'

Mr Everton wiped his mouth on his napkin and stood up as well. 'Right, I must be going too. You want me to take the boys back, Alex?'

'They can stay and help if they want. There's plenty to do and they can travel in the back of the van. It will be a bit uncomfortable, but there are plenty of clean sacks to sit on.'

Jim, as the oldest, answered for them. 'We can have an explore when we've finished, Dad, and Alex said he might be able to show us the airfield before we come home.'

Barbara and Alex waved goodbye from the front gate. Their brothers had been given the job of putting books on bookshelves. 'We've got about another hour of decent light, Babs, and then we'll have to go if the boys are going to see anything at the base.'

'I'm going to stay here tonight. There's so much to do, and the place is reasonably warm now. Do you mind going back on your own with the boys?'

His eyes darkened and he kissed her, his lips cold and his cheek scratchy against her face. 'Do we have anything to eat here? I can cadge something from home.'

She hadn't been suggesting they spend the night together, but he'd just assumed this was why she wanted to stay. Why wasn't she excited by the prospect of making love with him again? They were going to be married in less than three weeks and were already lovers — so what was the problem?

'Actually, Alex, I don't think it would be a good idea for you to stay. Only my grandparents know we've already slept together; I'd like to keep up the pretence with your parents and Clarissa, if you don't mind.'

He frowned and for a moment looked like a stranger, then he grinned and everything was all right again. 'Sorry, shouldn't have suggested it. I'm not sure I'm happy with you being here on your own — '

'I'm going to have to spend most of my time by myself, so I might as well get used to it. I've never been alone overnight; I'm rather looking forward to it.'

When he drove off with the four boys happily sitting in the back of the van, she was beginning to regret her decision. There was no telephone, so she couldn't even speak to anyone if she got worried. They had managed to put up the blackout curtains in the kitchen, drawing room and main bedroom. The old-fashioned internal shutters had all been closed in the other rooms and she hoped that would do.

There wasn't enough fuel to keep all the fires burning, so she decided to eat in the kitchen and then go to bed early. The house was unpleasantly quiet, the dark oppressive, and she jumped at every small noise. She was certain the place was overrun with rodents and she prayed they were mice and not rats. What they needed was a big tomcat — she would ask Alex tomorrow if there was one on the farm they could have.

At least the house had electricity and indoor plumbing (if they could make it work), and the kitchen wasn't quite so bad now there was a pretty tablecloth, a few knick-knacks on the windowsill, and a dresser overflowing with china. She couldn't use either the downstairs lavatory or the one in the bathroom, and one thing they hadn't brought with them was a chamber pot. She didn't even have a suitable bucket.

Tom had shown her the privy; this had been for the use of the outside men and stable hands. She would have to use that before she went to bed. She sat at the table listening to the clock ticking and made a list of things she would try and buy in Brentwood before the wedding.

A radio was a must; the house was too quiet and listening to 'Music While You Work' or 'ITMA' would make her feel as though she had company. Mrs Brown had packed a large box with edible goodies; there were various jars of jam and chutney, a few bottles of plums, and a large container full of eggs in isinglass. The boys would have to look after the new chickens, which were supposed to be her responsibility.

After all the hard work moving furniture and cleaning, she was exhausted. Thank goodness Alex hadn't insisted on staying; she didn't have the energy for what he would have wanted. She couldn't have a good wash as there was no water upstairs, and a china jug and basin were something else they hadn't thought to bring.

Her torch was on the table; she always kept it in sight. She decided to turn all the lights out and rely on the wavering beam. The back door was in a tiled passageway that ran alongside the kitchen and scullery. She gave herself a few moments to allow her eyes to adjust to the darkness, made sure she had some toilet paper in her pocket, and was ready to brave the cold and dark.

There was a decent moon, so she didn't need a torch to see. She remembered where the privy was and was relieved to find it relatively clean. She hoped she wouldn't have to rely on this primitive lavatory. She smiled in the darkness and decided she wasn't going to empty the bucket under any circumstances.

She paused in the shadow of the stables to listen to the owls hooting and the occasional bark of a fox in the distance. Just as she was about to return she heard male voices. She switched off her torch. If they were poachers she didn't want them to know she was there.

They were coming towards the stables. Why should anyone want to visit here so late? Her heart pounded and a wave of unwelcome dizziness engulfed her. She dug her fingernails into her palm and winced at the pain, but it did the trick and her head cleared. The momentary distraction left her no time to hide.

8

'Who the devil are you? Why are you spying on us?' She couldn't see the face of the man who snarled these questions at her. He was well spoken, so obviously not a poacher.

'Barbara Sinclair. I'm renting the Dower House from Mr Williams and was forced out here in the middle of the night because the WC isn't working.' She was pleased her voice didn't reflect her terror.

The second shadowy figure vanished into the darkness and the man who'd spoken so rudely came closer. 'I beg your pardon, Miss Sinclair. I had no idea my wife had rented out this house. I'm Sydney Williams, and I apologise again if I scared you.' He didn't offer his hand and she wasn't particularly reassured by his apology. 'Mrs Williams had no right to install you here. I want you out tomorrow. Do I make myself clear?'

'As I have already paid six months' rent, I've no intention of moving. If you don't want me out here at night then I suggest you get my bathroom working.' She walked away and didn't feel safe until she'd locked the back door behind her.

There was something sinister about Mr Williams and his invisible friend. Surely all legitimate business was conducted during the day? Amanda had told her he was a gambler and lived on his wits. Was he also involved in something less savoury? She wished Alex had come back; she certainly wasn't going to stay here on her own again until they were married. The unpleasant incident brought back unwanted memories of the murder.

She left her rubber boots on the mat and headed upstairs. She didn't even bother to make herself a hot water bottle; she just wanted to be in the safety of her bed and pull the covers over her head. Why did she seem to attract violence? She had just agreed to marry a man she didn't really know — would he turn out to be violent too?

The next morning she pulled on yesterday's clothes and didn't even bother to clean her teeth or wash her face. She needed a cup of tea and for Alex to come back. She couldn't deal with this on her own. Fortunately she didn't feel sick, and despite her worry about being evicted at any moment, she was actually hungry.

The range had, by some miracle, remained alight overnight and all it needed was riddling and more coal. The water remained a trickle, but eventually she filled the kettle and put it on. She peered round the blackout. It was still grey outside and wouldn't be light for another hour.

She decided to light the oil lamp and put several candles in candlesticks around the room, as the single feeble bulb wasn't enough to dampen her anxiety. Once the room looked more cheerful her mood improved. There was half a Madeira cake in a tin and that would do for breakfast. While she waited for the kettle she examined the surfaces for the tell-tale droppings of mice or rats and was surprised not to find any. The cake was delicious and the tea just right. Her night-time fears seemed silly; nothing was ever quite as bad in the morning.

A sudden banging on the back door sent her plate spinning across the table, and the tea slopped onto the cloth. She couldn't move. Mr Williams had come back and she didn't know what to do. Maybe he thought she was still in bed. If she kept quiet perhaps he'd go away.

'Barbara, please let me in. It's Clarissa. I know you're up; I heard you in the kitchen when I walked past.'

'Hang on a minute, I'm just coming.' She was weak with relief. She didn't think she was up to a confrontation with Clarissa's nasty father.

She groped her way to the back door — no point in switching on the light, as she would have to turn it off again in order to let Clarissa in. Before opening the door she pulled on her coat and shoved her feet into her wellingtons.

'Go into the kitchen, Clarissa. It's lovely and warm in there. I'm just going across the yard — I won't be long.' She stepped around the girl and ran across the cobbles, glad they didn't seem to be ice-covered this morning.

In the daylight she could see a shiny new padlock hanging on one of the wooden doors of the tack room. She was sure it hadn't been there yesterday. Mr Williams was obviously storing something valuable, and probably illegal, and didn't want her to know what he'd hidden.

Mrs Williams had eagerly taken Barbara's bank cheque for the rent and had agreed that the use of the stables was included, but for some reason she hadn't discussed this with her husband. The whole enterprise now seemed in doubt, especially moving Silver.

'I'm going to lock the door behind me. I don't want unwelcome visitors,' Barbara called as she came in. She kicked off her boots and draped her coat on a peg. Why hadn't Clarissa answered? The girl was sitting slumped at the table, her face pale and her lips a strange grey-blue colour.

'Are you feeling ill? Do you want me to run over and fetch your mother?'

'I'll be all right in a minute,' Clarissa said, her voice so quiet it was almost inaudible. 'I've taken my tablets. I'd like a cup of tea, please.'

Barbara added two spoonfuls of her precious sugar and placed the mug in front of her visitor. 'Would you like a piece of cake? I've got plenty.'

Clarissa shook her head and with shaking hands clasped the hot tea and took a few hesitant sips. 'Thank you, I'm beginning to feel better now. The doctor has told me not to get agitated, but sometimes I just can't avoid it.'

Now Barbara was fairly sure Clarissa was going to be all right, she poured herself another mug and sat down on the opposite side of the table. They drank in silence for a few minutes. The only sound was the clock ticking on the French dresser and the ancient range burbling and crackling.

'I've come to apologise for last night. My father had no right to speak to you like that; Ma and I are in charge of the house. It's in her name, you know.'

'I did wonder why Mr Williams didn't know anything about me being here. My arrangement with your mother includes renting the stables — I can't bring my horse here if your father is using the stables to store something secret. He was very angry when he thought I was snooping.'

'He's always up to something, usually some dubious deal or other, but we're worried that this time he's involved in something really bad. Definitely illegal and possibly dangerous.'

'Well, he's certainly got something locked away in the stables that he didn't want me to see, and also whoever he had with him last night made very sure I didn't see his face.' She smiled encouragingly at Clarissa. After all, it wasn't her fault her father was up to no good. 'Did he tell you what he said? He seems to think he can have me evicted.'

'Yes, he was ranting and raving this morning, threatening all sorts if we didn't get you to leave.' She pushed herself upright and spoke with more authority. 'Ma made it perfectly clear where he stood. He is a guest in her house, and if he doesn't like the way things are then he's the one who's got to leave, not you.'

'What did he say to that?'

'He went very quiet, and then sort of apologised and said he wouldn't bother you again. Ma told him he had to move his stuff from the stables immediately and he stormed off. I don't think he'll come round here, but I should try and stay away from the stables for a bit.'

'Until I can get something done about the plumbing upstairs, I've got to use the privy outside. One thing I didn't think to bring was a chamber pot.'

'Doesn't the lavatory work? How awful! We should never have let you move in without getting those things fixed. One thing I can do is find you a couple of pots. I'm pretty sure there's an enamel bucket with a lid, and a jug and basin that you can use, until things are sorted out.'

Clarissa drained her mug and stood up, her complexion almost normal now. 'Your money's an absolute godsend, Barbara. Without it I don't think we could have stayed here much longer. We were both terrified you would want your cheque back and find somewhere else after the way Pa behaved last night.'

'As long as I'm not going to be bothered by him again, and don't have to go outside in the dark, I'm very happy to stay here. However, I think it's probably better not to tell Alex what happened. He might get a bit overprotective and make a fuss.'

'Thank you for being so understanding. Ma will be very pleased. I'll go and sort those things out. If you would like to come over later this morning you can collect them. I promise my father won't be around.'

'I think I'll wait until Alex and the boys arrive; they should be here by nine o'clock. We're going to clean windows and paintwork today. I'm hoping Alex has found a plumber and a chimney sweep — I'm sure the range would pull better if the chimney was swept.'

Clarissa stood up with difficulty; she still seemed a bit shaky. However, she wasn't so pale and her smile was certainly brighter. 'I'll get Ma to put the kettle on — I think we've even got some coffee left, and Pa brought home a box of Quality Street the other day. I bet your little brothers would enjoy a chocolate.'

Just before nine, Barbara heard the distinctive sound of the old van rattling up the drive. The Dower House had lost its magic; the pleasure of having her own home had been crushed by her unpleasant experience the previous night. She'd no intention of staying here on her own again until she was married. In fact, she was in two minds whether to tell Alex she'd changed her mind and wanted to remain at the Grove. However, Clarissa and her mother desperately needed the rent and she didn't have the heart to back out of the arrangement.

There was no point in Alex and the boys coming inside; she might as well meet them in the yard and take them straight over to the Hall. She grabbed her coat and pushed her feet into her boots and rushed out. Alex jumped out of the van and she threw herself into his arms. 'I'm so glad to see you; I didn't know how horrible it was going to be on my own in a strange house.'

He kissed her and she forgot her fears. He made everything safe for her; she was worrying unnecessarily. 'Hang on, darling; we've got to let the boys out. They've got a surprise for you.' He kept his arm around her waist and guided her round the back of the battered vehicle, then turned the handle and opened the doors.

'Goodness, what's all this? I thought we brought everything over yesterday.' She laughed as the four boys scrambled out over the pile of boxes and bits and pieces. 'Where on earth did you all sit?'

David reached her first and pressed his face into her side. 'I don't like it without you being there, Babs. I don't want you to get married and move to this old place.'

'Why don't you spend every weekend here?' she said. 'Grandpa and Grandma will have you during the week whilst you go to school.'

167

She looked across at Alex; she should really have asked him if he minded before making this offer. He smiled and nodded. What a lovely man he was; she was so lucky to have found him. Some girls might wait a lifetime to meet the love of their life. Tom beamed and David hugged her. 'Well, that's settled. Now, tell me what you've got in the van?'

'It's things from our house, Babs. Mum had a good look round yesterday and sent all this to make your home more comfortable.' Ned giggled and nudged his brother. 'There's two potties with flowers in the bottom — aren't there, Jim?'

'Just what we need. I can't wait to get it all inside. However, Clarissa has invited us to have coffee with her.' She grinned at the circle of boys. 'Actually, she was going to try and find a chamber pot as the lavatory doesn't work.'

Alex slammed the van doors. 'Right, you horrible lot, you must be on your best behaviour. There will be no messing about whilst we're visiting.' He looked sternly at each of them and they all nodded. 'Good, glad we understand each other. Babs, we can't stay too long; we've got a lot to unpack and I have to be back at the base before dark.'

There was an overgrown path down the side of the house that led to the main drive and Barbara decided to take this, as she didn't want Alex to see the stable door with its shiny new padlock. As they emerged from the shrubbery Mrs Williams arrived with a large box in her arms.

'I'm so glad I caught you, Barbara. I'm afraid Clarissa has had to go back to bed. I'm sure she's told you she has a weak heart so must be very careful.' She handed the box to Alex. 'I've put in the things I thought you might need. I'm so sorry you can't come over for coffee today — perhaps next time.' Without waiting for a reply, she was on her way back to the hall.

Tom stared after her, shaking his head. 'She's a very strange lady, Babs. Why is she wearing her nightie outside?'

'Shush, that's not a very nice thing to say. And that's not her nightie, it's a frock.'

David shoved his brother in the back. 'I knew that. Grandma has a floaty frock like that. But it's not warm enough for the winter, is it, Babs?'

'Mrs Williams always wears floaty frocks, boys, and I expect she's got warm underwear on so she won't be cold.'

'Actually I'm glad we're not going to waste any time over there, Babs,' said Alex. 'It's going to take us at least an hour to empty the van. Come on, you lot. If you want to make a detour past the base again you'd better work really hard this morning.'

Eventually all the bits and bobs were inside and they congregated in the kitchen for a much-needed cup of tea. 'If I cut the cake into really thin slices, I think there will be enough for all of us,' Barbara said as they sat down.

'Mum sent a hamper; I left it on the front seat. I'll go and get it. I'm sure she put in a cake of some sort.' Whilst Alex was out of the room, Barbara spoke seriously to the boys.

'It's not fair to expect Alex to keep taking you to the base. If you've been once, then that will have to do for now. Fighter planes are weapons of war; their pilots are brave young men who don't want to be disturbed by children gawping at them.'

'We know that. We're not daft. Mum said the same, but Alex said seeing us was good for morale.' Jim nodded and then he grinned. 'We don't know what that means, but I reckon the men enjoyed showing us round.'

'It means they were cheered up by your visit, so forget what I said. I haven't seen the base myself, so maybe I'll get to see a Spitfire close up as well.'

There was more than enough in the hamper for elevenses and lunch. Mrs Everton had made sure none of them went hungry.

Once Barbara and Alex had rolled out the rug in the drawing room, and the boys had put out the cushions and ornaments, the room began to look familiar.

'Thank goodness the house isn't very big, Alex. It's going to be difficult just keeping this room and the kitchen warm. The dining room can be used in the summer, but until then we can put all the things we don't want — packing cases and things — in there.'

He stood up and put his arms round her, dropping a light kiss on her head. 'You seem a bit quiet this morning, sweetheart. Have you gone off the idea of living here? You could always stay at the Grove. It would be a lot easier for you and the boys.'

She was about to agree and tell him her doubts about Mr Williams, but something stopped her. Although he'd made the offer, he was tense and she guessed he'd only said it for her sake. 'I love it here. It will be our first home, and so much easier for you to come and see me if you get an hour or two off.'

His hold tightened and he lifted her from the floor. 'Thank you, darling. I hoped you'd say that. The boys can come over at weekends, and you can go back to see Doctor and Mrs Sinclair as well. I know I have to share you with your family, but living here will mean I get you to myself more often.'

171

Now was not the time to remind him about petrol rationing. He was so excited and really believed she would be able to move between the Dower House and the Grove as the mood took her. He could get petrol from the base, but Grandpa didn't have enough to waste it gallivanting around the countryside unnecessarily. He needed what he had to get to the hospital and see his patients.

The boys had been given the task of polishing furniture and had done a remarkably good job. Alex had scrubbed the hall, and the black and white tiles sparkled. 'I'll go and get lunch ready. It's soup and sandwiches. Can you find the boys and get them to wash their hands? That reminds me, what are we going to do about the plumbing and chimneys?'

'I forgot to tell you — a couple of the chaps who look after my Spit said they knew a bit about plumbing, and I'm going to bring them over at the end of the week. Are you going to come over again before the wedding?'

'I'm going to be too busy. I'll ask Mrs Williams to light fires before we move in. It would be wonderful if the bathroom was working, but we can manage perfectly well as long as it's not me who has to empty buckets.'

'Sorry, sweetheart, I can't promise to be

here even for such a delightful job as that. I've offered the blokes a couple of quid each — if they get it working, I'll give them extra.'

'And the chimney sweep? Is there someone in the village who could do it for us?'

'I've not had a chance to ask. I'll do it tonight when I go down for a beer.'

'What a hard life you pilots have — indoor plumbing, lovely warm accommodation, and a trip to the pub every night.'

'I've got night training with the two new bods from tomorrow — I'll be lucky if I get to see 'my lovely warm accommodation'.'

An hour later they were ready to leave and Barbara thought she'd better go and see Mrs Williams. 'I won't be long. By the time the boys are settled and you've driven the van round to the front I'll be ready. I must find out how Clarissa is; she was very poorly this morning.'

She hurried to the back door; the family were more likely to be in the kitchen than in the front of the house at this time of the day. She banged loudly and a few moments later the door was flung open. She recoiled, lost her balance and fell backwards onto the cobbles.

Mr Williams was immediately at her side. 'Are you hurt, Miss Sinclair? I didn't mean to startle you.' He was a different man from the

173

one she'd seen last night. He was smiling, his narrow features etched with concern.

'I'm fine, thank you. Just my pride has been hurt.' When he offered his hand she took it and he pulled her to her feet. 'Mrs Williams told me you were out, so I didn't expect to see you.'

'And after the way I behaved last night, I'm not surprised you reacted the way you did. I really do apologise. I'd had far too much to drink and had quite forgotten you were staying.'

He was charming — no sign of the aggressive man who had frightened her. Maybe she'd misjudged him. 'Please don't worry about it, Mr Williams. I've forgotten about it already. I only called to see how Clarissa was and to tell you that Alex will be bringing over some plumbers, and hopefully a chimney sweep, later in the week.'

'I should have arranged for those things to be done myself, it's very good of you to organise this. And my daughter is feeling much better, thank you, but unfortunately she's not well enough for visitors. I'll tell her you called by.' He nodded and smiled again. 'If you're quite sure you aren't hurt, then if you'll excuse me I must get on.'

Alex decided there wasn't time to make a detour to the base, and Barbara was so busy talking about their forthcoming wedding she had no time to dwell on what Mr Williams had told her. It wasn't until she was getting ready for bed that the significance of what had been said finally registered. Clarissa had said quite clearly that her father hadn't known about the Dower House being rented out. She'd also said her father had been furious about moving whatever he was hiding in the stables.

Mr Williams wasn't above average height, had slicked-back dark hair and was of slim build. She shivered. He might be small, but there was something about him that wasn't quite right. She wished she'd told Alex about what happened — she should warn him to be careful if he was going to be there at night.

★   ★   ★

Alex didn't enjoy the drive back to base in his open-top car — he would have to try and get the hood fixed or he would get frostbite. He reported in, dumped his bag in his room and headed for the officers' mess. Although he'd told Babs he was going to the pub, he didn't fancy spending any more time in his MG.

He was greeted with raucous shouts from his fellow officers. 'Shut up, you lot, or you won't get an invite to the wedding.' Bloody hell! Why had he said that? Now he would have to include everyone in the bar or look like an idiot. 'It's not going to be a big do — the Sinclairs are very grand and won't appreciate your usual sodding about.' He glared at them and they settled down. Being so tall was a definite an advantage in these circumstances.

'We'll be on our best behaviour, Alex. We wouldn't dream of letting you down,' Pete said. As he was the best man, he was already invited.

'I don't suppose we'll get a pass anyway, so don't look so worried,' Bob added. 'But you can't get hitched without your squadron being well represented. By the way, Wing Co was looking for you — he said would you toddle along and see him when you got back?'

There was already a brimming pint waiting on the bar. Alex looked at it sadly. 'Goodbye. I don't suppose I'll see you again.' Before he reached the door one of his mates had pinched his beer.

Fortunately the Wing Commander had his office in the same building as the mess. He wandered into the outer office and nodded at the NCO fiddling with a pile of papers at the desk. 'I'm expected. Don't worry, I'll show myself in.' He was given a sloppy salute which he returned in the same way, and with a cursory knock on the door walked in.

His commanding officer was a tall, thin man in his fifties, a veteran of the Great War, but he was a formidable leader and stood no nonsense from anyone.

'Ah, there you are, Everton. Got some good news for you — you've been promoted to Flight Commander. Good show — you deserve it, old boy. Your batman has got the stripes and is already sewing them on your uniform. You want to look your best for your nuptials, old chap.'

'I hope you'll be able to come to my wedding, sir, I seem to have asked the rest of the squadron and they'll need someone to keep them in order.'

'I'll do my best; I like to support my boys when I can. My wife always enjoys a wedding.'

Alex retreated, thrilled he'd been promoted but horrified he'd more or less doubled the guest list without even consulting Mrs Sinclair. He would use the public telephone in the corridor. Perhaps Babs could break the news? God knew how many people would now be coming — he'd not thought about wives and girlfriends. It could be another thirty people. His heart was pounding, his hands clammy. He'd rather fly a sortie than make this phone call.

Mrs Sinclair picked up the phone herself. He took a deep breath and launched into his apology and explanation.

'How absolutely splendid! Edward won't like it, but I want my lovely girl to have a big send-off. I rather think I shall invite most of the village as well. I'm sure they will all be willing to contribute something towards the wedding breakfast. Do you wish to speak to Barbara? She's upstairs putting the boys to bed, but I can run up and fetch her if you would like me to.'

'No, thank you, Mrs Sinclair. I don't need to speak to her tonight. I just remembered, could you tell her I've been promoted to Flight Commander?' This news went down very well with his future grandmother-in-law.

He replaced the telephone receiver and couldn't stop grinning. What an amazing family he was marrying into. Nothing seemed to faze them. Not only was his future wife the most beautiful, intelligent, honest and kind girl he'd ever met, but she was also incredibly rich. He couldn't believe how lucky he was — she would still be engaged to that Thorogood bloke if he hadn't decided to go to the New Year's Eve party.

After a few beers he was ready for bed; there was a lot to do tomorrow if he was to get up to speed with his new role in the squadron. He wouldn't have any time to himself for a few days, but somehow he had to find a chimney sweep and get his two erstwhile plumbers to Radcliffe Hall.

9

Barbara escaped to the stables, glad to leave the endless discussion about her forthcoming wedding to her grandmother and her friends. She couldn't believe how something that had begun as a simple family event had now turned into a village affair. Alex had invited his entire squadron, and their wives and girlfriends, and Grandma had invited all her friends and anyone in the village who had even the remotest connection to the family.

Joe was grooming Silver and looked up with a smile. 'I'll be done in a jiffy, miss. You thinking of going out again this morning?'

'No, it's far too cold. I wanted to talk to you about what happens when I get married.'

'Mum says you're likely taking your little mare with you. Will you have anyone to help out?'

'Actually, I've decided not to move her right away — things are a bit tricky over there and I don't have use of the stables at the moment.'

'That's all right, then; I can lunge her every day now you've shown me how to do it.' He scratched his head, transferring several pieces of straw to his hair. 'I reckon I'll have plenty to do here when she does go. Your grandpa's thinking of ploughing up the park and planting wheat or some such thing. He'll need me to help with all that.'

'I'll leave you to it, Joe. I just heard another car arriving and I expect I'll be needed.'

She'd been sick again this morning and was almost certain she was pregnant. That being the case, she wouldn't be able to ride for much longer, so it would be better if Silver stayed where she was. The mare would be far more useful pulling a cart here than standing about in a stable at Radcliffe Hall.

Her prayers had definitely not been answered this time. How could she look forward to the birth of a baby when she didn't know who the father was? She walked away from the house towards the ornamental lake, hoping she wouldn't be seen from the drawing room and called back.

John had straight fair hair and blue eyes like her grandmother, and Alex had conker-coloured hair and bright green eyes. Her hair was brown and wavy, her eyes hazel — she had no idea how these facts influenced the colouring of an unborn child, and this was hardly something she could ask Grandpa.

A wave of nausea made her regret her decision to walk so far. She wasn't sure if this second bout of sickness was caused by worry or her condition. She leant against a tree for a few moments until she felt better and then turned back.

On the way she tried to remember when she'd had her last period. Certainly not since at least two weeks before Christmas, and that was now six weeks ago. She wasn't entirely sure how due dates were calculated, but was fairly sure this was worked out from the last period. This would make her around two months gone, the baby due in September some time.

Thank God there had only been a week between her sleeping with John and Alex. There was no point in agonising about it; John was the only other person who knew what had happened, and he was safely in Canada and unlikely to even hear about the baby. She doubted she'd have any further contact with Uncle Bill and Aunt Irene; they would hate her for breaking their son's heart, and she didn't blame them.

As she'd feared, the drawing room was full of smartly dressed women — friends of her grandmother, all eager to discuss the wedding and offer their assistance. When the last lady had left she was exhausted.

'Barbara, my dear girl, is something wrong? Your grandmother and I are concerned you might be having second thoughts about this wedding,' Grandpa said.

'No, it's not that.' She closed her eyes and took a deep breath. She might as well get this over with. 'I'm pretty sure I'm having a baby.'

To her astonishment he chuckled and smiled at Grandma. 'It's not the ideal circumstances to be bringing a child into the world, but I think you'll make an excellent mother.'

'Aren't you shocked? I thought you would be ashamed of me for conceiving a child before I married.'

Grandma put her arm around her shoulders and gave her an affectionate squeeze. 'As Edward said, we would have preferred you to wait a little while, but there's a war on and you young people seem determined to make the most of every moment.'

'Elspeth and I thought there was a good chance you were pregnant. I'm afraid it's a myth that you can't conceive the first time. As we said before, Alex is a fine young man, and he'll make you an excellent husband. I expect you're worried about the inevitable gossip when you have the baby early, but if we don't mind, then you can ignore anyone else. Anyway, I'm damn sure there'll be other things to think about by September.'

'Grandpa, is there anything I need to do at the moment?'

'I tell all my new mothers the same thing: eat well, exercise frequently, and don't smoke or drink to excess. In my opinion, cutting out alcohol and tobacco altogether would be beneficial for both mother and baby.'

'As I don't smoke and rarely drink alcohol, I'm all right on that. How long will it be safe for me to ride?'

'Ride? You mustn't do that anymore, my dear,' said Grandma. 'All that bouncing can't possibly be good for the baby.'

Grandpa shook his head. 'Elspeth, I think Barbara can continue to ride for another few months. Good heavens, I've heard that women in their final trimester still hunt with no ill effects.'

'I told Joe that I might not be taking Silver with me. I hope that's all right? Before I got her she was used to pull a trap as well as being a saddle horse. I think I saw a pony cart in the barn; I'll ask Joe to clean it up and then take her out with that until I leave.' This way she wouldn't upset Grandma and her mare would still be exercised.

'I'm glad the wedding's already planned and nobody will know that you're pregnant,' said Grandma.

'I don't give a damn what anybody says;

this will be our first great-grandchild and I'm absolutely thrilled with the news. Where are you going to have the baby?'

'I haven't thought that far ahead, Grandpa. I expect they have an excellent medic at the base, and it might be impossible to get back here in a hurry. Anyway, if the bombing starts I'll come back here — but I hope it won't be until after September. Alex has petrol at the moment, but he says it's going to be restricted even for them from now on.'

'Well, we can discuss that nearer the time. You're obviously a healthy girl, and I don't anticipate you having any difficulty with either the pregnancy or the delivery.' He headed for the door. 'I've got paperwork to catch up on, so I'll let you get on with the details for the 14th.'

'I'm really sorry Alex invited so many of his friends, Grandma. Is it going to make things really difficult for you?'

'Not at all, my dear. Everyone's happy to contribute to the wedding breakfast. Mrs Brown is making the cake. I'm afraid it will be a sponge, as she used up all the fruit on the Christmas cake.' She reached out and picked up a pad of paper. 'There are several things I need to discuss with you, minor details about decorations and flowers.'

Barbara was glad to escape when her

brothers returned from school — there was just so much wedding planning one could take. She'd attempted to contact Alex at the base to congratulate him on his promotion but had been told he was unavailable for the rest of the week. The officious orderly who'd answered the phone had refused to take a message.

There was no point being upset; he was a serving officer and his duty must always come first. But she did wish she'd been able to tell him her news and warn him about Mr Williams and his unpleasant behaviour when they'd met the other night.

* * *

'I'm going to be off base this evening, sir. I have to organise the plumbers and chimney sweep,' Alex said to his commanding officer as they left yet another briefing.

'Go ahead, you've done bloody well this week. Your squadron's in damn good shape; the new blokes have got the hang of the night flying, thank God.' The old man rubbed his hand across his eyes and yawned. 'I wish I could say the same for the other lot. They're all over the shop. Last night was a bloody shambles — I'm surprised that idiot Soper didn't kill himself.' He slapped Alex on the

186

back and ambled off, looking every one of his forty or so years.

Bill, one of the mechanics, was waiting outside, holding an impressive bag of tools. 'Sid's bringing a van round, sir. We managed to borrow one for the evening.'

'Good show. I've got to get back smartish, so you'll have to lock up when you've done. Okay, I'll meet you at the gate in five minutes.' Using his MG with no hood was bloody horrible in this weather, but with his greatcoat and his scarf tied around his ears, he wouldn't freeze to death. He'd yet to locate anybody who was able to repair the hole, and the way some of the new blokes were pranging their Spits, no one would have time to look at his car.

Only two weeks to the wedding — he just hoped Babs didn't change her mind. His orderly had already sewn the new stripes on his best blues, so he had nothing further to do for the big day. He'd vetoed the idea of a stag night; he wanted a clear head on his wedding day. He'd got the ring and there wasn't going to be a honeymoon, so there was nothing left for him to organise apart from getting the Dower House ready for occupation.

It was a bugger having to work in the dark, but this was the only time the chaps could get away from the base. He'd managed to find a corner in an empty hangar in which to park his car, so he didn't have to waste time scraping the snow off the seats. She roared into life straight away and he reversed into the darkness and drove round to the gates, where the men were waiting in the van. He pulled round them and they tucked in behind for the short journey to Radcliffe Hall.

As he parked in the gravelled yard he was sure he could hear movement in the house. There were no other vehicles parked at the back, so whoever it was had come on foot. He vaulted out of the car and ran to the back door. This was unlocked, which was a good sign, as Mrs Williams had promised to let the sweep in. Still, this was a damn funny time to be sweeping the chimney — why hadn't the man come during the day?

He waited for the other two to join him before going in. 'There's somebody inside; I just heard him again. He's upstairs some-where. Dump your bag and come with me. I might need you if it's a burglar.'

'Can't think why any bleeder would want to rob this place, sir. It's too far out.' Bill's hoarse whisper was loud in the darkness.

'I'm hoping it might be the chimney sweep. I can't think of anyone else who would be creeping about upstairs,' Alex replied quietly.

He stepped into the darkness, the two men close behind, and directed the thin beam of his torch towards the stairs. Yes — definitely movement, and too surreptitious to be anyone legitimate.

He crept forward and was halfway up the stairs when the intruder appeared at the top. The figure was male, his clothes black and his face obscured by a scarf. Definitely not the chimney sweep. Alex took the final stairs three at a time and brought the man down with a rugby tackle. Bill and his mate threw themselves into the melee and between them they subdued the bastard.

'Right, sir, we got him. Are the blackouts up? We could do with a bit of light down here,' Bill said.

Alex couldn't remember where the light switches were and it took him a couple of minutes to locate one and click it down. The would-be burglar was a young man with black hair and a swarthy complexion, and he was muttering to himself in a foreign language. 'Take him downstairs, lads, whilst I see what damage he's done up here.'

A quick check of the bedrooms revealed nothing appeared to be missing — mind you, there was little worth stealing. There were no drawers open, no signs of a search for valuables. What the hell had the man been doing? There wasn't time to investigate further; they'd already wasted too much time already. He didn't want the bother of calling the local constable out when nothing had been stolen.

'Let the bugger go, lads. Check he's not got anything in his pockets and then shove him out. He's probably a gypsy — certainly looks and sounds like one.'

The man wasn't particularly grateful about being released. He seemed to hesitate at the door as if he didn't want to leave, but then Bill pushed him through and he vanished into the darkness. 'A bit strange the door was open, sir, and he just happened to wander in.'

'I know. Mrs Williams has a key; I expect she brought something over and forgot to lock up. The man was an opportunist burglar; probably a gypsy camp somewhere nearby. We need to get the plumbing sorted tonight, and we've wasted too much time already. Right, what you want me to do?'

'You're all right, sir — me and Sid can sort this lot out. You have a good look around and see if anything's out of place.'

Alex showed the two men the bathroom and left them to it. He returned to the front bedroom and stood in the door, trying to see what the intruder might have been doing before he'd been disturbed. The bed was smooth, the eiderdown untouched. Nothing had been moved on the dressing table either.

Then he noticed a smudge of soot on the fireplace and realised the sweep had been. That explained the open door; perhaps the vagrant had just wandered by and tried it, then finding it unlocked, had come in to see what he could find.

Pleased he'd found a reasonable explanation, Alex decided to tell Mrs Williams that she had left the door unlocked and he'd discovered a prowler in the house. He could push a letter through her door on his way out. There was no point in lighting the range; they could have a drink when they got back to base. The desk in the sitting room had writing paper and envelopes, so he would get on with the note whilst the men hammered and banged upstairs.

A couple of hours later, the lavatory was working and water flowed from the taps in the bathroom. He was assured that when the range was lit there would also be hot water. Sid and Bill seemed happy enough with a couple of quid each for their trouble. 'You two get back to base; I've got to take this letter across to the big house.' He looked at his watch. 'Bloody hell! I hadn't realised it was so late. It's going to be midnight before I get back.'

He checked all the fires were laid and ready to light, the range riddled, and the hods and baskets filled. When he and Babs arrived on their wedding night he wanted everything to be perfect. The larder was well-stocked with basics, and the housekeeper at the Grove was packing them a large hamper with the fresh stuff in it. He'd discovered there was a decent shop in the village, and a butcher's van called round once a week.

Things were going to be much harder for Babs than for him; she would be on her own most of the time and was going to miss her family. His sister Valerie and her husband Peter were only three miles away; they had a decent-sized farm just outside Romford. He hoped Babs would cycle over whenever she was lonely.

As he locked up he was trying to imagine what it would be like having a wife to love, protect and support, and one as young as Babs. She was so grown up he often forgot she wasn't even nineteen until March, but then Valerie had married at the same age and she and Peter were really happy.

He decided not to drive his car around to the front but cut through the stable yard and push the letter under the back door of Radcliffe Hall. The flagstones were slippery and twice he almost lost his balance. The second time he dropped his torch and was on his hands and knees searching for it under the hedge, when he heard voices approaching. He turned off the beam and crouched silently in the darkness. He recognised one of the voices and was damn certain it was the gypsy who'd broken into his house. Whoever he was talking to was responding in the same language — did this mean there was a gang in the area?

They were coming his way. He pulled his greatcoat tight around him and rolled under the hedge just as they arrived on the path. Why the hell had he hidden like this? He should have confronted them and scared them away. He was well over six foot and had been twice the weight of the man they'd captured earlier, so why was he skulking under a bush?

He was about to emerge when a third man joined them, and he was speaking in English. Alex lay still and tried to catch what they were saying.

'They're moving in on the 14th — we have to get everything out before they arrive. We're bloody lucky they haven't found the boxes already. Are you sure that RAF pilot didn't see you come down from the attic?'

'No, not see me. Not go in attic, not time.'

'Right, you two, push off and I'll contact

you when it's safe. Give me the key; you can have it back next time.'

They moved away and Alex thought he heard them say they would try again at the weekend. What the hell had they got up there? Had to be illegal, but whatever they were storing in his attic was going to stay there. First thing in the morning he would try and find a locksmith and get him to change the locks.

No point in taking the letter as he was pretty sure it had been the owner, Williams, who was the third man. When they'd gone he scrambled out from under the hedge and brushed himself down. One thing was certain — his darling girl wasn't going to sleep in that house on her own. In fact he was going to start looking for somewhere else. If he couldn't be there to protect her then he must make other arrangements, and pretty damn quickly too.

★   ★   ★

'Barbara, Alex is on the phone for you,' Grandma called from the study.

'I'm coming. I've not been able to get in touch with him all week and I'm hoping he'll have a few hours off this weekend.' She picked up the receiver. 'Alex? I'm sorry to

194

keep you waiting, but I had to take off my boots first.'

'I haven't got long, darling, but I need to tell you something that happened last night.' When he finished she was equally worried. She told him about her unpleasant meeting with Mr Williams.

'I don't like the sound of all this, Babs. There's something nasty going on at Radcliffe Hall and I don't think you should live there until it's sorted out.'

'There's something else. I'm pregnant. This means there's no point in moving Silver, so I don't know what I'll do with myself all day if I don't have her to look after.'

'I'm not surprised, and I am pleased. I think you'd better stay at the Grove for the moment, at least until this other business is settled. I was going to get the locks changed but instead I think I should inform the police.'

'I can't imagine what might be hidden in the attic; do you think Mr Williams is involved in burglaries and they're storing the loot up there?'

'What's this about loot, my dear?' said Grandma. 'I heard this morning that the Farley factory was broken into whilst it was closed. They only just noticed the discrepancies.'

'Alex, did you hear that? You must contact the police — there could be stolen munitions in our house.'

'Bloody hell! I'll get on to it right away, and let you know what happens. It's going to be rotten for Mrs Williams and her daughter if it's true.'

'Can you get away for an hour or two, Alex? I'd really like to see you. There's so much we have to discuss, especially about the baby.'

'I've got a four-hour pass on Saturday; I'll be in Ingatestone by ten o'clock. Could you meet me at the farm? I need to speak to my parents about something.'

She agreed. As long as it wasn't snowing she could drive the pony cart — the more practice Silver had the better. Alex hadn't sounded especially enthusiastic about the baby, but maybe he was preoccupied with whatever Mr Williams had been up to.

When she'd arrived at the Grove a few months ago she thought she'd left violence and unhappiness behind, but disasters seemed to be following her around. She'd lost her childhood friends, because she was certain neither John nor his parents would ever forgive her for what she'd done. She was marrying a man she loved, but was possibly carrying John's baby — if Alex found out he'd never forgive her. Now her new home was tainted by association with Mr Williams and his shady friends. What else was going to go wrong?

* * *

Barbara arrived at the farm before Alex. Her brothers had accompanied her, as they thought being driven in a pony cart would be good fun.

'Are we staying for lunch, Babs?' David tugged at her coat, impatient for a reply.

'Yes, we are. Here come the boys — do you think you four could unharness Silver for me and then put her in a box? Make sure she's got water and hay.'

Tom answered for his brother. 'Of course we can. Joe showed us yesterday and it's a piece of cake.'

She left the children to look after her mare and headed to the back door, surprised Mrs Everton hadn't been waving at her kitchen window as she usually was. The two Collie dogs were also absent, but Mr Everton was probably working somewhere on the farm, so they would be with him.

'Hello, Mrs Everton. It's me, Barbara — shall I come in?'

'I'm on the phone,' Mrs Everton called

back. 'It's Valerie. I won't be a minute. Make yourself at home in the kitchen.'

Barbara hooked off her boots and hung her coat on a spare peg, then dashed into the kitchen as the corridor was freezing, the cold seeping through her socks. She glanced at the clock ticking loudly on the windowsill — Alex should be here soon. Had he told his mother about the baby? If she was honest she would much rather not tell the Evertons. Let them think the baby was conceived after they were married. They must already think she was a bit flighty after almost being engaged to two men at the same time, and knowing she and Alex had slept together might put them off her altogether.

'Well I never! You won't believe the excitement that's been going on in Hornchurch.' Barbara rather thought she knew exactly what the drama was about. 'There's policemen all over the countryside, my Valerie says, and Mr Williams has been arrested. I don't suppose you'll want to be living there now.'

'Actually, Mrs Everton, the thieves hid some of the stolen goods in the attic at the Dower House and the rest in the stables. Alex was the one who informed the police.'

'Good heavens! Imagine that! I can't believe someone as grand as Mr Williams is a

198

crook. His poor wife and daughter — they must be feeling dreadful.'

'Clarissa has a weak heart; I hope the shock doesn't prove too much for her. She's a really nice girl and I'm hoping to become her friend.' Barbara took the mug of tea Mrs Everton held out and sat down at the scrubbed kitchen table. 'If the police have captured everybody, and taken everything out of our house and the stables, then I'm quite happy to live there as planned. I expect that's what Alex wants to talk about.'

An hour later there had been no phone call from him and he still hadn't arrived. Mr Everton came in from the fields expecting his lunch, which meant Alex was going to miss his meal unless he arrived very soon.

Dusk was falling; if she didn't leave immediately she would be driving the pony cart home in the dark. She called Tom and David down and said her goodbyes. 'I expect Alex is still giving his statement to the police. He doesn't have any more time off until the wedding, but I hope I can come over and see you again next week? And if Jim and Ned would like to come over after church tomorrow, that would be lovely.'

'They can come if they've finished their homework by then.' Mrs Everton smiled. 'And do visit if you have time, as I've got a few more bits and pieces sorted out for your new home.' She hesitated and her smile slipped. 'Perhaps you won't want them now, not after all this fuss.'

'I've paid the rent for six months so I'm jolly well going to live there, whatever Alex says. So whatever you've got for us, I'll be delighted to accept. I'll collect it next time I come. Thank you.'

Tom and David were so busy telling her about the game they'd been playing they didn't notice her absent-minded replies. Fortunately Silver had quickly adjusted to being driven and seemed to enjoy trundling along the lanes pulling the ancient cart, and didn't require her attention either.

Although she'd reassured Mrs Everton everything was fine, she was really worried about Alex's absence and the fact he'd not even bothered to ring. Being interviewed by the police couldn't possibly have taken all day, and he'd told her the phone in the officers' mess was always available.

He had suggested this hasty marriage, so he wasn't marrying her because he had to, but he hadn't seemed overjoyed when she'd told him his suspicions had proved correct and that they were going to be parents in the autumn. Was he having second thoughts? Had he realised he was marrying a girl he'd only known a few months, had never actually been on a date with, but who had slept with him the first time they'd been alone? Not forgetting, of course, she'd actually been engaged to John when she'd gone to bed with him.

For all his so-called wildness, he was a young man with principles and would never have offered to marry her if he knew her sordid secret. How could she have got herself into this muddle? If she hadn't been having a baby she would cancel the wedding, but now she had no choice — even her beloved grandparents would reject her if they ever discovered she didn't even know who the father of her baby was.

She swallowed her tears; she loved Alex and if it wasn't for the uncertainty about the baby's parentage, she would be overjoyed to be marrying him next week. Now she must hide her unhappiness and try and act like a young woman about to marry the man she loved. Next week she would be beginning her married life based on a lie and could never tell Alex the truth. How could a relationship based on deceit hope to survive, especially with the added pressures of living through a war?

10

Joe was waiting when Barbara guided the pony and trap into the yard; she left the boys happily helping him put Silver to bed. She hurried inside, hoping Alex might have rung and left her a message. Mrs Brown was in the kitchen, the puppies scampering about the floor being watched by Lavender. The enormous cat was purring encouragement, and whenever one of the dogs came near enough she batted them gently with a paw.

'There you are. Been quite a to-do this afternoon, miss, seeing as the vicar has had a funny turn and might not be able to marry you next week.'

'Golly! I do hope he's okay — he's not seemed particularly well these past few weeks. I'm sure we can find a substitute from somewhere, Mrs Brown. Are my grandparents in the study?'

'They are; asked me to tell you to go straight in and not bother about changing. Don't worry, I'll sort the boys out when they come in. Joe will go up with them; once your little mare is put away he's done for the day.'

Barbara didn't stop to put on her slippers,

but skidded along the polished floor to the study. Even with the thick curtain hanging across the passageway there were icy draughts from the unheated front of the house. No wonder the study door was firmly closed. When she'd first arrived she would have knocked, but now she charged in knowing she was welcome. 'Sorry if I'm late. I stayed on a bit longer, hoping Alex might eventually turn up. I've got news for you as well.'

Her grandfather had been talking on the telephone and he replaced the receiver as she came in. 'Bad news, my dear. The vicar has had a stroke — quite a serious one — and he won't be able to conduct the service next week.'

'Mrs Brown told me, Grandpa, and I think I have a solution. Alex could ask the padre from the base if he would do it for us.'

'Excellent idea! Well done, Barbara. Why didn't your young man turn up this afternoon?'

They were suitably horrified by the dishonesty of Mr Williams and his foreign friends, but unlike Mrs Everton they thought it would be perfectly safe for her to live there now the man was in custody. 'I certainly want to be there until the summer, Grandma, but I'm definitely coming here for the birth, if that's all right with you.'

'Sensible move, my dear. It's a bit primitive at the Dower House. Another thing you need to consider is that Hornchurch is likely to be a target for the Germans once the bombing starts. You would be a lot safer here, and I'm sure Alex would agree with me.'

'Alex and I have talked about this as well. I don't even know if there's an Anderson shelter at Radcliffe Hall, so we'd have to go in the basement if there was an air raid.'

'Why don't you ring the base and see if you can get hold of young Everton? We need to have a decision on the padre ASAP. You might also try ringing Radcliffe Hall and speak to Mrs Williams; she might not want you and Alex there if she knows he reported her husband to the police.'

This time, when she asked to speak to Alex, she was told to hold the line and a few minutes later he was there.

'My God, darling, I'm so sorry. There's been a frightful flap on all day and all leave was cancelled. It turned out to be a false alarm, not the Luftwaffe, but it's too late to come over now. They arrested that bastard Williams and it seems his wife and daughter were pleased to see him go. Everything has been removed from the attic and stables, the plumbing has been mended and the chimneys swept.'

'I wish you'd come over this afternoon; I didn't know if you'd told your parents about the baby — '

'God no! The fewer people who know, the better.'

'Good, that's what I thought. The vicar has had a stroke; do you think your padre would marry us instead?'

'I'm sure he would; he's coming anyway. Tell your grandparents not to worry; everything can go ahead as planned.'

'There's another thing. Grandpa's worried about air raids on the base — Radcliffe Hall is very close and might be hit by a stray bomb. Do you know if they have an Anderson shelter there?'

'Haven't the foggiest, Babs. It's something I should have asked when we were there. Now I come to think about it, I'm not sure I want you living so close to the base, especially not in your condition. Maybe you'd better stay where you are.'

Her answer was instantaneous. 'No, I want to be with you in our own house, at least until it becomes dangerous. I know I won't see a lot of you, but just knowing you're only a couple of miles away will make all the difference.'

'Are you sure?'

'Absolutely. I love you and I want to be

with you; I might not see you for weeks on end if I'm at the Grove.'

'I'm so glad you said that, darling girl, as I've just been talking to the CO and he says I can live off base if we get a phone put in. It's only five minutes by car, and we'll get a preliminary warning before we have to scramble. Obviously, when my squadron's on call I have to be here, but otherwise I can come home at night.'

'That's wonderful news. Will you be able to organise a telephone by next week?'

'The CO is pulling a few strings and it should go in on Monday; as there's already a telephone at the Hall they just have to run a wire from that. I've checked with Mrs Williams and she's quite happy to share a line with us.'

'Grandma seems to think the entire squadron has been invited. Is she exaggerating?'

''fraid not; in fact Pete has organised a coach to bring everyone. We all chipped in and there's a load of drink on its way — we raided the officers' mess. I don't want your grandparents to have to pay for everything. Mum says it's the groom's responsibility to pay for the alcohol and flowers. She's getting her cronies to decorate the church — have you organised your bouquet? Another thing

— who's going to be your matron of honour?'

She hadn't thought of that, and there wasn't enough time to find someone now. 'My brothers are going to walk down the aisle behind me. They won't be dressed as pageboys, but they will be very smart. I'm not carrying fresh flowers; you'll see why on Wednesday.'

She was smiling when she hung up. She'd been worrying about nothing, and despite all the problems her wedding to Alex was going to be perfect. There was no point in fretting about something that might not happen, so she was just going to enjoy being married to the man she loved.

⋆ ⋆ ⋆

Eventually Barbara's wedding day arrived. She'd slept soundly, which surprised her as this was her last night at the Grove. Well, that wasn't really true; she was going to be coming back as frequently as she could. The lovely gown was freshly pressed and hanging in her closet. She'd washed her hair yesterday so all she had to do was have a quick bath, put on her make-up, do her hair and get dressed.

Grandma had managed to persuade several local ladies to help out with the reception, and they had descended on the Grove to decorate the reopened dining room and drawing-room. Fires had been lit for the past few days and with so many people coming, it should be more than warm enough.

She would have liked Clarissa, Amanda and Harriet to come, but Clarissa wasn't well enough and the other two girls were unable to get leave. She would have no friends to support her, but she did have her family. Her side of the church was going to look rather empty as Alex and invited so many of his friends from the base.

It hardly seemed possible such a large event had been arranged in so short a time, especially so soon after the start of rationing. She decided she wasn't going to carry her gas mask today — she would leave it in the car and hope she wouldn't be arrested by an overzealous ARP. Come to think of it, Mr Everton didn't take his with him when he was on the farm, and she hadn't seen Alex's gas mask for ages. It seemed silly to have to take her identity papers, ration book and gas mask to her own wedding.

There was a soft tap on the door and her grandmother came in dressed in an absolutely splendid suit from Norman Hartnell. 'Lilac looks lovely on you, Grandma. I hope you're going to be warm enough.'

'I shall wear my mink, Barbara dear, but

I'm worried you are going to be frozen. We married in June and my gown is not really suitable for February.'

'I can put a rug around my knees in the car; that should be enough. I'm too excited to be cold. I wanted to come down and look at what you've done. Do you think it would be all right for me to go down in my dressing gown when there are so many people here?'

'Perfectly suitable. The women from the village who are helping Mrs Brown are in the kitchen, and there's nobody about apart from your grandfather and the boys.'

Barbara hastily pulled on her serviceable all-enveloping dressing gown and followed her grandmother downstairs. 'I don't want to put on the dress until the very last minute. I hope you're going to have time to help me?'

'I am indeed, my dear, I can't tell you how much I'm looking forward to today. Are you feeling at all nauseous? It would be most unfortunate if you were sick in the church — there would be a lot of raised eyebrows.'

A few months ago her grandmother would never have joked about something so serious, and now they talked about everything. She was going to miss her grandparents and her brothers, but Grandpa had promised to bring them over next weekend. He hadn't seen the

209

Dower House fully furnished and she couldn't wait to show him how comfortable it looked.

The vast entrance hall was flooded with sunlight from the glass rotunda in the ceiling. A huge log fire burned fiercely in the grate, and there were half a dozen attractive arrangements of flowers and leaves placed about. The drawing room had been transformed — the furniture had been removed and the carpet rolled up. There were chairs around the edge of the room, and enormous bouquets on either side of the double doors leading to the grand dining room.

'The flowers are beautiful,' said Barbara. 'Did they come from Mrs Everton?'

'They did. She's done a splendid job arranging them. What do you think, my dear? Do you like the way this looks?'

'I do. There's plenty of room for people to talk to each other. With so many coming, finger food will be perfect; then the ladies only have to worry about their handbags and a glass. They won't need to balance a plate as well.'

'We're putting on a splendid buffet, my dear. There's a whole salmon, three large ham joints, and various potted meats and terrines. There will also be canapés taken around on trays, and there are a dozen tables laid up for those who wish to have a knife and fork meal.'

'I can't believe you've managed to find so much food now all luxury items are rationed. Mrs Brown told me the cake has a sponge base as she couldn't find enough dried fruit for anything else.'

'With vol-au-vents, sausage rolls and the biggest sherry trifle you've ever seen, there will be more than enough. I think you'd better have your bath, Barbara — the car's coming to collect you in a little over an hour.'

★ ★ ★

Barbara stood in front of the mirror, scarcely able to believe her eyes. 'I feel like a princess, Grandma. I don't recognise myself.'

Her grandmother dabbed her eyes with her lace-edged handkerchief. 'You look so like your father, my dear. He would have been so proud of you. To think six months ago we didn't even know you existed, and now we have two wonderful extra grandchildren as well.' She adjusted Barbara's veil and stepped back with a watery smile. 'I think we should have the photographs taken in the drawing room — there's a charming young man, another friend of Alex's, waiting to take your picture. He's already done Edward and me

211

with the boys; now he must do some of all of us and some of you on your own.'

The next twenty minutes were filled with endless pictures, then David and Tom left with Grandma and Barbara was alone with her grandfather for the first time that day.

'There's still time to change your mind, my dear girl. If you think this is a bit of a rush and would rather wait until after the baby is born, we'll support you.'

'I've never been more certain of anything in my life; I'll never love another man the way I do Alex. I hate to say it, but he could be killed at any time. I know there have been several fatalities already at the base and the fighting hasn't even started.' She swallowed a lump in her throat. 'He might be lucky and survive the war, but if he doesn't, I'll have no regrets. Every day we can spend together will be wonderful.'

'In which case, your carriage awaits. The last time I saw that gown was on my own wedding day — I must say, it looks just as splendid on you as it did on Elspeth. Once this bloody war gets going you must promise me you'll come back here where it's safe.' His voice was gruff; he was as moved as she.

'I promise I won't take any risks with our baby's health or mine. Alex will tell me when it's time to leave Hornchurch.' She was holding the train over her arm and this made it impossible to put on her coat. He draped it over her shoulders and collected her gasmask along with his own. He looked handsome in his smart double-breasted suit, snowy white shirt and grey silk waistcoat. He was even wearing a bow tie.

As the car, a Bentley hired for the day, drove through the village, people stood on the kerbside and waved. Barbara thought this was how royalty must feel. She shrugged her coat onto the seat and pushed the rug to one side. The chauffeur opened the door for Grandpa and then hurried round to do the same for her.

'I say, Babs, you look like a film star. You want us to hold your traily bit?' Tom asked as he rushed up.

'I want to hold it too,' David said peevishly.

'You can have one side and Tom can hold the other. Remember, you must keep up with me or you'll pull my veil off.'

She slipped her arm through her grandfather's and he led her briskly through the wicket gate and up to the church. He paused at the doors and she heard the padre ask everyone to stand. The organ groaned into life when she walked down the aisle to the strain of Mendelssohn's 'Wedding March'. Alex was standing to attention at the front, another blue-grey clad officer next to him. As she approached he turned and his eyes widened, and then he smiled with such joy she almost stumbled.

The wedding service passed in a blur. She made her responses when asked and held out her hand for Alex to push the gold band onto her finger. It wasn't until Alex put his arms around her to give her the traditional kiss that she realised she had just promised to love, honour and obey a man she loved, but barely knew.

Everything seemed unreal — the off- key organ music, the smiling congregation, even the man standing beside her. She had been swept along by events ever since that dreadful night when her lunatic mother had attacked her and she'd left Crabapple Cottage. She'd bounced from one disaster to another, and by far the worst was sleeping with Alex on New Year's Eve. If she hadn't done that she wouldn't be standing here beside him, no longer Miss Barbara Sinclair but Mrs Barbara Everton.

Her brothers had been officially adopted by her grandparents and were now Sinclairs. They had shared the same name for less than a month. She wanted to run away, take off the ring and give it to Alex, but she couldn't do that. A saying popped into her head: '*You have made your bed, now you must lie in it.'*

She blinked back tears and smiled at her husband. This was a feeble effort but it seemed enough to satisfy him. She prayed that loving him was going to be enough to see her through the difficult months ahead.

'I can't believe I've just married the most beautiful girl in the world. You've made me so happy, darling, and I promise I'm going to make you the best husband.' He pulled her hand through his arm and led her down the aisle into the watery sunshine, where the photographer was waiting to record the event for the family album.

'I hope he doesn't take too long; I'm desperate to spend a penny,' she whispered to Alex.

He laughed and shouted to his friend who was wielding the camera. 'It's too damn cold to hang about out here, Brian. You can get all the photos we need at the reception.'

The Bentley was waiting, engine purring, and wonderfully warm inside. 'Thank you; I'm sure all the guests will be delighted to be spared a long wait outside in this weather,' Barbara said. 'I just hope everything's ready at home. We're arriving a bit sooner than they will be expecting.'

'Doesn't matter if they're not. I need a drink — preferably something very strong to steady my nerves.'

She looked at him in surprise. 'Were you nervous? You didn't look it or sound it. I was in a daze throughout the ceremony, and then all I could think of was that I needed to go to the loo. I think it's because I'm pregnant. I never had this problem before.'

'You look so slim nobody could possibly guess, and I'd forgotten until you just mentioned it. How are you feeling? I can remember Mum was sick a lot in the beginning — have you had any more of this morning sickness lark?'

'I wouldn't call it a lark,' she said, giggling. 'But no, I was sick a couple of times and sometimes feel a bit dizzy, but apart from needing to rush off every five minutes, I'm absolutely fine. Although I've missed two periods now, I don't think a doctor can confirm the pregnancy until I'm three months. Hopefully I won't start to show until the summer.'

He gently drew her into his arms and she forgot her reservations and lost herself in the excitement of his kiss. The car turned into the drive and pulled up in front of the house. This was the first time she would have been in through the front door. Was this a good omen?

The chauffeur opened the door and she

slid out, being careful to keep her beautiful gown from the ground. Alex arrived beside her. 'Here, sweetheart, let me hold your skirt. I don't want you to trip over.'

The front door opened as they arrived and Mrs Brown was waiting to greet them. 'Welcome, Mr and Mrs Everton. You look ever so nice, madam. That dress might be a bit old-fashioned, but I reckon it's the prettiest one I've seen in a long time.'

'Thank you, Mrs Brown. Alex would like a large whiskey and I'd like a cup of tea, if that's possible.'

Barbara shot off down the corridor to the downstairs cloakroom and after spending a frustrating few minutes struggling with her long skirt, she eventually emerged to find Alex standing anxiously outside the door.

'I was getting worried, Babs. You took so long in there.'

'It's not so easy with a long dress, train and veil, but I'll have to get used to it. I thought you were desperate for a drink?'

'Not until I was sure you were okay. Before we go into the drawing room, darling, there's something I need to say to you. I know this has all been a dreadful rush, I know you wouldn't have married me today if we hadn't slept together, but I knew the moment you walked into the yard that I had met the

217

woman I was going to spend the rest of my life with.' He grinned and for a moment looked like his younger brother. 'You would have married me eventually. It's just happened a bit sooner than you wanted. You do love me, don't you?'

'Of course I do, and if we hadn't got married today we might never have got married. Being a fighter pilot is a very dangerous profession . . . ' Her voice trailed away. What had made her say something so dreadful on her wedding day?

His eyes blazed and he pulled her almost roughly into his arms. 'Thank God you understand — that you realise I could be killed. It makes things so much easier between us. However long we might have together, I want to leave you with happy memories, no regrets on either side.'

She gulped and tried to swallow back her sobs but failed miserably. His understanding, his kindness, and her earlier doubts overwhelmed her. He held her close while she cried, stroking her back and murmuring words of love and encouragement. Eventually she stopped and blew her nose noisily on his handkerchief. 'I can hear cars arriving. I must look dreadful. Are my eyes terribly red?'

'No, nothing a quick splash of cold water won't cure. Stay there, I'll sort it out.'

She leaned against the wall taking deep, steadying breaths. She must forget how she'd come to be in this position and look to the future — she was having a baby in seven months' time and this must be her priority. Hadn't she said the same to Grandpa? She and Alex were in love and this was all that mattered. They must make the most of every day just in case something dreadful happened. She pushed the thought of Alex dying to the furthest corner of her mind. The idea of a world without him didn't bear thinking of.

'Babs, are you okay?' He was beside her with a cold, wet cloth. Not waiting for her answer, he began to wipe her face as if she were a toddler. She rather liked being looked after; she'd not had much of that in her life. 'There, all tickety-boo. Just in time; I can hear your grandparents coming in.'

'Is my lipstick smudged? In fact, do I have any left on?'

'Plenty — and your eyes are sparkling and your cheeks are rosy. The picture of a radiant bride.' He grabbed her hand and rushed her to the entrance hall, where she was greeted with relief by her grandparents.

'Thank goodness, Barbara,' said her grandma. 'We thought we would have to greet your guests without the bride and groom.'

'Sorry; I'm here now.' She saw her brothers huddled against the wall. 'Behave yourselves until everyone is here — why don't you get something from the buffet to keep you going?' They were looking a little forlorn, as if they'd only just realised how different their lives were going to be now their big sister was married. Her suggestion was greeted with shrieks of excitement.

'What can we have? We don't know what everything's called,' Tom said as he jumped up and down.

'You can have whatever you like, but only a little, just a taste. Take Jim and Ned with you — I'm sure they'll want something too.'

Mr and Mrs Everton joined the line and the procession of guests commenced. Less than half the guests had arrived when the boys charged off upstairs to play. They must have eaten enough to keep them going. Joe was directing traffic outside with the help of a couple of his friends who were glad to earn a pound each for their trouble.

Barbara was astonished by the number of people who trooped past, most of whom she didn't know; all the young men were in uniform and most of those were RAF. 'I'm going to have to go to the cloakroom again soon, Alex. I don't think I can stand here until everyone is in.'

'Don't worry, my dear girl — these are the last of them. You can scoot off as soon as they've gone into the drawing room,' her grandfather said.

Grandma was in her element. Resplendent in her lilac suit and matching hat, she nodded and smiled and shook hands like a queen. Barbara had never seen her so animated. 'Alex, do you think this is the first time they've had a big party here since my father left all those years ago?'

'Probably. They didn't have much to celebrate before.' He bent his head and whispered in her ear. 'They'll have the christening in October, but that won't be as big an event as this. At least, I hope it won't.'

The final guests vanished into the already crowded drawing room and Alex went to fetch the boys down so the photographer could take the official pictures. The family gathered on the front steps whilst the man set up his tripod. Barbara was shivering by the time he'd finished but was glad Alex had arranged for them to be done.

'Let's get the speeches over and done with, Barbara my dear,' said her grandpa, 'and then we can do the cake-cutting and everyone can relax and enjoy themselves with no further interruptions for formalities.'

'I'm glad the bride doesn't have to make a

speech — that would have ruined my day.'

The best man was amusing and not too rude. Alex just thanked her grandparents and his parents for everything, and then it was Grandpa's turn.

'I know I should have spoken first, but I wanted to end the proceedings with what I have to say. When my son died it was the darkest day of our lives; neither Elspeth nor I ever thought this place would be a real home again. Then Barbara came into our lives and everything changed — she brought with her happiness and joy, and also her brothers. I want to introduce them to you, as they are now legally our children.' He beckoned to the boys and they rushed up to him, nudging and giggling with excitement. 'This is Thomas Sinclair and this, David Sinclair. Take a bow, boys.' A spontaneous round of applause greeted the brothers and they grinned and waved. 'Today we have not lost a grand-daughter, but gained an excellent grandson-in-law.' He raised his brimming glass to Alex. 'Please raise your glasses to the happy couple, Alex and Barbara Everton.'

11

After Barbara had circulated around the reception three times, she was exhausted and more than ready to slip upstairs to remove her wedding gown and change into something more practical. When she'd packed her clothes she'd decided to leave all her smart items behind; she wouldn't need them at Radcliffe Hall. She'd also put in clothes that were loose-fitting; though she didn't show at the moment, in a few months she was bound to be bulging at the front.

Grandma had suggested she and Alex spend their wedding night at the Grove, but the possibility of using the bed she'd shared with John with her new husband had appalled her. Therefore they were leaving shortly for the Dower House.

Just taking two large suitcases made it seem like a holiday, not a permanent removal. When she was changed into her slacks she stretched out on the bed. David had been strange all day, not his normal self at all, and she had a horrible feeling he wasn't going to adjust to this second upheaval in less than three months. Although the boys seemed

223

pleased to be adopted by her grandparents, she'd not really sat down and talked to them about it. She sat up and scrambled off the bed. There was something she could do about this and it would make the move less distressing for all of them.

Downstairs she searched for her grandfather and discovered him hiding in the study, smoking a cigar and clutching a glass of whiskey. 'Grandpa, I want the boys to come to us every weekend. It'll be like they are weekly boarders at Brentwood School, and that way they won't feel left out of things.'

'I think that's an excellent idea, my dear, as long as you remember your promise to move back permanently when things get too lively at Hornchurch. There's a perfectly good bus service between Brentwood and Hornchurch; the boys can catch the bus to you on Friday night and go to school from there on Monday morning.'

'I haven't got time to pack their things before Alex and I leave today. Do you think Grandma will mind doing it for me? I'm leaving half my clothes here and Tom and David can do the same. They've got a spare set of everything they need for school.'

'What is it you want me to do, my dear?' Grandma joined them with a tray of sandwiches and a much-needed pot of tea.

'I'm sure you haven't eaten or drunk anything since breakfast, Barbara, so sit down and have something now. You can tell me what you and your grandfather are planning whilst you eat.'

Her brothers were overjoyed at the suggestion, especially David. One person Barbara hadn't discussed her plans with was Alex — but she was pretty sure he wouldn't mind. After all, they would have Monday to Friday together when he wasn't on duty.

The Bentley was to take them to their new home. The suitcases were loaded and the guests gathered in the hall to say goodbye. The party showed no signs of slowing down, everyone determined to stay until every scrap of food was eaten and all the alcohol consumed.

'It's a good thing your pals are going home in a coach, Alex,' said Barbara. 'I don't think any of them could drive safely.'

'Our squadron's not on call until Friday, sweetheart, so they've got plenty of time to recover from their hangovers.' He kept his arm firmly about her waist as he guided her through the press of people. She'd already said a tearful farewell to the boys and her grandparents and she wanted to get this difficult departure over with before she broke down.

Some wag had tied tin cans to the bumper

of the Bentley and a few minutes later they were clattering down the drive. The glass partition between them and the driver was closed; finally they could talk without interruption.

'You look exhausted, darling. As soon as we get home you can lie down whilst I unpack.'

'I am tired, but I'm also a bit sad to be leaving the Grove. I've been so happy there, and I thought I would be with my grandparents until the war finished.' She turned to him and smiled. 'Which reminds me — David and Thomas are going to live with us at the weekends and here during the week. It's all arranged.'

He frowned. 'It didn't occur to you to ask me first? I was hoping to spend the few months before the baby comes with you, not have to share you with two boys.'

'I'm sorry you're not happy about it, but only two months ago David and Tom were abandoned by their parents; it's not right for them to be away from me so soon. Anyway, they'll only be here at the weekend, so we'll have all week together.'

'As it's a *fait accompli*, there's not much point in arguing, is there? In future, Barbara, I need to be consulted before you make decisions for both of us.' He turned away and rested his head against the seat, closing his eyes so she couldn't continue the conversation.

He wasn't being very nice; she thought he'd understand how important the boys were to her. John had said they would be his responsibility too, but Alex obviously didn't feel the same way. She moved across the car until she was pressed into the far corner, leaving an empty space between them. Why was she thinking about John when she had just married Alex?

She pressed her face against the glass and tried not to cry. John must have had her letter by now and his parents would have received the ring. He would be devastated at her betrayal. What would he do when he eventually discovered she had had a baby so soon after marrying Alex? Would he turn up on the doorstep demanding to see the child, saying it could be his?

'Darling, I'm so sorry, I'm a rotten bastard to talk to you like that on our wedding day. Of course I'm delighted to have Tom and David as part of our family. Please, Babs, look at me.'

She sniffed and reluctantly turned her head, not ready to forgive him, her thoughts full of John and how he wouldn't have been sniffy with her.

'Bloody hell! I've made you cry, and today

was supposed to be the happiest day of your life.' Without giving her a chance to refuse, he scooped her up and pulled her into his lap. 'I love you so much, my darling. I can't believe my luck. I've been out with a lot of girls but never met anyone as beautiful, intelligent, kind or brave as you.'

He looked so wretched she stretched out and kissed him. His passionate response pushed her doubts away — as long as they loved each other everything else would fall into place. They arrived at their new home breathless and hot and Alex had to carefully arrange his jacket to cover his embarrassment.

'Look, there's smoke coming out of several chimneys — did you arrange for someone to light the fires?' Barbara asked.

'Yes, Mrs Williams said she'd get her daily woman to do it, and there are one or two other things I've arranged as well. We're going in the front door this time, so I hope the wretched key works. It took ages to open it the other day.'

They ran hand in hand down the garden path to the front door and Barbara waited impatiently for him to turn the key. Fortunately it moved easily and the door swung open. He spun round and snatched her up in his arms.

'I'm supposed to carry you over the threshold the first time we go in, so here goes.' He stepped into the immaculate entrance hall and the first thing she noticed were the flowers.

'Put me down, I want to see. It's lovely and warm in here and these are so beautiful. Where did they come from?'

Before he could answer, their driver arrived with the first of the suitcases. Whilst Alex directed him to the bedroom, Barbara ran around the house like a five-year-old. All the rooms were warm, with a fire in every grate, and all had at least one vase of flowers. She headed for the kitchen and stopped in delight when she saw the room. The long table was covered with a crisply starched damask cloth and laid up with beautiful cutlery and china for dinner. Where had all this come from? The range was hot, the water worked perfectly and the pantry was groaning with food.

Alex appeared at the door with a hamper of goodies from Mrs Brown. 'Do you like it? Mum and Mrs Sinclair organised it for us.' He took the food into the pantry and she followed him.

'I love it. I can't believe Grandma managed to do this without me noticing. Do we have a telephone yet?'

'We certainly do — there's a handset in the

hall and one in the bedroom. It's a party line, but that shouldn't make any difference.'

She flung herself into his arms and he hugged her. 'Thank you for doing this, Alex. I was a bit miserable earlier but now I'm really happy to be here. I don't want to lie down . . . '

His eyes darkened and he kissed her hard. 'Why don't we both have a lie down, darling girl, and finish what we started in the car?'

She nodded and, with her still in his arms, he turned and charged down the passageway and took the stairs two at a time. Fortunately the bedroom door was open and he tossed her on the bed, landing with a thump beside her.

'You're mad, Flight Commander Everton, but I love you just as you are.'

'And you're my lovely wife, Mrs Everton, and I want to spend the rest of the night making love to you.' He propped himself on one arm and smiled at her in the particular way of his that made her fizz inside, then stroked her face. The roughness of his fingertips on her cheek made her pulse race.

She giggled and rolled away to stand on the far side of the bed. 'I don't know much about this making love business, but I think it's usual to do it without clothes.' Keeping her gaze fixed on him, she slowly unbuttoned her cardigan and tossed it into the air. Her blouse followed and she was standing in her slacks and brassiere. She couldn't quite bring herself to unfasten this with him watching so turned her back.

The bed creaked and he was behind her, his hot breath on the nape of her neck. 'Let me help you, darling, and then you can do the same for me.'

★   ★   ★

The room was dark when she woke up in his arms, relaxed and satisfied. The first night they'd spent together before had been wonderful, but this had been even better. Being married to him, being in their own bed, removed all the worry about being discovered. She stretched and he stirred beside her.

'Mmmm . . . how do you like being a married woman, sweetheart? I'm finding marriage is absolutely spiffing.'

She poked him and laughed. 'Spiffing? You're beginning to sound like one of Amanda's friends. Are they all very posh in the officers' mess?'

'Most of them are public schoolboys, but they are all very bright chaps. You can't become a pilot without passing umpteen tests.' He ran his fingers down her spine and nibbled at her ear. 'What the hell are we talking about that for? I can think of a lot better things to do.'

'That's quite enough of that, thank you. I'm absolutely starving and there's all that lovely food downstairs waiting for us. Go on, get out of bed and draw the blackouts so I can get up.'

'Are we going to get dressed? Hardly seems worth it when we'll be coming back to bed as soon as we've eaten.'

'You might want to come back, but I intend to make some telephone calls and listen to the wireless in my very own sitting room after supper.'

She lay in bed listening to him muttering and swearing as he groped his way across the room, bumping into furniture and stubbing his toes. The fire had burned down; they must have been in bed for hours.

'There, you can switch the bedside light off now, Babs.'

Light flooded the room and she looked up. She couldn't breathe. He was standing with his back to her by the window, and she'd never seen anything so beautiful. His shoulders bulged with muscle and his back tapered to his waist. His buttocks were firm, quite unlike a woman's.

He turned and his expression changed. Hectic colour flooded his cheeks and in two strides he was across the room and back in bed with her. By the time they'd taken a bath together it was far too late to make telephone calls.

'I'd better go and check the fires downstairs, darling, and I'll do the blackouts as well. You stay in bed; it's warmer there.' He shrugged into his dressing gown but ignored his slippers. He padded across the room, blowing her a kiss before he left.

Whilst she was waiting she decided to change the sheets; they were rumpled and rather unpleasant. Alex had already rekindled the fire and the room smelt of applewood. She found her nightie, part of a negligee set Grandma had insisted she needed, and quickly pulled this on. She put his pyjamas on the end of the bed, hoping he would wear them. Being naked was lovely when you were making love but a bit sticky and cold when you were trying to sleep.

Her stomach growled, and she rather wished she'd gone downstairs with him to find something to eat. She wandered around the bedroom checking everything was in its place, smiling at the photographs of her brothers, grandparents and Silver. She decided to start unpacking the suitcases and was so engrossed that she didn't hear him arrive.

'Leave that until tomorrow. I've brought us some supper. Do you want to eat it in bed or sitting by the fire?' He put an enormous tray down on the fireside rug. There were vol-au-vents, sausage rolls, sandwiches, fairy cakes, a bottle of champagne and a pot of coffee.

'By the fire; we can sit on the rug. It smells delicious — I can't believe you've even heated things up. Those sandwiches look freshly made. I'm very impressed; I didn't know you were a dab hand in the kitchen.'

'There's a lot we don't know about each other, but we've got the rest of our lives to learn. Would you like champagne or coffee, or both?'

'I'll have half a glass with you, but a whole mug of coffee, please.'

They talked and munched contentedly until dawn, when they eventually fell into bed, and this time they were both too tired to do anything but sleep.

Barbara was woken by someone hammering on the door — it sounded like an emergency. She nudged Alex but he just grunted and turned over. She would have to investigate herself. Her unglamorous dressing gown was found amongst the clothes in one of the suitcases and she pulled this on, before hurrying to the window which overlooked the front door.

She drew back the blackout curtains and pushed up the window, then poked her head out and called down. 'Hello, we're not up yet. Who is it?'

A man she'd never seen before stepped into view and stared up at her in astonishment. 'I say, are you Mrs Williams? I got an emergency call. I'm Doctor Simpson.'

'This is the Dower House. You want Radcliffe Hall itself. If you continue around the corner you will see it in front of you.'

He waved and apologised for disturbing her and ran back to his car. She had an awful feeling about this. Clarissa must be really ill if the doctor had been called out in such a hurry. 'Alex, we must get up at once. The doctor has just been here; he must have been looking for Clarissa. I want to see if there's anything I can do.'

This time he woke up, rubbed his eyes and yawned. He looked years younger with his hair tousled and his cheeks unshaven. 'God, that's awful. I don't know if there's anything we can do, but we must certainly offer to help.' He was dressed and in the bathroom shaving before she'd had time to find clean underwear. No doubt being in the RAF had

235

speeded up this process.

'I don't need any breakfast; I'm full after our midnight feast,' Barbara told him as she hastily pulled on the clothes she'd worn yesterday.

'Leave the tray; I'll take it. You're not supposed to be lifting heavy things.'

'Thank you. I'll just clean my teeth and so on and be downstairs. Do we want to light the fires everywhere again today?'

'No, that was a one-off for our wedding day. We can spend the day in the kitchen and light a fire in the sitting room this afternoon.'

He rattled off downstairs with the tray, leaving her to use the bathroom. After all the passion during the night it seemed strange to be talking about something so mundane as lighting a fire. Somehow she'd thought being married would be more romantic; maybe it would have been if they'd had a few days away somewhere for a honeymoon.

She pulled the bed straight and ran down to join him for a quick cup of tea before they went up to the hall. He was stripping the table of the unused crockery and cutlery when she got down. 'When do you have to report back to base?'

'Tomorrow morning, so we have today to get settled in. Should I have left this? You look a bit put out.'

'After your mother and my grandmother went to so much trouble it seems a shame we didn't use it. Maybe we can lay up again tonight and cook ourselves a delicious dinner.' She drank a few mouthfuls of her tea and put it down. 'That tastes a bit funny. Is the milk off?'

He sniffed the jug and shook his head. 'No, it's fine. Mum went off tea when she was expecting Ned; perhaps you're doing the same. Shall I make you something else?'

'No, thanks. I think we'd better get going. I still haven't rung to say thank you, but it will have to wait until we get back.'

She hadn't bothered to put on her hat and gloves, and regretted it — the sun was out but the wind was bitter. Alex took her hand. 'Let's run. We don't want to stand about out here.' Without waiting for her agreement he set off, and she had no option but to go with him. They took the route past the stables as this led directly to the back door.

He knocked loudly, but when no one answered he opened the door. 'Hello, it's Alex and Barbara. We wondered if we could do anything.'

Nobody answered. 'Close the door, Alex. We'll go and find them. I don't think, in the circumstances, Mrs Williams will mind.'

She vaguely remembered the layout of the house from New Year's Eve and headed for the main staircase. The sound of voices coming from the drawing room must mean Clarissa was downstairs and not in her bedroom.

'We should have knocked on the front door; Mrs Williams would have heard us then,' said Barbara. 'Should we creep out?'

'Don't be daft, Babs. We're here now.' He strode over to the drawing room door and knocked loudly. 'Mrs Williams, it's Barbara and me. We wondered if you needed us to do anything?'

Immediately the conversation stopped and there was the patter of feet on the parquet. The door opened and Clarissa stood there looking perfectly fit. Seeing their stunned expressions, she laughed. 'How kind of you to come. It's not me who needed the doctor, but Ma. She fell off the stepladder and she's broken her ankle. Come in, Doctor Simpson is just putting a temporary splint on.'

'I'm so glad it's nothing worse than that. We thought you were unwell.' Barbara was so relieved to see her friend she stepped forward and hugged her.

'Is there an ambulance coming?'

'No, Alex, I have to get her there myself. I say, do you think you could take us? Pa's car has half a tank of petrol, but I'm afraid I don't drive.'

'Of course I can. If you give me the key I'll bring it round and make sure it's running okay.'

'Come in, Barbara, Alex; don't stand about in the freezing hall. It's much warmer in here,' Mrs Williams called, sounding remarkably cheerful for someone who'd just broken her ankle.

Clarissa led them into the room that was only marginally warmer than the entrance hall. Mrs Williams was sitting on the sofa with her right foot up and the doctor was making the final adjustments to the temporary splint.

'I'm so sorry about your accident, Mrs Williams, but what were you doing up a stepladder?' Barbara asked.

'There's a mouse nesting behind the picture rail over there and I was trying to poke him out with a stick.' She gestured vaguely towards the corner, where a stepladder was leaning rakishly against the wall. 'I was doing really well when the little bugger poked his head out, and I was so startled I fell.' She laughed. 'I think he's won this round. We must get a cat, Clarissa darling, as your father's no longer with us to forbid it.'

'Mrs Williams, could you tell me where the car keys are? I'm going to take you to the hospital to get your ankle set.'

'Last time I saw them they were hanging on a hook on the French dresser in the kitchen. It's so kind of you, and I do apologise for missing your wedding yesterday.' She smiled sadly. 'Actually, we were rather hiding from all the unpleasantness. Clarissa wasn't unwell at all.'

'We understand, and I don't blame you.' Barbara turned to the doctor, who was packing his bag. 'Will Mrs Williams have to stay in overnight, Doctor Simpson?'

'I should think so. It's a compound fracture and will need to be set under general anaesthetic. They'll want to keep her in until they're sure she's fully recovered from that.' He was remarkably young for a doctor, but seemed competent enough.

'In which case, Clarissa, you had better pack a bag for me — and please don't forget to put in my reading glasses, darling.'

'Would you like me to make you a cup of tea or something to eat whilst you wait for Alex to get the car going?'

'How kind, but no thank you, Barbara my dear. However, I should be eternally grateful if you could help me hop to the cloakroom.'

'Absolutely not, Mrs Williams. You must manage with a chamber pot. Also, absolutely nothing to eat or drink — is that clear?'

Having issued his orders the doctor nodded, picked up his bag, said his goodbyes and disappeared.

'My dear, how embarrassing this is. Perhaps you could — no, you wouldn't know where to find what I need. At least you can make sure your new husband doesn't come in.'

'Don't worry, Ma, I'll get the pot whilst Barbara moves that screen over here. It will give you a bit of privacy.'

Barbara folded the shutters across the windows and arranged the chipped Chinese lacquered screen in front of the sofa. Mrs Williams was shifting uncomfortably, her need obviously becoming desperate.

'Here you are, just in time by the look of it,' Clarissa said cheerfully.

'Can you manage on your own? Remember, your mother mustn't jar her ankle.'

Clarissa and her mother both assured Barbara they would be fine without her help, and she retreated to the hall just as a powerful car pulled up outside. She ran to open the front door just as Alex jumped out of a sleek black saloon. She was astonished when he told her it was the same make as his little sports car.

'I don't understand why Mr Williams has such a luxurious car when he can't even

241

afford to put food on the table.'

'None of our business, sweetheart, but I expect this was bought with his ill-gotten gains. The car has a heater and I've got it on full blast. I'll go in and get Mrs Williams. Let's hope it doesn't stall. I won't be long — why don't you get in the front and keep warm?'

She did as he suggested, not sure if she was enjoying his cosseting or finding it a bit too much. A few minutes later he came out carrying the patient and, with Clarissa supporting her mother's injured ankle, he carefully manoeuvred Mrs Williams onto the back seat. 'There you are, hope I didn't hurt you.'

'No, you did splendidly, young man. I do apologise again for bothering you the day after your wedding. I'm sure there are things you would rather be doing than ferrying an old lady to hospital.'

Barbara smothered her giggles and didn't dare meet his eye. Clarissa scrambled in beside her mother and Alex slammed the door and ran round to get in the driver's seat. 'Rush Green Hospital it is, then. We should be there in half an hour, but God knows how long it will take to get you admitted in the emergency department.'

'There is no need for you to wait, Alex,

Clarissa can stay with me and take a taxi home when I'm settled.'

'We're not abandoning you, Mrs Williams, and we're certainly going to take Clarissa home. In fact, why don't you be our first house guest?' No sooner had Barbara spoken than she regretted her words.

'I wouldn't dream of it, but thank you for asking. Actually, I've brought my own overnight bag and intend to find a B&B somewhere nearby. I'll find someone to collect us when Ma's allowed out.'

In a surprisingly short time the patient was admitted, and Barbara and Alex were on their way home. 'I'm really sorry I asked Clarissa to stay, but it seemed the right thing to do. I'm relieved she isn't coming.'

'So am I. Tonight I'm going to impress you with my culinary expertise whilst you sit with your feet up and listen to the wireless.'

'Alex, I don't need to put my feet up. I'm not unwell, I'm having a baby. However, I'll be delighted to hand over the cooking to you. Another thing I didn't know you could do.'

'Your brothers told me you're a good cook, and actually I'm not bad either. Mum was only too happy to teach me the basics, but I'm not sure what my dad thought about it. He can't even make a cup of tea that's drinkable.'

'I'll go and unpack whilst you do whatever you're going to do in the kitchen. When I've finished I'll come down and do the table so it looks as pretty as it did last night. That reminds me, I must make my phone calls first.' The car purred along the road, eating up the miles, and they turned into the drive mid-afternoon.

'I'll drop you off here and then go and put the car in the garage. We'd better hang on to the key; whoever is going to collect Mrs Williams and Clarissa will have to call here for it.'

Barbara went in the back door which, in their hurry to leave, they had forgotten to lock. She didn't want to go in until Alex got back just in case someone was in there — she was being silly, but after he had found that intruder last week she'd been a bit nervous.

She waited on the doorstep, her hands and feet slowly going numb, and then he arrived in the yard.

'Babs, what on earth you doing out here?'

'We didn't lock the door and I don't want to go in until you've checked there's nobody in there.'

'Sorry, that was my fault. Stand inside whilst I check, I'm absolutely positive there's nothing to worry about, but I can see how upset you are.'

He thundered up the stairs and then in and out of the bedrooms and raced down again. 'I told you, the beggars who came in last time are in jail. I shouldn't think there are any other criminals in this area. Let's go into the kitchen and have some of that soup and a hot drink before you go upstairs. You'll need to thaw out as it's a bit parky up there.'

The rest of the day passed pleasantly and by the time Barbara had sorted out the clothes, appetising smells were wafting up the staircase. She hadn't done the table yet. This would be the first proper meal they had shared as husband and wife, as having soup and sandwiches didn't count.

She remembered something she'd said to herself just after she'd met Alex last year — she had fallen in love with a man who she wasn't sure she actually liked. She liked John, but she wasn't in love with him. She glanced at the large bed and her lips curved. She was quite certain she had made the right decision. Liking someone wasn't enough to make a good marriage. Also, she'd revised her opinion of Alex ages ago. He was the kindest and most caring man, and she jolly well did like him as much as she liked John.

12

Barbara woke the next morning to find Alex had already left for the base, but he had written her a romantic note saying he'd ring if he couldn't return that night. She didn't relish the prospect of spending the day alone, especially as Radcliffe Hall was empty. Both her bicycle and grandpa's old one were in the shed. She wondered if Alex had cycled instead of using his car.

The room was freezing; they hadn't bothered to light the fire last night when they'd tumbled into bed. She hoped all this love-making wouldn't harm the baby, because she didn't want to give it up until she absolutely had to. She grabbed her dressing gown and scooted into the bathroom for a strip wash; the day was far too cold to have a bath. Living at the Grove had been so luxurious she was going to find it a bit primitive here, until she got used to having no central heating.

Already the linen basket was full, but strangely nothing of Alex's was in there — she was certain he'd changed his shirt and underwear, so he must have taken it back to the base for his orderly to wash. He was being very considerate. She hoped this wasn't just a temporary thing, as she was beginning to like being spoilt.

By the time she'd sorted out the range, finished the washing-up from the delicious dinner last night and tidied up, she was ready for some breakfast. The idea of spending the day alone still didn't appeal to her. It was fine and cold outside; maybe she would get out her cycle and explore the area — although she really should write thank-you notes for all the wonderful wedding presents they'd received. They had brought only half of them to the Dower House, and her grandparents would bring the rest when they came on Saturday morning.

The sudden clang of the telephone startled her and she slopped her drink on the table. She rushed to the entrance hall and snatched the receiver up. 'Good, I thought you might be out. Sorry I left without saying goodbye but I didn't want to wake you.'

'Alex, I didn't expect to hear from you this morning. I thought I'd go for a bike ride. I don't want to be cooped up in here all day.'

'Why don't you go and see Valerie? The place is easy to find and I don't reckon it's more than two miles. Give her a ring to make sure she's in. I've written all the numbers you might need on the pad by the telephone.'

She flicked through and saw his sister's number. 'That's a good idea. I'll do that. I hope nobody rings up to ask for the car key whilst I'm out, but I'm sure Clarissa doesn't expect me to hang about all day on the off chance. Are you flying today?'

'That's what I'm ringing about. I've got to go to Biggin Hill to collect a new kite, so I doubt I'll be back tonight. Will you be all right on your own?'

She was tempted to say no, but there was no point in worrying him as there was nothing he could do about it. She must get used to doing things for herself; she was a married woman and would be a mother in a few months.

'Of course I will. I've got plenty to do and lots of books to read. Tom and David will be coming tomorrow and I've not got their room ready yet.' There was an awkward pause. She wanted to tell him she loved him and missed him but the words didn't come easily, especially over the phone.

'Don't overdo it, darling, will you? I've got to go. I'll try and ring you again tonight. I love you.'

'I love you, too. Don't worry, I'm not going to do anything silly.'

She replaced the receiver and wiped her

eyes with her sleeve. This was only the beginning — how was she going to manage when he was actually flying a live sortie and could be shot down at any minute? As far as she knew, Hitler and his Luftwaffe weren't expected to attack just yet, so they must make the most of the time they had together and not think about what might happen in the future.

Valerie must've been standing next to the phone, as she picked it up immediately. She was thrilled to hear from Barbara and immediately invited her to come over for lunch. The detailed directions she gave made the journey seem simple enough. After carefully locking the back door Barbara headed for the shed, noticing the MG had gone. Perhaps Alex didn't realise there was a bicycle for him too.

The lane was a bit muddy and she was glad she'd decided to wear her gumboots and tuck her slacks into them. She was able to see over the hedge into the fields. In several she saw the thin green blades of winter wheat poking through the black soil, in another a field of dispirited cows. She waved to a group of Land Girls trudging across the lane clutching various tools; they looked as if they were going to do some hedging or ditching. A backbreaking job, and one she'd expected to be doing at some point, but now everything had changed and she would be exempt from war work.

Valerie was in the yard when Barbara pedalled in. 'You've made good time. I just came out to collect the eggs; I didn't expect you for another half an hour.'

Barbara dismounted and leant her bike against the wall so she could hug her sister-in-law. 'It's no distance at all. I hope you'll come over and see me when you're not too busy. It only took me twenty minutes; I think I could walk it in less than an hour.'

'I should like to come and see where you and Alex are living. Come in, I'll collect the eggs later on.'

'I'd love to help. Shall we do it now?'

Fortunately the hens were free range and there was no smelly henhouse, as the chickens laid their eggs in the barn. Although Barbara didn't have morning sickness, she was finding strong smells made her feel a bit queasy.

After a great deal of rummaging in the straw in the enormous barn, they'd collected more than two dozen fresh eggs. 'I enjoyed that,' said Barbara. 'I'd intended to join the Land Army, but now I'm married I must think of something else to do.' The farm was of a similar size to the Evertons' but had more livestock and was less arable. 'How are you managing? Have you lost your labourers?'

'Two of them have been conscripted already, but the other one's too old to be called up. We've put in for Land Girls but they haven't got that organised yet.' She grinned as she led the way inside. 'You could always come and give us a hand if you want.'

How was Barbara going to refuse without revealing her condition? 'I'd love to, but it might be a bit tricky as my little brothers are going to live with us half the time, and there's holidays and half-terms and things to think about.'

'Anyway, the offer's there. It would be lovely to see you more often.' Valerie rubbed her stomach protectively. 'I'm expecting a baby in August, and as I had a miscarriage last year, I need to take things easy. So you see, I'm going to need help with the chickens and so on.'

Barbara had no choice; it would seem mean not to agree to help out. 'I'm really sorry, and please don't tell anyone, but I'm in the same condition.'

Valerie shrieked and grabbed Barbara's hands. 'I knew it! I don't really want you to come over and work here; I was trying to push you into telling me. Peter and I were pretty sure you were pregnant too, but it's not the sort of thing you can ask someone who's just getting married.'

'It's all a bit embarrassing. We got carried away on New Year's Eve. Alex asked me to marry him before I knew for sure. He didn't want me to think he was doing it because he had to. My grandparents know, and I suppose now that you and Peter do as well, we'd better tell your parents. Will they be horrified?'

Valerie shook her head. 'Of course not. Everybody can see you're head over heels in love, and the baby won't be all that early. Sit down, I'll make us a cuppa.'

'Not for me, thank you. I've gone right off tea. I like hot water so I'll have that, please.'

'I can't tell you how happy I am about this — the babies will be born around the same time and with you living so close, they can grow up together. Mum will be absolutely thrilled. She's already knitting like a maniac.'

'Baby clothes will be more fun than knitting balaclavas for the WVS. I've done loads and can't say I enjoyed the experience. I prefer to sew, although I'm not very keen on that either. I like to be outside.'

Peter came in for his lunch and greeted Barbara as if he'd known her for years. 'You could have knocked me down with a feather when Alex told us you were moving in so close. My Valerie gets a bit lonely away from her mum. Having you almost next door will be grand.'

Over meat pasties and vegetable soup they moaned about the difficulties caused by rationing, the lack of farm labourers and the danger of living so close to an airbase. Barbara was sorry to leave and promised to come over the following Monday. Peter wouldn't let Valerie cycle or walk in her condition.

There was a young man in khaki sitting on the front steps when Barbara pedalled up the drive. He jumped to his feet as soon as he saw her. 'You must be Mrs Everton. I've come for the key to the car so I can go and collect Mrs Williams and Clarissa from the hospital. I've been sitting here for an hour.' He didn't introduce himself and glared at her as if it was her fault he'd had to wait.

He was scowling, and she gave him her best stare in return. 'I'm sorry you had to wait, but I wasn't going to stay in all day on the off chance somebody came round. Stay there and I'll get it for you.' She jolly well wasn't going to ask him in — not when he'd been so grumpy.

She pushed her bike down the path at the side of the house and propped it against the wall, then grabbed the car key from the hook in the kitchen and unbolted the front door. He held out his hand and she tossed it to him. He didn't respond. 'How is Mrs Williams?' she asked.

'She's broken her ankle, how do you think she is? I take it you're going in to light the fires and get everything ready for them?'

She bristled. 'No, I'm not. I'm her tenant, not her housekeeper.' She slammed the door and bolted it firmly behind her. How rude he was — the worst kind of toffee-nosed, arrogant young man. He reminded her of the one she'd met at the New Year's Eve party. Why did these men, who had been given everything by their doting parents, sometimes turn out like this?

The house was considerably warmer than outside and the range was burning well. Barbara would make herself something to eat and take a book to bed; she'd had more than enough exercise for one day, and hearing about Valerie's miscarriage last year had made her a bit worried about her own pregnancy.

She would get up early, sort out the bedroom for the boys and then make some soup and an egg and bacon pie for lunch. She'd come back with a dozen fresh eggs and intended to make good use of them. Perhaps she was being a bit mean not going over to the house and making sure everything was ready, but it really wasn't her job. Then she remembered Clarissa telling her they had a daily woman called Ada Hughes who lived in the village. Perhaps she would cycle down and ask her if she could come and sort things out — it wouldn't take long and shouldn't do her any harm.

She had no idea where Mrs Hughes lived, but was sure someone would be able to tell her the address. She asked a young woman pushing a pram bulging with small children and was told the house she wanted was next to the church.

This was somewhere else she ought to investigate. She wouldn't be able to go to the Ingatestone church now she was living here and, whatever her feelings about religion, her brothers ought to go every week. The church stood on a hill and she was a bit breathless when she arrived at her destination.

She had been directed to a row of recently built terraced cottages. She was halfway up the path when the door opened and a woman in her forties with the most startlingly orange hair flung open the door. 'Well I never. Who do we have here? I'm not expecting any visitors, I can tell you.'

'Good afternoon, Mrs Hughes. I'm Barbara Everton and my husband and I have just moved into the Dower House at Radcliffe

Hall.' How silly she sounded, as if she were a member of the royal family, not an ordinary girl. 'I'm not sure if you know, but Mrs Williams has broken her ankle and will be coming out of hospital this afternoon. I was rather hoping you might be able to light a few fires and perhaps make them something to eat?'

'Well I never did! Poor things, and after all the fuss with Mr Williams too. You wait there, Mrs Everton. I'll just get me hat and coat. My Bertie has a long shift at the marge factory and won't be back until late.' She vanished and Barbara returned to her cycle, determined to have a look at the church she had heard so much about. Sure enough, there was an impressive sculpture of a horned animal; she was fairly sure it was a bull's head. This must be where the village got its name from. St Andrew's was bigger than the church at Ingatestone but about the same age — she wasn't too good at dates, but the building must be hundreds of years old.

Ten minutes later the cleaning lady appeared from behind the house pushing an ancient bicycle. 'Thank you for coming, Mrs Hughes. I'm sure Mrs Williams will be pleased. I was thinking that maybe the Chesterfield in the drawing room could be made up for her to sleep on, as I doubt she'll be able to go upstairs very easily.'

'Fair enough. I reckon she'll be on crutches for a few weeks. She told me you was coming to live next door — full of it, she was. A real lifesaver your rent is, I can tell you.'

They pedalled back to the hall without further conversation. Barbara called out as they were nearing her house, 'Do you have a key? If not, I have one you can borrow.'

'Yes I do, love. Makes sense, as I'm in and out of here most days. Ta ever so for fetching me. I could do with a bit extra, what with everything being so expensive and rationing and all that. TTFN.'

Barbara hoped Mrs Hughes had a decent torch, because she'd be going home in the dark and didn't have any lights on her bicycle. Barbara dumped her own cycle in the shed and let herself in. She paused just inside the back door and breathed in the aroma. Yes, the place definitely smelled like home. It seemed strange to have so much room. Somehow the Grove, although huge and with more than a dozen bedrooms and countless other rooms, had never seemed overlarge because there was so much going on all the time.

She was too tired to do any cooking tonight; she would just have to get up early in the morning and get things done before the visitors arrived. The house was secure, the range banked down for the night, and she had a hot water bottle and large mug of cocoa to take upstairs with her.

The bedroom was unpleasantly cold, but it would be too extravagant to light the fire now. She must get someone to fill up the log store and cut her sufficient kindling to last the winter — there might be a national shortage of coal, but surely there were enough dead trees around that nobody wanted? She would ask Grandpa tomorrow if he knew anyone who could do this for her. Maybe Joe could do it and bring it over in the pony cart?

She scrambled into bed in her warmest nightgown and kept her dressing gown and socks on. Her hands were warm from the heat of the cocoa, and the hot water bottle was tucked securely in the small of her back. This would be her second night of sleeping on her own in the house — she'd better get used to it, because Alex was likely to be away more than he was home in a few months.

The phone on the bedside table rang, the sound so loud in the silence that Barbara almost fell out of bed in fright. She quickly put down her half-empty mug and stretched out to grab the receiver. 'Hello, Barbara Sinclair — sorry, Barbara Everton here.'

'I rang earlier, darling,' came Alex's voice.

'I was getting really worried, as Valerie said you'd left her house hours ago.'

She quickly explained where she'd been and he ticked her off for overdoing things. 'I'm absolutely fine, and I'm in bed now curled up with a book. As it's only eight o'clock, I shall get plenty of rest before I have to do anything else tomorrow morning. Will you be able to come over, even for a short time, this weekend?'

'I'm ringing from an airfield in Kent. I've been in the air most of the day and am absolutely knackered. I'm about to fly back, but will be on duty until Sunday morning. I might be able to wangle a couple of hours then.'

She swallowed the lump in her throat. 'That's wonderful. I'll have the boys here all weekend so I won't be lonely, but I do so want to see you. I really miss you, Alex. This bed seems to be too big just for me.'

His rich, dark chuckle made her smile. 'Believe me, darling girl, I'd much rather be in it with you than freezing my backside off in a Spitfire.'

'I wish you didn't have to fly at night. It must be far more dangerous — '

'Don't think about it, sweetheart. Just pretend I'm warm and cosy in the mess, drinking beer.'

When he hung up her cheeks were wet. She seemed to be crying all the time at the moment. Was it because of her condition? She would have to ask Grandpa when she saw him tomorrow. She wiped her face on the sheet and snuggled down under the eiderdown — she didn't want her cocoa now but would heat it up for breakfast.

The book no longer interested her, so she turned out the light and settled down, hoping to fall asleep quickly and not think about Alex flying home. She ran through the conversation and wondered why she couldn't use endearments as he did. Somehow the words 'darling', 'sweetheart' and 'my love' just didn't come easily to her. She wanted to call him 'darling', but just couldn't. Maybe her abusive childhood had damaged her in some way and she would never be able to talk to Alex in the loving way he talked to her.

She fell asleep eventually and woke the following morning feeling more optimistic. She hadn't heard the car bring Mrs Williams and Clarissa back yesterday and didn't have time to go across and make sure everything was okay. If she finished her chores before the family arrived she would ring and check they were both all right.

The room for her brothers was clean and tidy; all she had to do was make the beds.

There was a full bookshelf and the large trunk crammed with toys as well as those she and Alex had put in the dining room downstairs — more than enough to keep them occupied over a weekend.

Their bicycles would be useful for going to Church on Sunday mornings; she must ask Grandpa what he thought about bringing them over. It might be possible for them to cycle back and forth once the weather improved, but it was almost eleven miles and that might be too much for them.

The fire was laid and the guard hooked to the wall; there was no need to light it until after lunch. Grandma would prefer to sit in the sitting room and not the kitchen, so Barbara put a match to the kindling and hurried into the kitchen to bring the range to cooking heat so she could put the soup on to simmer, and the quiche in to bake.

Should she ring Mrs Williams, or go over there? She wasn't quite sure how to connect to the other half of the party line, but jiggled the rest a few times and there was definitely a dinging noise at the other end.

'Is that you, Barbara?' Clarissa asked.

'Yes, I wasn't sure how to get you to pick up the phone, but what I did obviously worked. How is your mother? I didn't hear the car and wasn't sure if you were back.'

'Horrible Henry collected us and we were home before dark. I'm really sorry it had to be him, but I couldn't find anyone else at such short notice. His mother is a sweetie. His father died in the last war, and she has spoilt him dreadfully. He wouldn't have come if she hadn't insisted.'

'I'm glad it wasn't just me; I thought he was so rude. You haven't told me about Mrs Williams.'

'That's another thing. Thank you so much for going down and fetching Mrs Hughes. She had everything ready and is going to come in every day to cook until Ma's back on her feet. The consultant said it was a nasty break but should be completely better by the spring.'

'I'm so glad to hear that. I can't come over to see you today, as my family are coming any moment now. I don't think I told you, my brothers are going to live here at the weekends so I'll be busy until they catch the bus on Monday morning.'

'Are you going to church tomorrow? If you are, I'd like to walk with you. Would that be all right?'

'That would be lovely. I noticed when I was there yesterday that matins is at eleven o'clock. How long do you think it would take us to walk there?'

'Twenty minutes if we take a shortcut. I'll meet you outside your house at twenty past ten; that should give us ample time to get there.'

Barbara hung up, confident she was coping with her new role as wife and surrogate mother. The only thing she hadn't managed so far was the laundry. There must be a copper somewhere; she would look for it on Monday. The soup was ready, the cheese scones and the quiche in the oven, and all she had to do was lay the kitchen table.

She glanced at the handsome clock on the French dresser, a wedding present from Mr and Mrs Everton. Her first guests should be here any minute. There had been no phone call from the base, so she wasn't worried that Alex might have crashed on his way home. She couldn't expect him to be ringing her up every five minutes; the telephone should really be for emergencies only.

There was a mirror in the entrance hall — another present — and she checked her lipstick wasn't smudged and her hair was neatly restrained by the tortoiseshell combs. Satisfied there was no flour on the end of her nose, she went into the sitting room and threw half a dozen logs on the fire. The room was almost warm enough to sit in and looked very smart.

She went to stand at the window. She didn't want to miss the car when it arrived, and she'd only been there a few minutes when she saw it approaching. She ran around to the front door and had it open before the car had crunched to a halt. Grandpa wound down the window and shouted out to her: 'Do we leave the car here? Won't it be in the way?'

'No, it's fine up against the hedge like that. If the doctor comes to see Mrs Williams there's bags of room to get past. Remember the little turning you've just passed takes you around to the back, so you can park in the yard like last time. It will be easier to bring things in through the back door, but Grandma, I want *you* to come in through the front.'

She stood back to allow her to step into the entrance hall. 'How pretty, Barbara, and the flowers look lovely. What a transformation! Quickly, my dear, close the door — all the heat is escaping.'

'I'm so glad you like it. I feel as if I'm playing at being a grown-up in an extra-large doll's house. I didn't know housework could be such fun.'

'I'm afraid the novelty will soon wear off. I can't think of anything more tedious.' Grandma had never had to do any housework so she was probably biased.

'Let me show you what we've done. I'm afraid it's rather cold, as I don't have enough fuel at the moment. I'm hoping Joe can cut me some logs from the Grove and bring them over in the pony cart, and then I'll be able to light all the fires.'

'What a good idea. I don't know why we didn't think of that ourselves. We want you to be comfortable here, my dear. I couldn't bear to think of you living in a cold house.'

Barbara thought it better not to mention the primitive plumbing or the fact that she would have to do the washing herself and put it through the mangle. 'I can hear the boys coming in, so the conducted tour will have to wait.'

'Before you rush off, Barbara, there's something I need to talk to you about. David has started wetting the bed — Edward says it's nothing to worry about, that he'll get over it when things settle down. There is a rubber sheet in his suitcase.'

'I thought he was a bit subdued at the wedding. I think there's been too much change in their lives. They have changed their names to Sinclair to be like me and I've changed my name to Everton — no wonder David's confused.'

'When you think about it, Barbara, it has

265

been a very difficult time for them. Perhaps it would be better if they lived here permanently and just visited us on the occasional weekend?'

Barbara was about to agree but remembered what Alex had said about discussing things with him first. Also it would be really selfish to take the boys away from her grandparents, as they were so enjoying having a houseful. 'Shall we see how things are after a week or two? The Grove is so much more luxurious than here, and they have the Everton boys to play with. I think they'll want to stay where they are during the week.'

Grandpa insisted on carrying all the boxes and suitcases upstairs himself with the able assistance of Barbara's brothers. Lunch was a triumph, and during the afternoon they all helped with the unpacking. By the time her grandparents were ready to leave, the boys were settled in. She even managed to surreptitiously remake David's bed, putting the rubber sheet underneath a draw sheet so she could easily slip it off in the middle of the night if necessary and leave him with a dry bed.

Alex turned up just as Grandpa drove away. She watched them have a quick conversation through the car window, and then the MG disappeared down the narrow lane that led to the rear of the Dower House. Tom and David raced to the back door to greet him. They both seemed in good spirits and she hoped she was worrying unnecessarily about David's mental state.

'Sorry I'm so late, darling, but the good news is I don't have to be back until midnight.' Alex's mouth was icy after driving in an open-top car, but Barbara revelled in his kiss and things might have gone further if her brothers hadn't been watching.

'That's wonderful. We're in the middle of a game of Monopoly. You can have Grandpa's hand.'

'That's not fair, Babs. Grandpa's winning — I want to have his hand,' David whined.

'Why don't you boys find something else to do?' Alex suggested. 'If you start setting up the train set in the dining room, I'll give you a hand after I've thawed out and had a cuppa.'

This suggestion went down well and the boys went away happily to start unpacking the trains — this had been their Christmas present from their grandparents.

'Thank you. David is a bit upset by all the changes; we're going to have to be careful over the next few weeks.'

'He's not been himself since we told him we were getting married. Poor little chap. It's very hard for him losing you so soon after arriving in Essex. Why don't we have them here permanently?'

'Grandma suggested that as well, because he's started wetting the bed.' She stopped and smiled. 'Oh dear, that sounds as if she's trying to get rid of him because of the extra work. You know what I mean; she wants him to be happy. I said we'd wait and see how he was in a few weeks before making that decision, but thank you for offering.'

Once safely in the kitchen away from childish eyes, Alex pulled her into his arms and they spent an exhilarating quarter of an hour in a passionate embrace. Eventually he released her, his cheeks flushed and his eyes dark. 'God, I love you so much. It's going to be bloody hard leaving here tonight.'

'The boys go to bed at eight o'clock, so we can do the same.' She was as eager as he to tumble into bed and take their lovemaking to the next step.

13

The boys settled into their new routine and David no longer seemed as disturbed by the changes in his life. After a few weeks, living with their grandparents during the week and their sister at the weekends was working perfectly. Barbara returned to the Grove whenever she could and always visited her in-laws at the same time. Being married wasn't as hard as she'd expected; in fact both she and Alex had adjusted to their new roles as well as the boys had. Barbara was now four months pregnant but still didn't need maternity clothes; she was just leaving the top button of her slacks undone and wearing a loose blouse and jumper. Nobody, so far, suspected her condition.

When the boys had their Easter holiday, Barbara spent it with them at the Grove; there was far more for them to do there and she enjoyed not having to do any housework or laundry. The summer term was underway and her world seemed far removed from the violence of war. If it wasn't for the fact that Alex was on duty more than he was at home, she could almost believe nothing horrible was ever going to happen.

The weather was suitably springlike and Alex now used the bicycle to dash backwards and forwards from the base. After a particularly harsh winter, Barbara was enjoying the sunshine and most days she saw Clarissa or cycled over to see Valerie. She was enjoying the novelty of having two close female friends. One morning she was sitting in the kitchen of Radcliffe Hall waiting for the midday news to come on.

'Alex hasn't been home for a few days. Is there a flap on?' Clarissa asked as she pushed over a mug of hot water.

'He's not saying much. I don't think they're allowed to talk about it, but I'm sure you're right, and that's why I want to hear the news.'

The wireless crackled and the plummy voice announced it was the Home Service, and then the news bulletin followed. When it finished, Barbara's hands were clammy and she felt sick. 'It's really started, hasn't it? The phoney war's over. Now Hitler has occupied Denmark and Norway, it can only be a matter of time before he starts marching across the rest of Europe. I hope Alex isn't sent over there — it's so far away, I'd never know whether he was safe or not.'

'It's not going to be safe anywhere once the

bombing starts. At least we have a decent shelter to hide in. Pa insisted we had a lavatory, proper beds and furniture down there.'

'I ought to come and have a look. Is it very damp? The one at the Grove is tiny and dismal; I'm sure nobody will go down there unless there's a bombing raid directly overhead. The water drips down the walls and you can't leave bedding there, but have to take it with you when the siren goes.'

'No time like the present. Ma's having another driving lesson this morning. She's getting really good at it.' Clarissa laughed. 'Not that we have much petrol anymore. At least you have your bicycles. We've tried to get hold of one, but no luck so far.'

'I've got my old one at the Grove. I'll get Joe to bring it over in the pony cart for you. I can't believe how well your mother has got over her broken ankle; she hardly has a limp now.'

Clarissa didn't bother to lock the back door; since her father and his unpleasant associates had been arrested, there was no need. The shelter had been built at the back of the house, no more than a few yards from the back door. It had been sunk into the ground as all Andersons were, but there the resemblance ended.

'Goodness me! This is positively luxurious — not only comfortable bunks to sleep in, but a table and chairs. And is that a paraffin stove right at the back with the meat safe and larder?' Barbara was very impressed.

'Yes, we can prepare basic meals down here. We have a stack of tins and tea and condensed milk, so we could be down here for several days and not starve.' At the bottom of the concrete stairs was an alcove with a heavy curtain. Clarissa pulled it aside with a flourish. 'Voilà! All your needs are catered for. Not as good as a flush lavatory, but a chemical toilet is a lot better than a bucket and chuck it. The Elsan system works really well; whatever they put in the stuff stops all the nasty smells.'

'It even has a wooden seat with a lid — and real paper, not torn-up newsprint.' Barbara was finding it a bit claustrophobic despite it being twice the size of the one at the Grove. 'I've seen enough, thank you. I'll know where to come if there's an air raid.' She scampered up the steps into the April sunshine, pleased to be outside again. She really didn't like being underground and prayed she'd never have to spend any time in the shelter.

'I'd better get back,' said Barbara. 'I promised Grandma I'd finish knitting the scarves for the sailors by the weekend. Although I'm no longer an active member of the WVS, at least I can still do a bit for the war effort.'

'Barbara, if you don't mind me asking, are you having a baby?'

'I didn't think I showed yet. How did you guess?'

'You don't drink tea anymore and you didn't like being in the shelter. Congratulations, you'll make a lovely mother. Have you told the boys?'

'No, we thought we'd wait until a lot nearer the time — no need to worry them yet.'

'I should think they'll love being uncles. Will I see you tomorrow?'

'Valerie's coming here for a change. Peter has to take a load of hay somewhere nearby so he's dropping her off. Why don't you come over and meet her? She's expecting too.'

'Golly! I think I'll give it a miss. I'm not over-fond of babies myself, and two expectant mothers would be a bit much for me.'

Although she said this with a smile, Barbara detected something sad in the comment. She decided to walk into the village and see if they had any vegetables. On the way she considered Clarissa's remark; her friend found being around anyone pregnant difficult because she'd never be able to have children herself. She would make an effort not to talk about babies with her in future.

★ ★ ★

On Friday, when Barbara walked down to meet the boys from the bus, Tom was more excited than usual and danced around her, desperate to give her his news.

'You'll never guess, Babs, but we're going to be in the school play. We're being evacuees — the play is supposed to be showing parents why children should be sent away somewhere safe. Mr Barclay said half the children who left London last year have gone home again.'

David grabbed her hand like a lifeline and his face was pinched and grey. 'Will they send us away when the bombing starts? Everyone says Hornchurch is going to be a target because of the base at Sutton Farm.'

'Of course not, David. We'll all live at the Grove, where it's going to be perfectly safe. Don't worry, I won't let anyone take you away from me.' She put her arm around his shoulders and drew him close.

'Do you have a lot of lines to learn?'

'I've got about twenty, and David's got quite a few as well. We've got to start learning them this weekend. Do you know, Babs, we're going to be doing this play to all the parents and other people as well. It's going to be jolly good fun.' Tom's gas mask bounced as he hopped from one foot to the other.

'Grandpa, Grandma and I will definitely come, but I'm not sure whether Alex will be able to. He's very busy at the moment.'

Tom nodded wisely. 'Sir was saying the Germans are getting ready to invade Europe. I expect Alex will have to try and help the French.'

Barbara was shocked he was so knowledge-able, and so matter-of-fact, about what was coming. 'I'm sure your teacher was right, but I don't want to think about it and I don't think you should either. Let's just enjoy every day before all the unpleasantness begins.'

They were just sitting down to tea when the back door banged and Alex strode in. Barbara flung back her chair and threw herself into his arms. Ignoring the boys, they kissed passionately — it had been far too long since she'd seen him.

'Are you staying the night, Alex, or do you have to get back?'

'Twenty-four hour pass, sweetheart, but I'm pretty sure this will be the last one for a while. We'll talk later. I'm starving; I hope there's enough tea for me.' He ruffled the boys' hair as he walked past and pulled out a chair next to hers.

'We've got meat pasties, mashed potatoes and cabbage, and then baked apples for dessert.' She laughed as she handed him his cutlery. 'I'm afraid there's not a lot of meat in the pasties, but they still taste very nice.'

Alex was brilliant with the boys, and before they tumbled into bed they were both almost word-perfect and had also done most of their homework. This would make the rest of the weekend so much easier. Nagging the boys to get this finished was stressful for all of them.

Barbara was waiting for Alex in their bedroom, eager to hear his news but rather dreading what it might be. She was still dressed; she wanted to talk before they made love. He came in and quietly closed the door. Her breath caught in her throat. She loved him more every time she saw him; if anything happened to him she didn't know how she'd be able to carry on.

He was across the room in two strides and pulled her roughly into his arms. 'Please, don't look at me like that, darling girl. I know what you're thinking and it breaks my heart.'

His chest was pounding, his arms tight around her, and her tears soaked his shirt. He rocked her gently until she recovered and then carried her to the bed and put her on it and flopped down beside her fully clothed. 'It's going to start any day, Babs. The squadrons at Hornchurch will be in the front line, and once it all kicks off we'll be moved about a lot — you won't know where I am, or anything else.'

She blew her nose and rubbed her cheeks dry. Getting in a state wouldn't help him or the baby. 'I'm sorry to be such a wet blanket. I seem to cry at the slightest thing nowadays. Don't worry about me; when things get tough I'll move back to the Grove.' She snuggled into his arms and he pulled the eiderdown over them. 'Can you tell me what's going on at the base, or is it hush-hush?'

'That bastard Hitler is about to turn his attention to Holland, and when they fall the Jerries will be straight into France. I'm certain our base will be told to send squadrons over to protect our troops and help the French.' He was stroking her hair as he spoke. 'The wing co is worried they won't have enough pilots — they can't train them fast enough. The new bods we're getting have so little airtime they'll be shot down straight away.'

'I'm so proud of you — you're so brave. I think the RAF are all that stands between Hitler and us.'

He didn't answer and she rolled over and raised her head. He was sound asleep and he was still wearing his uniform. She slipped out of bed and quickly undressed, put on her nightie and got under the blankets, leaving him with the eiderdown. At least he wasn't wearing his shoes, even if he had everything else on.

She was woken during the night when he started to remove her unromantic nightdress. Sleepily she raised her bottom and he pulled it over her head, then his warm hands began their magic. They made love as if it might be the last time they did so — silently, passionately — and together they reached new heights. When Barbara climaxed he joined her in release; and they fell asleep, hot and sweaty, still intimately entwined.

At dawn Barbara untangled herself and pulled her discarded nightdress on before heading for the bathroom. She pushed open the window and leaned on the windowsill, listening to the soaring chorus of waking birds. At times like this it was hard to comprehend they were in the middle of a war. She turned at a slight sound behind her. David was standing there looking at her with his head tilted sideways and his eyes scrunched up.

'You're getting very fat, Babs. I can see your big tummy.'

She sighed. She had no choice; she would have to tell them about the baby and hope for the best. 'How clever of you to notice. I'm not fat, exactly. I'm going to have a baby in a few months, and you and Tom will be uncles. Isn't that exciting?'

'An uncle? None of my friends are an uncle. I'll be able to swank about this. I bet Grandpa and Grandma will be pleased.' He frowned and scratched his head. 'Will Ned and Jim be uncles too?'

'Of course they will. You could form a gang and call it the Four Uncles.'

'I think that's a smashing idea. I'm going to tell Tom.' He scampered out of the door and then rushed back in again. 'Will it be a boy?'

'I've no idea. We'll have to wait until the baby arrives before we know that.'

There was no point in going back to bed; the boys would want breakfast now they were awake. Barbara wanted to wake Alex and spend every precious minute with him, but he'd looked so tired yesterday she left him to sleep. He didn't appear in the sitting room until mid-morning when she was playing cards with her brothers. He kissed her thoroughly and then turned to grin at the boys, who were pulling faces at them.

'Morning, lads. Sorry I'm down so late. I thought we could cycle to the base this morning and you could have a look at my new Spitfire.'

'When? Can we go now? Is Babs coming too?' Tom chucked his cards on the table and rushed over to Alex, David right behind him.

'Hang on, I've got to have some breakfast first. Are you going to come, darling?'

'Absolutely. I'll make a picnic and we can have it afterwards. It's a glorious day, more like June than the middle of April.' She stood up and pointed to the scattered cards. 'Put these away please, boys, and then you'd better check your bicycles don't have flat tyres.' She left them tidying up and followed Alex into the kitchen. 'The boys know about the baby, so you'd better ask your parents to tell Ned and Jim. Tom and David are so excited at the thought of being an uncle, they're bound to talk about it at school — and even though your brothers are in different classes, I'm sure they'll hear about it.'

'Good, I'm glad everybody knows now. Did you say when the baby is due?'

'Of course not. I don't look over four months. Let everybody think the baby is due in October, not September. Can you turn the wireless on? There'll be a news bulletin soon.'

Whilst she made Alex some toast, he fiddled with the knobs until he found the Home Service. 'David has been trying to tune this into another channel again. I'll tell him to leave it alone as we need to have it where we can listen to the news.'

They caught the end of 'Music While You Work' and Barbara was busy buttering bread for the sandwiches when the newscaster began his broadcast. She swayed and grabbed the edge of the table in shock. Hitler had bombed the low countries, flattened many of their cities, and was now storming across Europe towards France.

'My God, how horrible. Those poor people. Imagine being bombed and then occupied by the Germans.' She collapsed on a chair, unable to continue. Alex was at her side in a second and offering her comfort. Then the telephone rang.

'Bloody hell! I'm sorry, sweetheart; I expect my leave has been cancelled.' He shot out of the kitchen and she could hear him speaking quietly to someone on the other end. She looked at the pile of sandwiches and her eyes filled. There would be no picnic today — maybe no more this year.

He returned looking grim. 'Sorry, I've got to go. Take the boys over to Valerie's; they'll be so disappointed not to come to the base, but they'll will enjoy a picnic at the farm.'

He didn't say when he'd be back, but from his expression she guessed this could be the last time she saw him for a long while. She mustn't cry. She wanted him to leave sure she was coping on her own, and not worrying about her or the boys.

'That's a good idea; and I'll ring your parents later as well.' She swallowed the lump in her throat and stepped into his arms. He crushed her close; his kiss was fierce and he stared at her as if imprinting her face on his memory. She couldn't speak; she was too choked.

'I've got a photo of you in my cockpit and one in my pocket, next to my heart. I love you, darling girl. Knowing you are waiting for me, carrying my child, will keep me strong.'

His eyes glittered and he kissed her one last time, and then without another word strode out. She couldn't make her legs move to follow him and wave goodbye.

She did her best to remain cheerful; her brothers enjoyed the outing to the farm and fell asleep immediately, exhausted by all the fresh air and exercise. She was equally tired, but couldn't sleep and desperately wanted the comfort of Alex's arms around her in the big, empty bed. There had been no planes taking off from the base, but she was sure they were all on alert, ready to go to France when the word came through.

Around midnight she had almost decided to get up and make herself a hot drink when she felt a strange sensation in her tummy. For a moment she was disconcerted, then she placed both palms across the small mound that was the baby. There it was again — the baby was kicking, as if reminding her that however dreadful things were, she was carrying a new life inside her.

14

The flap at the base didn't turn into action and Alex was able to sleep at home three nights a week. Although the news from France was dire, life continued pretty much as usual. Then in the middle of May things changed. After the normal Monday morning rush to get the boys organised and on the bus, Barbara was cycling home when she was hailed by a group of ladies she knew from church.

'Mrs Everton, have you heard? The Prime Minister has resigned and that Winston Churchill has taken over.'

'No, I didn't have time to listen to the news this morning. I think Mr Churchill will make a better Prime Minister; he seems to know more about fighting than anyone else. With Hitler marching towards the channel, we're going to need someone strong in charge.' The group nodded and agreed with her. She smiled and made her excuses, saying she was expecting Alex to ring at any moment and needed to be at home.

She still found it strange to be addressed as Mrs Everton instead of being called by her name, but being married had raised her status and she was now a member of the local WVS and WI. Her advancing pregnancy was now an accepted topic of conversation and, as she was still barely showing when dressed, the ladies of the village assumed the baby was due in October. She certainly didn't contradict them.

Clarissa was waiting outside the back door when Barbara pushed her bike into the shed. 'Barbara, you look exhausted. Should you be cycling around in your condition, especially when it's so warm?'

'I'm fine; a nice glass of water is all I need. Come in, I'll make you a cuppa. I want to put the wireless on — Chamberlain has resigned and I want to hear more about it.'

With the windows open there was a pleasant through breeze and the kitchen, despite the range always burning, wasn't too hot. They listened to the bulletin in silence. Clarissa drained her cup and pushed it over for a refill. 'I think a coalition government is a good idea. There's no time for party politics at the moment.' She laughed. 'Golly, don't I sound grown up? Actually, I came over to invite you to supper tonight. Ma is having the park turned over to farming, and some men from the Ministry of Agriculture are coming to stay for a couple of nights to explain what she has to do. We thought you'd probably understand what they wanted, as Doctor Sinclair has already started ploughing up his grounds.'

'I'd love to come. Alex is on duty so I will be on my own anyway. Would you like me to come over and help with the meal?'

'If that's all right, it would be really helpful. Mrs Hughes has sciatica and we've got nobody at the moment. You know how useless we are in the kitchen.'

'I've just got to mangle my washing and hang it out and then I'll come over.'

Her friend left shortly afterwards and Barbara finished her chores, hoping the phone might go before she went to the Hall. If Alex did get a moment to ring she would much prefer to speak to him alone, but at least he could still reach her — having a party line with Mrs Williams did have that advantage.

She was halfway up the drive when someone yelled her name. She spun around to see Alex pedalling furiously towards her. She forgot her promise to help Clarissa and her mother and ran back to greet him. He dumped his bicycle and caught her as she arrived, swinging her around like a child. 'I've only got a couple of hours, but I just had to see you. Do you have to go to the Hall right now?'

'I can go later. I didn't say exactly when I'd be over. I'm invited to supper because they want me to cook it for them.'

He collected his bike without releasing her hand and wheeled it into the hedge and let it go.

'Nobody is going to steal this rattletrap so I might as well leave it here. Pete managed to get you some coffee; I know you haven't had any for ages.' The back door was unlocked; she never bothered when she was only going across to the Hall.

'I heard the news this morning. Is that why you've come over in such a rush? Is there something else that wasn't mentioned on the bulletin?'

'Not really. It seems Lord Beaverbrook is going to increase production of fighter aircraft, which is great — but we barely have enough pilots to fly the ones we've got, so I hope they are planning to train a lot more.'

'Do you think there's going to be an invasion? I'd hate to be living on the channel coast at the moment, especially as all our army is in France.'

'I don't want to talk about anything apart from us. Seeing you is the one time I can forget about this bloody war and what's coming.'

'I've decided to have the baby at the Grove.

Seems silly to have it here, and I don't know if you're going to even be based at Hornchurch by then. Mrs Hughes's son is a pilot, a non-commissioned officer, and his squadron has moved three times already this year.'

'I think we're going to stay based here, but there will be dispersal points for the squadrons on duty once things start and we have to sleep there. I gather conditions will be pretty primitive. I suppose my squadron could be moved to Gravesend, Rochford or even Croydon, depending on circumstances, but I won't be sent overseas, at least not at the moment.'

'I thought we weren't going to talk about the war. Let's try again. Joe's coming over tomorrow with another load of logs — we're going to have enough for the winter after this lot.' She frowned. 'Good grief! I probably won't even be here next winter, so why am I filling up the log store?'

He answered with his back to her. 'Doesn't matter. Even if we're not here next winter, we'll be back some time — this bloody war can't last forever.'

She watched him grind the beans and then carefully tip the coffee into the bottom of the jug. He added the water, stirred vigorously, then tipped some milk into a saucepan to heat. It didn't matter what he was doing — even something as mundane as making her a pot of coffee was a visual pleasure. As they spent so little time together, every snatched moment was precious, and she was sure he felt exactly the same way. There was a flutter of movement in her tummy.

'The baby's moving — I don't think you can feel it yet, but it won't be long before he's kicking properly.'

'That's amazing. You think the baby's a boy then? I wonder if he will have my red hair. He's bound to have green eyes — at least I think he is.'

This casual comment about the baby's possible colouring ruined the moment. She pushed back her chair and clapped her hand over her mouth as if she felt sick, and ran upstairs to the bathroom. They did both have green eyes and as far as she knew, no one in his family had blue eyes or blond hair. She didn't know a lot about how these things worked, but remembered someone telling her there had to be a particular eye colour or hair colour on both sides of the family for the baby to inherit those things.

Her mother had blue eyes and so did Grandma, so blue eyes were perfectly possible if John was the father. Her mother was also fair-haired. Her stomach lurched and she just made it to the lavatory in time. Before she could regain her feet, Alex came in and handed her a glass of water to rinse her mouth and a wet flannel to wipe her sweaty face. His actions reminded her of John; he had done the same for her a couple of times in the past. For as long as she could remember she had been plagued by bouts of nausea, usually brought on by emotional stress.

'I thought you'd got over the morning sickness, sweetheart. Has this been happening a lot?' He gently stroked her back and then put his hands under her arms and lifted her to her feet.

'No, I've not been sick for a while. I expect it was something I ate, and nothing to do with the baby at all.'

He reached around her and pulled the chain. 'Do you want to lie down? You look rather washed out.'

'I want to come downstairs and have my coffee. I'm fine now — in fact I might have some toast as well.'

He hugged her and kissed the top of her head. 'I wish I was able to be here with you all the time — '

'Even in peace time you would be away, wouldn't you? You're a regular member of the RAF. I expect I'll just have to get used to life with a husband who puts his duty first.'

'I won't always be in the RAF. I only joined because I could see the writing on the wall and had a pretty good idea this lot was coming. I signed on for nine years and I'm halfway through my stint. I can't think about the future until the war's over, but now I'm married to a woman of means, things could be very different for us.'

'What do you mean? Do you want to set up a business or something?'

'Actually I'd like to go to university, study architecture or maybe civil engineering — what do you think?'

'That would be wonderful. I've a horrible feeling a lot of engineers and architects are going to be needed later on.' She wanted to kiss him but thought he might not like it after she'd just been sick, even though she'd rinsed her mouth out thoroughly. 'You have to go back soon; let's go and drink the coffee and make some toast.'

When he cycled off she waved until she couldn't see him anymore, not sure if she was relieved or sad that he'd gone. She really ought to be going over to help Clarissa and her mother, but decided to take a long walk first and try and make sense of the muddle in her head.

Should she tell Alex the truth? If the baby

was born with blue eyes and fair hair, would that mean her secret would be instantly revealed? She was pretty sure all babies had blue eyes when they were born, and some children started off fair-haired and became dark as they grew up.

If her grandparents or Alex asked if she'd slept with John she wouldn't be able to lie about it. Perhaps if Alex was prepared for the possibility that the baby wasn't his . . . No, if he knew he might leave her. What about John? Presumably he knew she'd married Alex, but if ever he discovered she'd been pregnant at the time he would put two and two together and know the baby could as well be his as Alex's. The baby might be born with red hair, and then she would have ruined her marriage for nothing.

She paused to lean on a wooden gate and stare across the meadow. Whatever happened, one thing she was certain of — her grandparents would stand by her. She must think about the good things in her life: the fact that she was healthy, her brothers were happy, that she had loving grandparents and a generous trust fund which meant she would never have to rely on anybody else's money to live comfortably.

Her hands clenched and a stab of pain in her palm jerked her back to the present.

There was a large splinter embedded in the soft flesh at the base of her thumb, and removing it produced an impressive quantity of blood. She wrapped her hand in her hanky and turned for home. Her lips curved; when had the Dower House become her home and not the Grove?

Mrs Williams was overjoyed to see her. 'My dear, we were so worried you might be unwell and not able to come and help. Clarissa saw Alex leave an hour ago.'

'I'm sorry. I went for a walk. I'm here now and we have plenty of time to get everything ready. Show me what you've got in the pantry and I'll come up with a menu.'

Once the food was ready to go in the oven, the table laid and several vases of summer flowers put out to decorate the entrance hall, Barbara thought she'd done her bit. It wouldn't make any difference if she came to the meal or not; they'd only invited her so they could ask her to cook it for them with a clear conscience. She couldn't understand why two such intelligent women didn't make more of an effort in the kitchen.

'If you don't mind, Mrs Williams, I'm going to go home. I'm not feeling very well and I'm afraid I won't be able to join you for supper after all.'

They didn't try to persuade her to change

her mind, which rather confirmed her suspicion. She would curl up with a book in the sitting room and listen to the wireless for an hour or so and then have an early night. The news was grim: German troops were advancing at lightning speed and now occupied both Holland and Belgium. Rotterdam had been bombed almost to extinction. Although there was nothing said in the bulletin about the danger to the British troops, it seemed obvious they could well be trapped if something wasn't done about it.

★　★　★

The further Alex pedalled from the Dower House, the easier it was to push Babs and the baby to the back of his mind. If he was going to survive the next few months he had to focus entirely on his job — the men in his command were relying on him. There was no time for sentiment at the moment. He skidded through the gates and parked his bike with a heap of others. Nobody seemed to bother which bike they took; he wasn't even sure the one he was riding was the one that used to belong to Dr Sinclair.

He checked in and was told the CO was looking for him. He checked his office but the pretty young WAAF told him he was waiting in the mess. (The recent arrival of these women in Air Force blue had proved popular with the men.) Thank God! It couldn't be anything urgent. He strolled to the mess, stopping to greet friends and exchange pleasantries before he spotted his commanding officer. He didn't salute — nobody bothered much with that sort of thing here, leaving all that rigmarole to the Army.

'Good show, Everton. Need a word.' He pointed to a quiet corner and slouched over whilst Alex bought himself a pint of beer before joining him. 'Keep this under your hat for the moment; don't want to lower morale. I've heard things are bad in France; Lord Gort and the French tried to link up with the Belgian Army, but those bastard Germans got through our lines and there's bloody chaos out there. The Nazis have all but destroyed the squadrons in France. God knows what's going to happen next.'

'Will they send us out to replace those that are lost?'

'I don't know, but Fighter Command has kept the Spitfires out of the battle so far. Our job is to protect Britain from a German attack, but we can't leave those poor sods unprotected from the Luftwaffe, can we?'

Alex drank half his beer before answering. 'No we can't. The entire British Army is in

France at the moment. If they're defeated there's nothing to stop Hitler invading.'

'Anyway, old fellow, thought I'd better fill you in. I've let the other chaps know. The balloon's going up any day and all leave is cancelled indefinitely. Make sure your men are ready when the word comes; some of them have only got a few hours' experience in a Spitfire.'

'Shall I organise a few mock sorties? Dogfights without the ammunition? None of us have had experience of the real thing.'

'Bloody good idea. I'll leave it to you then. Let your boys be the bandits; a flight can try and catch you. No need to go up at night; we've already lost two buggers doing that.'

Alex went in search of Pete and then sent word to the rest of the squadron that they would be scrambling at dawn. He might as well make it as authentic as possible.

The next few days were spent in dawn patrols and everyone was getting jumpy. The British Expeditionary Forces were fighting for their lives in France, Calais was blockaded, and the only port left for the poor sods to escape from was Dunkirk.

Dispersal points had been set up away from the base, and Alex's squadron was the first to move to one. The conditions were primitive, the rations disgusting, and there were only tents to sleep in.

Operation Dynamo was the code word for the evacuation of the troops, and Alex was expecting to be in action at any moment. Finally the order came. There was no let-up; one sortie followed another. Alex sometimes led B flight across the channel and behind the beaches in an attempt to intercept any German aircraft that were coming up to attack the soldiers on the ground. His squadron also had to escort the Blenheims as they tried to bomb strategic points around Dunkirk.

By Thursday they were three days into the operation and he was too tired to think straight. He'd lost one man so far from his command, but A flight had lost two. He stared down from the cockpit at the sea below. In every direction was the flotilla of small ships ferrying the stranded troops from the beaches to the larger vessels waiting in deeper water. These were ordinary folk, fishermen and retired sailors, doing their bit for Britain. He was proud to be part of this extraordinary event and determined not to be shot down if he could possibly avoid it until all the soldiers were safely home.

By Tuesday the evacuation was over. He couldn't remember the last time he'd had a hot meal, changed his clothes or had any decent kip. God knew how many sorties they'd flown from Hornchurch — it must have been hundreds, but only three planes had been lost, and those all in the first sortie.

After the last flight he had fallen headfirst from his Spitfire, rolled across the wing and sprawled inelegantly on the grass. He had been too tired to get up; his Mae West had pinned him to the ground and it took the combined efforts of his two ground crew to heave him to his feet.

'Up you come, sir. There's transport waiting to take you back to base; you can have a nice hot bath and sleep in your own bed tonight.'

'Thanks, I can just about stagger across the field. I couldn't have kept going without your help, boys. You did a grand job.'

Somehow he pulled himself onto the back of a lorry in which a dozen other pilots were already sat. Nobody greeted him; they were all hollow-eyed and grey-faced with fatigue. He collapsed against the canvas and dozed until he was shaken awake by his orderly.

He hadn't washed or shaved for more than a week; he must stink to high heaven and look like a tramp, but he didn't care. He was alive — he had survived, and when he was called on again to fight he would be better prepared and more experienced.

'I'm too bloody tired to do anything but sleep. Unless there's another flap on, don't call me for six hours.' He yawned, his jaw cracking loudly. 'In fact, just leave me to it. I'll send for you when I need you.' He staggered into his room and collapsed on the bed intending to pull off his flying boots, but was asleep before he did so.

★   ★   ★

The roar of planes landing and taking off at the base from dawn till dark meant Barbara was reminded several times a day that Alex was risking his life. She decided to move back to the Grove for a few days, at least until the evacuation at Dunkirk was over. Her grandparents were delighted and Grandpa said he would drive over to fetch her immediately. She rang Clarissa and told her she was going to be away for a while.

'Good show. I wish I could do the same. Shockingly noisy at the moment, isn't it?'

'It isn't just the noise, Clarissa. It's impossible to relax for a minute knowing Alex is in one of the Spitfires. I've cancelled the milk and I don't suppose I'll get any post anyway. I'll ring when I get back. Don't overdo it. I'll see you soon.'

Barbara was waiting outside the front door when her grandfather arrived. She didn't need to take a suitcase as she had more than enough clothes at the Grove. She had the passenger door open before he could get out. The trees shook and she closed her eyes, waiting for the planes to vanish into the sky. 'When we decided to live here I'd no idea what it was going to be like when the base was fully operational.' She slammed the door and embraced him. 'I can't tell you how pleased I am to see you, Grandpa. I can't wait to get home and spend some time with you and the boys.'

'Elspeth and I were going to suggest it might be better for you to live with us at the moment. Damn dangerous place so close to a base, now things have started.'

'I'll certainly stay until Alex tells me it's safe to return. Valerie, my sister-in-law, says The Ministry of Agriculture is intending to provide a tractor for every farm. I hope that doesn't mean the Everton horses are going to go.' Her eyes filled at the thought of those magnificent animals being sent to the knacker's yard.

'Don't worry, my dear girl; Mrs Everton says they have more than enough hay to feed them.' He patted her on the knee. 'Everything a bit emotional, I expect. It's absolutely normal in your condition.'

'The baby is kicking and I don't feel sick very often. In fact I feel absolutely splendid at the moment, apart from being insane with worry about Alex.'

'It won't be so bad when you can't hear the planes. It's much quieter at the Grove. By the time they fly over us they've gained sufficient height not be so noisy.' He changed the subject. 'You'll hardly recognise the puppies — Buttons now has a long, curly coat and is the size of a spaniel. Patch is much smaller and looks more like a terrier. It's hard to believe they came from the same litter.'

'I expect that they're living outside; the cat won't want them in her basket now.'

He chuckled. 'Not a bit of it. Every night they curl up together as before. By the way, your mare is proving a godsend. Joe has her out every day with the trap; she's really taken to being in harness again.'

'I was going to go and see Silver before coming in, but I don't suppose she's there at the moment.'

'No, I'm pretty sure Joe's gone to the Everton's to collect something or other this morning. Don't look so despondent, my dear; you will have ample time to spend with her before you return to Hornchurch.'

In a little over three months everything had

changed here, and she'd not been part of it. Of course being married to Alex meant her loyalties must be to him, that her home was wherever he was, but she missed her brothers and grandparents and found it hard to reconcile the two sides of her life. The baby fluttered inside her — being an adult was so much harder than she'd expected.

Her grandmother had cancelled her visit to Brentwood especially to be there when Barbara arrived. 'You look positively blooming, my dear. Pregnancy suits you. Have you thought of any names yet?'

Barbara kissed her and shook her head. 'No, we've had so little time together and there's always something else to talk about. Also, most of Alex's leave has been at the weekends when the boys are with us.'

'I've asked Mrs Brown to serve lunch on the terrace. I don't believe you've eaten outside since you came here last year.'

'There's so much I haven't done. I did so want to live here and join the Land Army, and look where I am now — I'm stuck on my own with a baby on the way and a husband who could be shot down at any moment.'

'My dear girl, we'd no idea you were so unhappy living at Hornchurch. Stay here until the baby's born; let Edward and me look after you.'

Barbara was ashamed of her outburst. 'I'm sorry, Grandma. I'm not unhappy, not really. It's just not the way I thought my life was going to be. I love Alex, and I don't regret for one minute marrying him or having this baby. I just wish it had all happened next year, not right now.'

Grandpa guided her through the French doors and indicated a comfortable rattan chair on the terrace. 'Sit down, Barbara. You are getting overwrought; it won't do you or the baby any good.' Obediently she sat and he patted her shoulder. 'Good girl. Now listen to me. It doesn't matter that you're married, you will always be our granddaughter — the Grove will always be your home. You can come and go as you wish; Alex will be only too pleased to know we're looking after you so he can concentrate on doing his job.'

She sighed. He was right; she was being silly. 'I'll stay for the time being, Grandpa, but I must go back if things calm down. Alex can cycle to the Dower House when he has an hour or two free, but it's too far for him to get here.'

'Fair enough. You must put your young man first, of course.' He didn't sound too convinced by this statement and she smiled.

'Edward, that's enough, you're upsetting Barbara. She loves Alex and will want to spend every available minute with him.' Grandma didn't say what they must all be thinking — their time together could be very short indeed if this wretched war went on too long.

'Doesn't the park look strange with wheat growing where there used to be grass? What's happened to all the deer?'

'They still have ten acres of woodland — they'll come to no harm,' her grandma answered. 'Now, my dear, what would you like to eat?'

The conversation turned to safer topics and the *al fresco* lunch was enjoyed by all of them. 'Do you mind if I go for a nap?' Barbara said. 'I've not had much sleep since Tuesday.'

'Do you want me to call you later?'

'Of course, Grandma. I intend to walk down and meet Tom and David. Could you please call me half an hour before then?'

Her old room was unchanged — everything exactly where she'd left it. It seemed to be welcoming her back. She kicked her shoes off and flopped onto the bed. She wouldn't be so anxious and emotional if things were as they should be. If only she'd not allowed John to make love to her, everything would be so different. She would be brimming with happiness and not knotted up with worry.

15

Although the Spitfires flew constantly over-head, the noise was not so deafening and Barbara didn't flinch every time they passed. By the weekend she was feeling more relaxed and for the first time joined her grandparents to listen to the nine o'clock news. When the bulletin ended they sat in silence for a moment, absorbing what they'd just heard.

'Thousands of little boats have gone to the rescue of our troops. Isn't that a typically British thing to do?' Grandma said.

'They will have to abandon most of their equipment — what good is an army without tanks and weapons?'

'Grandpa, those things can be manufactured. We can't replace the lives of those who die there. I think we turned defeat into victory.'

'Hardly that, Barbara my dear. Hitler will control the whole of Europe and the next thing that will happen is an invasion of Britain. However, I concede that rescuing hundreds of thousands of our men is good for morale, and I think that's almost as important as winning the battle.'

She didn't want to think about it anymore

and scrambled to her feet. 'I'm going up now. Good night. I'm looking forward to attending church tomorrow after what I've heard about the new vicar.'

Her grandparents laughed; the curate who had been brought in to minister to Ingatestone was so nervous he frequently lost his place and had dropped his sermon from the pulpit. He then reassembled it in the wrong order but continued to read and was completely unaware his congregation were trying not to laugh.

'It's certainly a more interesting experience than previously, but I doubt it will ever be as funny as the time he lost his sermon.'

'Edward, don't make fun of the poor young man. We go to church to give our thanks to God, not to laugh at the vicar,' Grandma said with a smile. 'Good night, my dear. Sleep well. Oh, I forgot to tell you, the Evertons are coming to lunch tomorrow — Tom and David asked if they might see their friends.'

'I was going to take the trap and go and see them, but it will be lovely to have them here instead.'

★ ★ ★

The service the next morning was uneventful, and Tom and David were disappointed

Barbara had not seen anything funny. 'He didn't even give us the wrong hymn number today. Never mind, Tom; we don't go to church to enjoy ourselves.' That was a silly thing to say, but too late to retract it now. 'Ned and Jim are coming soon. What are you going to do after lunch?'

'Didn't you say you were going to finish the tree house, Tom?' Grandpa said.

Barbara and her grandmother walked ahead, leaving the boys discussing the finer points of carpentry. Hearing them so happy just confirmed the decision Barbara had come to during the night. 'I think the boys are better off here; they have their friends and far more to do. Now David has got used to the idea of me being married, I think he could cope without having me around so much. What do you think, Grandma?'

'I think we should ask them, let them decide. Anyway, we're hoping you're going to move back as well. I think it's going to be very dangerous living so close to the base once the air raids start.'

'If Alex is agreeable, then I think I'll come home. I do get a bit lonely in that house by myself. If he was in the Army and not the Air Force, he'd be posted away and I'd never see him. I'm lucky being able to talk to him on the telephone and to see him occasionally.'

'Would you like to have a rummage about in the attic and see what we can find for the baby? I'm certain I didn't get rid of the cradle or the perambulator that I used for your father. Mind you, they'll both be bit old-fashioned. Perhaps you'll want to buy something new.'

'I can't think of anything better than using the same things that were used for this baby's grandfather. I don't think we should buy anything new if we can manage with what we've got. It's not the expense, but after seeing all the 'squander bug' posters I'd feel guilty if we didn't try and reuse everything.'

Over the next few days Barbara managed to find a complete layette in a trunk; all she needed to do was wash the little vests, nighties and cardigans. They still hadn't found the bassinet or the pram, and she was in the attic on Wednesday evening poking about when the roar of an approaching aeroplane almost deafened her.

She ran to the tiny window and peered out. A Spitfire, belching smoke from one engine, was heading directly for the house. Too late to take evasive action, she clutched the metal bars at the window and prayed the plane would miss the house and the pilot be able to land without killing himself.

The damaged fighter flew so close to the roof it sounded as if half the tiles had blown away. But somehow the pilot kept it airborne long enough to crash-land in what was now a wheat field. She spun and raced through the attic, cracking her head painfully and barking her shins a couple of times on boxes before hurtling down the narrow staircase and onto the nursery floor.

The front door was already open when she reached it and she could hear shouting from the front of the house. She rounded the corner to see that Grandpa and her brothers had reached the crashed plane before her. As she ran towards it Grandfather shouted a warning.

'Stay where you are, Barbara — this could go up at any time. We've got the pilot; he's not too badly hurt.'

She skidded to a halt, too breathless to scream at her brothers to get away from the plane before it blew up. What was Grandpa thinking, letting Tom and David take such a risk? Her heart was banging so hard she couldn't hear. Why was it taking so long? Grandpa and Tom had the pilot's arms and together they managed to pull him from the cockpit. David helped his brother and the four of them staggered away not a moment too soon.

The pilot was dragging his right leg behind him, but apart from that he seemed comparatively unharmed. They were no more than fifty yards from the Spitfire when it exploded in a ball of red flame. The blast lifted the group from their feet and sent Barbara staggering backwards to land with a painful thud on her bottom. By the time she'd scrambled up, the others were on their feet as well, looking remarkably cheerful.

Tom yelled at her, 'Babs, we saved the pilot. Are you all right?'

'I'm perfectly fine. Grandpa, what do you want me to do?'

'We'll put him on the terrace — he'll be better out here in the fresh air. Can you get my bag?'

She ran indoors to do so and met Mrs Brown in the corridor. 'Mrs Brown, we've got an injured pilot here. If you could take this out to Doctor Sinclair, I'll ring the base and let them know he's landed safely.'

The phone was answered immediately and she explained what had happened. 'The pilot has a broken leg, I think, but my grandfather's a doctor and he's looking after him. Do you want us to take him to hospital, or will you send someone to get him?'

'Hang on a minute, miss. I'll speak to the adjutant.' The phone went quiet for a moment and then a voice she recognised was on the other end.

'Is that Barbara Everton?' She agreed that it was. 'Good show. I'm delighted to tell you Flight Commander Everton is safe. He's sleeping, totally knackered like the rest of the pilots, but I'm sure he'll contact you when he gets up. Been bloody difficult here these past ten days, but we've come off lightly. Three men lost and half a dozen injured.'

'Please could you tell Alex I'm living at the Grove, but I'll come back to Hornchurch when things have calmed down a bit.'

'Righto. Now, about your pilot. I assume it's Pilot Officer Benton — if you could ship him to Rush Green, that would be splendid. We'll transfer him to St George's — we're using that as an RAF hospital now.'

Grandpa had already put a splint on the pilot's broken limb, and the young man was sitting up and drinking a cup of tea. He wasn't someone she recognised. 'The adjutant asked if we could take you to Rush Green Hospital. I hope my grandfather has enough petrol in his car.'

'That'll be splendid. Rotten luck, coming down like that in your field. My own bally fault — I was forced to land in Dover yesterday and the mechanic said he wasn't quite sure about the starboard engine. Should

311

have waited until it was checked.' He rubbed his eyes and yawned. 'I just wanted to get back to base. It's been a bit hectic lately.'

'I should think it has been, young man. Shame to have crashed after all the excitement's over, but at least you got out of the plane with only a fractured leg, and it's not too bad either.' Grandpa gestured at the smouldering remains of the Spitfire. 'Will your lot come and remove that or shall I have to do it?'

'No idea, Doc. I'll ask the wing co next time I see him. I don't suppose there's anything to eat going spare, is there? I'm absolutely starving.'

'Mrs Brown has gone to make you some sandwiches; I expect you'd like another cup of tea as well,' Barbara said.

Whilst he was munching his way through his snack, she had time to talk to her brothers and her grandfather. 'Alex is safe and catching up on his sleep. I asked someone to tell him I'm living here for the moment. Now that I know you two want to live here all the time, I'd prefer not to move back to the Dower House permanently, but I'll have to see what Alex says before I make a decision.' David and Tom were more interested in the remains of the Spitfire and paid little attention to her remarks. 'Boys, don't go near the plane — it's far too dangerous.'

'Course we won't, Babs — not 'til it's cooled down.' Tom smiled eagerly at the injured pilot. 'Do you think we would be allowed to have a bit of the plane when it's cold?'

'Don't see why not. There'll be someone along to salvage it in a day or two, but they won't miss the odd scrap of metal.'

'The four of us have already started to collect things, Babs — bits and pieces to do with the war. We'll have the best collection at Brentwood School by the end of the year.'

'That's a jolly good idea, Tom, but promise you won't go near that Spitfire until Grandpa says it's safe.'

They nodded and her grandfather turned to the injured man. 'Pilot Officer Benton, I'm afraid it's going to be a rather uncomfortable ride, so I'll give you a shot of something once you're in the car.'

The young man shifted uncomfortably and Grandpa chuckled. 'Hang on, we'll find Joe. I think that between us we can get you to the cloakroom before we leave.'

Barbara wasn't certain she could trust her brothers to stay away from the smouldering wreck, so she suggested they cycle over to see Ned and Jim and tell them about the crash. When they returned, her grandmother was waiting to hear what she'd missed whilst out at her meetings.

Her brothers were so excited at the prospect of collecting souvenirs from the crash the next day that she had no time to wonder why Alex hadn't contacted her. The blackened ruin remained an eyesore in the middle of the freshly planted park, and the local policeman had visited to warn them to keep an eye out for looters. An ancient man from the village was employed to replace the tiles — fortunately most of those removed by the Spitfire were intact and no permanent damage had been done.

As the policeman cycled away Tom grabbed her hand. 'Are we looters, Babs? We've all taken a bit from the Spitfire.' He looked really worried.

'I suppose you are, so I should keep quiet about it. PC Squires isn't really interested in you four; he wants to make sure nobody takes the plane away and sells it for scrap metal.'

David grinned. 'If all the boys in my class came over here to collect a souvenir there'd be nothing left. They would have to arrest all of us, wouldn't they, Babs?'

'Which is why I told you to keep quiet about your treasures. Have you any home-work to finish? It's almost bedtime.'

They trooped unwillingly inside and

vanished upstairs, grumbling about having too much rotten homework to do. She left them to it and joined her grandparents in the drawing room. Both sets of French doors were wide open and the room was full of evening sunlight.

'There you are, my dear. Have the boys gone to bed?'

'No, Grandma, they have a bit of maths homework to finish. I'll go and check on them in half an hour.' She wandered across the room to stare at the Spitfire. 'I hope Alex is okay. I don't think I should ring the base again unless it's an emergency.'

'Young Benton told me Alex lost two of his men, so I expect there's a lot of red tape involved with all that,' her grandfather said.

'It's hard to believe Hitler's only twenty-two miles away from the coast — do you think he'll invade soon?'

'I'm sure he'll be thinking about it, but there's nothing we can do, so try not to worry. Come and sit down, Barbara. We're eating *al fresco* again tonight; seems a pity to waste the good weather.'

'It's wonderful to be able to use all the house. I suppose we'll have to shut down this end again next winter.' She curled up on the sofa next to her grandmother and accepted a glass of lemon squash. 'I don't suppose I'll have this again either — lemons, oranges and bananas have already vanished from the shops.'

'I expect someone will manufacture a cordial of some sort to replace what we don't have. Did you hear that? I think there's someone outside.' He put down his sherry and stepped out onto the terrace. 'Good evening, how did you get here? I didn't hear your car.'

Barbara was on her feet and through the door before the visitor answered. Alex was here. She didn't stop to ask how he was, just flung herself into his arms. He crushed her against him and they stood silently embracing for several minutes before she was able to speak.

He held her at arm's length, gazing at her intently. 'Darling girl, I never thought I'd see you again. It was a bloody miracle any of us survived the carnage.' She was about to answer when he stiffened. 'Someone had a split-arse landing out there. Who was it?'

'Pilot Officer Frank Benton. He broke his leg and is in hospital somewhere. Grandpa and the boys got him out just before the plane exploded.' He didn't react to her dramatic explanation.

'Surprised I didn't hear about it, but I've been organising funerals and contacting

316

relatives for the two bods who were killed in my squadron.' His voice was bleak; he gathered her close again and rested his chin on the top of her head. 'I suppose we were bloody lucky, really; only half a dozen planes damaged and three shot down. We'll be ready for the bastards if they try and invade.'

'I hope that's not going to happen before the baby's born — '

'So do I, but let's not talk about that. I've got a two-day pass — are we staying here or going back to Hornchurch?'

'Whatever you want to do, but I agree with my grandparents that it would be far safer for me to be here when things start getting unpleasant. Also, Tom and David don't want to come to us at the weekend anymore; they much prefer being here with all their friends.'

'Fair enough, and although I like the idea of having you close by so I can nip over if I get the chance, on balance I agree with Doctor Sinclair — you'll be better off here when the balloon goes up. Let's stay here tonight, and then we can go and see my parents tomorrow and ask Dad to give us a lift back to Hornchurch.' He kissed her again. His mouth tasted of engine oil. 'I suppose we'd better go in. Are the boys still up?'

'I was just going up to tell them to go to bed. Why don't you come with me?'

Alex shook hands with her grandparents and then bounded up the stairs beside her to the nursery floor, where her brothers threw themselves into his arms. She swallowed a lump in her throat — only then did she realise how worried the boys had been about him.

'Did you see the Spitfire in the garden? We nicked bits for our collection — the policeman said we're looters and could be arrested.' David was dancing around, obviously delighted at the prospect of being considered a villain.

'I'm proud of you both — you're very brave boys and deserve to have a bit of the plane as a reminder. But you need to get washed and get to bed; it's nearly nine o'clock and you have to be up to catch the bus tomorrow.'

'Will you come with us in the morning? We can tell our friends you were at Dunkirk saving our troops.'

'Yes, of course I will. Now get yourself organised. Your sister needs to put her feet up.'

She left them to it; after all Alex had been putting his brothers to bed for years. There was something she needed to ask her grandmother before he came down. She found her outside, looking mildly irritated at the delay to their evening meal.

'I'm so sorry; Alex will be down in a minute. Grandma, would it be all right if I make up a bed in a guest room? We need a double. I don't want to squash up in my single bed even for one night.'

'I've already done so, my dear. I've put you both in the Green room. I'm disappointed Alex is whisking you away. What have you decided about that?'

A wave of nausea engulfed Barbara. It would be far worse to sleep in her room — in fact it would be impossible, but the guest room was also full of memories she'd rather forget. The Green room was in the main part of the house, the room John had slept in when he'd stayed at Christmas.

'Are you all right? Do you feel sick?'

'I'll be fine in a minute, thank you, Grandma. I often feel a bit peculiar when I haven't eaten.' She pulled out a chair and sat down at the table before speaking again. 'I'll move back when things get dangerous, but I'll stay there until then. I can catch the bus to Brentwood and then get the local one here when I want to come home for a day or two. I still don't know how Alex got here tonight, but he certainly hasn't got his car as he's hoping to persuade Mr Everton to take us home tomorrow.'

The evening passed too quickly and her grandmother suggested they retire early before they needed to use a torch. Her grandparents had their rooms next to hers at the back of the house, but the guest rooms were at the front where they had slept before the war.

Alex walked beside her up the grand staircase, his arm loosely around her shoulders. 'I'm not surprised you want to live here. It makes our home seem a bit basic.'

'I don't want to stay here permanently, just whilst there's a war on. I do like living at Hornchurch, but I hope that when all this is over we can buy something of our own.' She glanced at him to see how he took this suggestion. 'You don't mind that I have so much money, do you?'

He laughed. 'Don't be daft, sweetheart. I've already told you, it's every man's dream to marry a beautiful, rich woman. To be honest, you know I don't want to stay in the RAF, so having your financial support will mean I can retrain.'

'Are you still thinking of being an architect or civil engineer? As you love flying, perhaps you could be a commercial pilot.' The last glimmers of light made it possible to see across the gallery and down the spacious corridor.

'Which room are we in, Babs?'

'The second door. It's very luxurious, and we have our own bathroom.' She pushed open the door and saw the bed had been turned down and a small vase of roses placed on the bedside table. 'Grandma did this for us — wasn't that kind of her?'

'It's hard to imagine us at their age, isn't it?' He tossed his jacket on a chair and his tie followed. 'I suppose one day we could be living here, but I'm not sure I'd really want to live in a house so big it needs staff to run it.'

'Actually, I think they might leave it to the boys. They are both legally Sinclairs since the adoption went through, and I'm not anymore.'

'Are you regretting it already, darling girl?' His smile had the usual effect on her pulse. His shirt was unbuttoned and she couldn't take her eyes from his naked chest. Even from this distance a sprinkling of russet hair was visible.

She slid down the zip at the side of her frock and reached down to grab the hem before slowly pulling it over her head. She was only wearing her bra and knickers underneath. Her intention had been to show him how much she wanted him but the reaction she got was quite different.

In two strides he was beside her. 'Look at

that — I didn't realise you had an actual bump. It hardly shows under that dress.' He flicked her frock onto the floor and then gently ran his hands over her distended stomach. 'Your breasts are bigger too. It's been too long since we were together like this, darling. I'm missing the changes in you.'

'The baby's kicking now, mostly when I'm lying down in bed.' She unhooked her bra and stepped out of her knickers — being embarrassed in front of him was a thing of the past. 'We can still make love. I asked the midwife when I saw her the other day; she said it's up to us when we stop, as we can't hurt the baby.'

She settled back on the bed and waited for him to join her. They hadn't bothered to draw the blackouts and he was silhouetted in the final rays of light filtering through the window. He was thinner, but still looked magnificent in his birthday suit. He joined her on the bed but instead of kissing her he rested his hand on her bump.

'Is he kicking now? Will I be able to feel it?'

'He only does it when I'm relaxed, and with you naked beside me I'm finding it very difficult to do that.'

His response was immediate. His hands began to stroke her in all the usual places and soon she forgot everything and was swept away by passion. Eventually they lay together, pleasantly hot and sweaty, and completely satisfied.

'Quickly, darling, put your hand on my tummy. He's really going mad at the moment.'

'My God, I felt him. That's totally amazing. Makes me realise what we're fighting for, what this war is all about.'

'I notice we both call the bump *he*. Is that because you want a boy more than a girl?'

'Not at all. I don't care what we have as long as you and the baby are healthy. Would you prefer a boy?'

'No, I don't mind either. But I do think I'm carrying a boy.' She paused, lost in thought for a moment. 'If we do have a boy, I'd like to call him after my father, Charles Edward Sinclair. Is that all right with you?'

'That's fine — I like it. Charles Edward Sinclair Everton has a real ring to it, don't you think? Just in case we're both wrong, what about a girl's name? Any ideas?'

'None at all; I'll leave it to you. There must be a family name you'd like to use.' She rolled over and slipped on her nightie. 'I'm just going to the bathroom; I need to clean my teeth and things.'

'So do I, but I neglected to bring anything with me. I hitched a lift most of the way and walked the rest. I should have gone back to my billet and packed an overnight bag, but if I had I wouldn't have got my lift.'

'You can use mine when I've finished, and you can shave at home.'

When they were back in bed, snuggled together like two spoons, he kissed her ear and whispered softly, 'Tonight was the first time you've called me darling. You can't believe how happy that's made me.'

'I know. I think I'm finally getting rid of my inhibitions. Growing up the way I did, being constantly belittled and beaten, has made it difficult for me to say what I feel.'

'That's all behind you, sweetheart. I'll never let anyone hurt you again.'

'I wish I could protect you from danger, but I'll just have to rely on your exceptional ability as a pilot. I know you're the best on the base, because you keep telling me so.' He laughed and with a small sigh was instantly asleep. She envied him his ability to do this; lately she had been lying awake for hours — partly because she was getting indigestion, but mainly because she was not only terrified he would be killed, but worried about what might happen in September.

He was so excited about being a father she could hardly tell him now. He'd never asked her if he was her first lover, just assumed he was. She should have enlightened him on New Year's Eve, but that would have made her seem like a girl with no morals, which was definitely untrue.

It didn't seem right to pray her baby might be born with red hair and green eyes when there were so many more worthy causes which needed divine intervention. Instead she asked God to keep Alex and John safe from harm and to give her the courage to deal with whatever happened in the future.

16

Barbara returned to the Dower House, and because things remained quiet at the base she decided to stay. Germany had occupied the Channel Islands and the country was anticipating a full-scale attack at any moment. The only topic of conversation in the village was everyone's determination to fight for their country.

Her brothers stayed for the half-term weekend, but this would probably be the last time they would come to her. Then in July the news announced that the Luftwaffe bombers had begun to attack convoys in the channel and British ports.

A couple of weeks later Alex had the evening off and they were sitting in the garden. 'This is it, darling — I think it's time for you to go back to the Grove. I need to know you and the baby are safe.' He patted her enormous bump affectionately.

'I'll start packing up tomorrow and as soon as I'm ready I'll arrange for Joe to come and collect everything. We only arranged to stay for six months anyway and that's almost up. I don't think there's any point in hanging on to this place, do you?'

He shook his head. 'Absolutely not. When this lot's over we can buy something, but you might as well be with your family until then as I'm not going to get any leave once the raids start.'

'Are you saying that I won't see you until the war's over? That might be years.'

'No, don't be silly. I'll get some evenings free. We don't fly at night as we can't see where we're going.' He grinned. 'Mind you, we've been sent up a few times to accompany the bombers, but it's bloody daft — unless there's a full moon you might as well not bother.'

'I don't know how you can joke about this; I think you pilots have a very strange sense of humour.' Her stomach heaved as the baby appeared to somersault inside her. 'Look at that! I'm sure we must be having a boy; I can't believe a girl would kick so much.'

'You and Valerie look like Tweedledum and Tweedledee. If we didn't know when the baby was conceived I'd think you were due next week, like her.'

She heaved herself out of the deckchair and pulled his hair as she walked past. 'Someone in the village suggested I was having twins — I hope they're not right. I've got six weeks left.'

'Twins? Is that possible? I thought there had to be a family history and there's certainly none on my side.'

'And not on mine either. Grandpa thinks I've either got a lot of water or this is a very big baby. Your mother said you were nine pounds — that's enormous.' She pulled a face and attempted to straighten her maternity smock but even this was becoming embarrassingly tight.

'I don't think you should do much packing. Could you ask Mrs Williams or Clarissa to help you?'

'I'll give them a ring; I need to tell them we're not staying on, so I'm hoping they might suggest their daily woman could help. Clarissa seems to have been avoiding me since I got so huge, so I doubt if she'll come.'

Alex and she weren't sleeping together anymore because she found it difficult to rest unless she was propped upright. He usually stayed until she fell asleep and then cycled to the base. It had seemed strange at first not being able to make love whenever she saw him, but their relationship had strengthened as they spent more time talking and planning their future.

She'd all but forgotten her worries about the baby's parentage and had convinced herself Alex was definitely the father and the baby would be born with unmistakable auburn hair. The more they talked about what they would both do once the war was over the easier it became to ignore her secret.

When she woke the next morning she rolled out of bed and picked up the telephone. She asked the operator to connect her to the Grove and her grandmother answered the phone.

'Grandma, I'm going to need Joe and the pony cart to help me move back. I'm going to ask Mr Everton if he can help as well.'

'Edward and I were talking about this last night; we wondered if there's any point in bringing back all the old bits and pieces we dug out of the attic for you. It might be some time before you, Alex and the baby can set up another home, and I'm sure you'll want to buy your own things when you do.'

'I hadn't thought of that. I'll have to check with Mrs Williams if she minds if we leave the furniture here. It would make moving back a lot easier. I'm going to ring them next.'

'Now the boys have broken up they are eager to have you home again. We've got lots of ideas about how to make you feel a bit more independent — if Alex does get any time off I'm sure you'll want some privacy. I won't explain on the telephone, my dear; we can talk about it when you come. However, I will tell you that I've finished relining the bassinet and we've managed to buy you a lovely new pram.'

'That's wonderful — I can't wait to see them. Thank you so much. I'll ring when I'm ready; if I'm not bringing the big stuff I think Joe will be able to manage everything. I'd rather not ask Mr Everton to use any of his precious petrol if I can avoid it. I hope Alex will have fuel to put in his car, otherwise even if he does have a few hours free we won't be able to see each other. It's too far for him to cycle to the Grove.'

Getting dressed was now a chore and she hadn't seen her toes for several weeks. Keeping her knickers in place was also problematical, and she'd taken to using safety pins to avoid an embarrassing accident. This meant she had to leave herself plenty of time to go to the loo, otherwise there would be an accident of a different sort.

At least the weather was so warm she only needed underwear and her smock, as she didn't have any cardigans that fitted. She examined her ankles. Grandpa told her that any swelling was a bad thing and she was to let him know at once if this happened. She'd already removed her wedding band just in case her fingers became swollen, but so far both ankles and hands were more or less normal.

Valerie was enjoying every minute of her pregnancy and insisted on discussing at great length what might happen when their babies were born. The last thing Barbara wanted was to be reminded of what she was going to have to do in order to hold her baby in her arms. If she were honest, she disliked being pregnant and couldn't wait to get her body back. The wriggling bump inside her should have filled her with maternal joy; instead she found the sensation unpleasant.

Once she was back at the Grove she'd ask Grandpa if she was an unnatural mother and if she was in danger of rejecting the baby when he or she was born. Alex was so excited about being a father she couldn't discuss this with him. She waddled downstairs and headed to the kitchen. When she got there she didn't fancy anything to eat, so she returned to the hall to make the phone call to Mrs Williams.

Clarissa answered. 'Clarissa Williams, Radcliffe Hall.'

'Hello, it's Barbara. I need to speak to Mrs Williams about the lease and things.'

'Barbara, I was just on my way over to see you. Ma managed to get some coffee and I know you can still drink that.'

'Coffee? I haven't had any for ages. Please, come over at once.' She laughed. 'I don't suppose you've got any cake? Alex ate the last of mine and it's too hot to bake today.'

'Actually, Mrs Hughes made a carrot cake — heaven knows what it tastes like as it doesn't have any eggs in it. Shall I bring that over?'

'I should love a piece, thank you. That's strange; I don't have much appetite for anything apart from cake and rhubarb.'

Twenty minutes later her friend arrived with the promised goodies. The kettle was boiling and the coffee pot ready. During the hot weather both the front and back doors were left open to get some fresh air through the house, so Clarissa walked straight in.

'Ma says you can have it all; Mrs Hughes is making us an apple cake instead.'

'Golly, that's generous of you. You must take some of my sugar ration; it's not fair if I have yours.' Barbara quickly made the coffee and cut two generous slices of cake. 'It smells wonderful. Who would have thought that cake made from vegetables would be so appetising?'

'Here, let me carry the tray. I take it we're going into the garden?'

'Absolutely — it's too hot inside. I left the deckchairs out, and there's a small table to put the coffee and cake on.' She inhaled the rich aroma of the freshly ground coffee and sighed happily. 'I can't tell you how good that smells. Alex brought back some hideous concoction that was supposed to be coffee made from chicory and acorns — quite disgusting, but he seemed to enjoy it.'

They sat in companionable silence, enjoying cake and coffee for a few minutes before Barbara broached the subject of the move. 'Alex wants me to move back home, Clarissa, so I won't be renewing the lease at the end of the month.'

'We didn't think you would, and to tell you the truth I'm relieved. Ma and I intend to move over here and rent the big house. It's far too big for two of us and too expensive to keep warm in the winter.' She glanced over her shoulder as if she feared she might be overheard. 'Actually, the real reason we want this house back is that some bigwigs want the hall for their headquarters.'

'How exciting. I'm so pleased our moving out isn't going to be a problem for you. We don't really want to take back the furniture we brought over; would it be all right if we left it here?'

'Perfect; then we don't have to buy anything. They want the house as it is — we can't even use the smart shelter once we move so we're going to have to get a Morrison. I can't see that hiding under a big metal table is going to be much help, but that's what we're going to do until we can get a shelter built for ourselves.'

'I'm going to start sorting things out today — I was rather hoping I could employ your wonderful Mrs Hughes to give me a hand. Do you think she might be prepared to help?'

'I'm sure she will — she's a good sort. She's hoping whoever is taking the Hall will continue to employ her — we won't need her every day when we're living here.'

The familiar roar of Spitfires taking off made conversation impossible for a few moments. 'I bet you'll be glad to be living somewhere quieter, Barbara. I'm used to it now, but out here it's absolutely deafening. Do you think the balloon's gone up?'

'Alex told me he won't have any more free time, so I suppose it must have. It's horrible to think how many civilians will die once the bombing starts — and that's without the soldiers, sailors and pilots who will lose their lives protecting us.' The church clock struck eleven.

Clarissa jumped to her feet, almost upsetting the tray. 'I'm sorry, I've got to go. I'm supposed to be in the village in half an hour for some boring meeting with the vicar's wife. It seems the busybodies want to evacuate the local children again but the mothers are against it.' She shrugged. 'They might be safer in Dorset but they certainly won't be happier. Ma's sending me as her representative — God knows where she is at the moment. I expect she's with her lover.'

This casual announcement of her mother's adultery shocked Barbara rigid. 'Is she thinking of getting a divorce?' Instead of being offended her friend laughed.

'I shouldn't think so. Ma's man friend is incredibly rich — just the ticket at the moment as we have no visible means of support.' Barbara attempted to heave herself out of the deckchair but Clarissa shook her head. 'Stay where you are, have another piece of cake and finish the coffee. I'll pop in and see you tomorrow, hopefully with Mrs Hughes in tow.'

'I think I will, being the size of a house has made me incredibly lazy. Thank you for coming, and tell Mrs Hughes the cake's quite delicious.'

Barbara closed her eyes and dozed; the only sound in the garden was of bees and birds. Her lips curved. She'd had quite enough of the birds and the bees this year; although she'd love to have several children, she wished it was possible to have them without being pregnant. Would she feel more in tune with her body if John was not in the equation? She hated deceiving Alex but she couldn't tell him now, not when he needed to be fully focused on fighting the Germans.

The sudden roar of a second squadron taking off ruined the moment. At least there would be no more noise until the first lot returned to refuel and rearm.

Should she have another slice of cake or wait until teatime? She shuffled upright in her deckchair in order to pour herself a second mug of coffee. Good God! How stupid she was — if Alex had known about John he would never have offered to marry her. In fact he would probably have been as shocked at her loose morals as she had been by Clarissa's revelations about her mother. Which would have been better — being an unmarried mother with a clear conscience, or a happily married woman with a secret?

The cake and coffee no longer appealed to her. She collected the tray and took it back to the kitchen — she would reheat the coffee this evening and the cake could go in the tin. The last Spitfires to leave the base might well have been Alex's squadron; he'd told her he would be on standby, but she was certain all planes had now taken off. There must be something big going on for all of them to be scrambled at the same time.

Being so close to the base had seemed like a good idea a few months ago, but now she couldn't wait to be further away so she didn't know when Alex was flying. She ought to make a start on the packing but decided to wait until Mrs Hughes was there to help. Maybe she would put her feet up on the sofa and read a book. Grandma had told her several times to make the most of the next few weeks, as once the baby came she wouldn't get any sleep or time to read a book at all.

The planes always returned in ones and twos although they took off in formation. She'd given up trying to count them in, just praying Alex would return safely. When the telephone rang an hour after she'd turned the lights out her heart jumped into her mouth and for a moment she was frozen to the bed. Was this the call every wife dreaded? Somehow she rolled across and picked up the receiver. 'Barbara Everton, the Dower House.'

'Darling girl, I'm absolutely knackered, it's been a bloody awful day. I'm back at the base having a few repairs done to the kite, so thought I'd give you a ring. I don't know when I'll get another chance — we're going to be flying half a dozen sorties a day until we've stopped the Nazis.'

'I'm so glad you're safe, darling, but please don't worry about me; just concentrate on staying alive. I've stopped listening to the news as I don't want to know how awful things are.'

'Sorry, there's a queue of blokes waiting to use the phone. I love you, take care of yourself.' The line went dead before she could respond and she swallowed the lump in her throat. She loved him so much and hadn't had a chance to tell him tonight. Never mind, he was safe until tomorrow and she was wide awake and for once the baby was quiet. Coffee and carrot cake seemed like an excellent idea.

Mrs Hughes was only too happy to help and the trunks and cases were packed and ready to be transported by the end of the week. The pony cart was on its way and Barbara walked across to Radcliffe Hall to say her goodbyes and hand over the keys.

'It's been lovely having you next door, Barbara. I hope we don't lose touch,' Clarissa said.

'Of course we won't. It's not going to be easy getting together but I'm sure we'll manage somehow. Mind you, once the baby's born, according to my grandmother I'm not going to have a minute to myself.' She grinned. 'I'm pretty sure my father was looked after by a nanny, so I don't quite know where she's getting her information from.'

Clarissa laughed. 'Why don't you wait here and have a final cup of coffee? Don't look so surprised; I told you ma's friend can get anything she wants.'

'I'd love some, thank you. Now I've handed over the keys, the house is yours anyway. Mrs Hughes has stacked my boxes and things on the front porch so I don't need to go in again.'

'Have you spoken to Alex recently? From the amount of activity in the sky today all the pilots must be exhausted. The German bombers and fighters seem to be getting closer every time — did you watch the dogfights yesterday?'

'I can't bear to. I know the Luftwaffe is made up mostly of Nazis, but they're still human beings and I hate to think of them being shot down in flames.'

'Don't let Alex hear you say that — he's risking his life to keep those evil Germans out of Britain. There's no time for sentiment in war, Barbara.'

'I know you're right, but being pregnant seems to have made me more emotional and less rational. I shall be jolly glad when this baby comes and I can do my bit for the war effort. Grandma seems keen to look after the baby for me once he's weaned, so I'm going to finish my first-aid course and then I'll be able to do something worthwhile.'

'Good for you. Don't let anyone stop you. I don't know much about babies but I'm pretty sure as long they're loved and fed they won't really mind who's looking after them — at least not in the first few months.'

Mrs Hughes had finished for the day and Mrs Williams was elsewhere, so they had the house to themselves. Barbara was draining her second cup of coffee when the unmistakable sound of the air raid siren echoed across the fields. She shot to her feet, dropping her cup on the floor, but was unable to think what she should do next.

Clarissa grabbed her arm. 'It's an air raid; we've got to get down the shelter. Come on, I can hear the plane coming.' She guided Barbara outside, where the noise of an approaching bomber was unmistakable.

'I can't believe it's really happening, that there's an air raid . . . ' Barbara stumbled into her friend as a deafening explosion tore the afternoon air apart. She glanced over her shoulder and saw clouds of thick black smoke a few miles away.

'Don't worry, Barbara — that will be the margarine factory, not the base.' Clarissa bundled her down the steep stairs, pausing for a second to switch on the light. 'Right up the end; I'll shut the door. We'll be safe enough in here.'

* * *

Alex was dozing on one of the camp beds at the dispersal point where he'd been for the past two hours. He'd overheard the telephone orderly talking to operations earlier — he'd told them the squadron was now at readiness with twelve aircraft.

The light outside was almost bright enough to fly, so things could kick off at any moment. So far the Luftwaffe were keeping their activities to the channel, but the odd Hun took a chance and headed for London.

Most mornings began with a German weather recce and although the squadron would be scrambled, they were unlikely to catch it because it would be too high.

Waiting was the worst part. Alex found it difficult to sleep, but some blokes managed. Others played chess or read a book, but he was too keyed up to relax. He was half asleep again when the bloody phone went. He jerked upright and stared at the orderly. Was this it? The man grinned and nodded and everyone relaxed again. 'The NAAFI van will be here a bit late, sir. Shall I spread the word?'

'Do it.' Alex yawned and swung his booted feet to the ground. 'I could do with a cuppa; let's hope it gets here in time.' One of the men wandered over to the door, opened it quietly and went out. No one was asleep now; everybody was tense, waiting for the next phone call which would send them scrambling for the planes.

The telephone rang again and this time the orderly turned to Alex. 'The squadron leader would like a word with you, sir.'

'Right, Ops say there's a plot over Gris Nez and it looks like it's coming this way. Okay, old boy?'

Alex put the phone down and turned to his men. 'Pete and Fred, on standby. Call yourself Green Section. On your way.' The next call was for the two to scramble and Alex watched the airscrews begin to revolve. Then they turned and taxied into the wind, opened up the throttles and raced away.

It wouldn't be long before the telephone rang again and he had to scramble. The call came. 'Squadron scramble — bandits — Angels ten.'

Alex was first out of the door and raced for his Spitfire. The ground crew already had the engine fired and he grabbed his parachute from the grass and started to put it on. The rigger had pulled the trolley clear and Alex stumbled around the starboard wing and on to the walkway. The fitter nipped out of the cockpit and heaved him in.

Once inside he felt calmer. The Sutton harness straps were fastened at shoulder and leg, then the door closed and Alex pulled on his helmet, mask and R/T and was ready to taxi. He gestured for them to pull the chocks away and released the brakes. The ground crew clung on to the wingtips until the last moment. He was ready to go. All his previous nervousness evaporated and he led his flight down the runway and into the air.

He glanced around to check the squadron was in the air, and smiled. It had taken less than four minutes to get airborne. The R/T crackled and Control came on.

'KL leader, this is Sapper. Thirty approaching Dover at Angels twelve. Vector 120. Over.'

'Sapper, this is KL, message received and understood, over.'

'KL, bandits include Messerschmitt 109s. I say again, many snappers. Over.'

His squadron would have heard the same message and his response. Control would keep him informed of any changes until they had a visual. His nervousness had gone; he'd settled into battle mode. He turned on the oxygen and then saw them. 'Sapper, KL here.

Tally Ho! There are no more than thirty of the bastards.'

He could see the enemy like a swarm of insects hovering on the horizon. The bombers were protected by the ME109s. These were the invaders, the enemy: they had to be destroyed. 'Right, Green Section, here they come. Green Section, break into them. Break starboard — break, for God's sake.'

He needed to pick a target. There was a Dornier on his own and no 109s in sight. It was hard to distinguish friend from foe, but he homed in on the bomber he'd selected. He concentrated, keeping it in his sight. The plane was getting big. He had to concentrate — he'd only get one chance. He steadied the Spitfire and pressed the gun button — and was deafened by the sound.

He couldn't tell which were enemy tracers, or which planes had been hit. There was an explosion in the enemy's cockpit. He had to keep firing, praying he wouldn't crash into his target. At the last moment he broke off, pushed his stick hard over and missed a fatal impact by seconds.

He had survived, but he was shaking and the Dornier was in flames. Before he realised, he was several thousand feet below the main fight and travelling at a frightening speed. The R/T was screeching with instructions that he ignored. This was do or die — a fight to the death.

Two Spitfires flashed across in front in pursuit of a 109 and he continued to climb looking for a second target, eager to get back into the battle. The radio screamed a warning about further 109s above and, as he watched, the Germans turned towards him. He flew in a wide circle and at top speed he headed back into the fray. A single Heinkel 111, back from some mission of his own, was attempting to reach the coast.

Alex wasn't going to let him go. He ignored the return fire and got a steady burst into the fuselage and starboard engine. There was smoke coming from somewhere — that was a good sign. He climbed and turned to attack from the rear and this time he was certain he'd got the kill. The Heinkel was done for. He fired a further few rounds into the crippled aircraft but his guns stopped. He had run out of ammo — time to go home.

As he banked there was a flash and a loud explosion from behind. He was surrounded by enemy aircraft. He'd been hit — bounced from the rear. He'd ignored the golden rule — never stop looking. Unable to return fire, Alex realised he was going to die . . . and it served him bloody well right.

He dived, hoping to shake off the two 109s,

but they pursued him relentlessly. Then a couple of Hurricanes flashed past and his attackers veered off. He was safe. He hoped his rescuers got home safely; they didn't deserve to die because of his stupidity. Keeping well away from the chaos above him, he headed for home.

After the most terrifying and exhilarating two hours of his life, he was back in Hornchurch. He had a large hole in his starboard wing and several smaller ones. His Spitfire would be grounded for a day or two, but he doubted he'd get even a few hours off to see his darling girl. But he was fighting for king and country, so family considerations had to come second. As he approached the base there were other aircraft circling, so he wasn't the only one returning safely, thank God! He checked in with control and then waited his turn to land.

After the aircraft touched down he undid his oxygen mask and pushed back his helmet. The cold air from the slipstream felt marvellous. Several other planes landed behind him — as far as he could see everyone had returned from the sortie safely.

As he wearily pushed himself from the cockpit his ground crew looked concerned. 'Are you okay, sir? Looks like you been in a bloodbath.'

Alex glanced down and saw his jacket was covered in blood. He hadn't felt anything — where was he hit?

'I reckon it's your arm, sir. Not as bad as I thought.' He shook his head. 'This Spit will have to go away, sir — too much damage for us to fix here.'

'Not to worry, lads. I'm sure they'll find me something else to fly in the meantime.'

Alex dropped his parachute on the grass and headed to the first-aid tent to get his arm seen to. He needed a few stitches and was told to take the rest of the day off, but to report for duty the next morning.

This was the best news he could have had. He'd go and see Barbara. He sauntered over to the dispersal hut, eager to hear how many kills they had made between them. As he stepped into the room conversation stopped and a chill ran down his spine.

The orderly sidled up to him. 'I beg your pardon, sir, but the adjutant wants to speak to you.'

'Okay — any idea why?'

The man shook his head. 'Not really, sir, but it's an emergency. That's all I know.'

17

The shelter was damp and despite the many extras Mr Williams had installed, the place still smelt unpleasant. Barbara hesitated on the second step, unwilling to descend into the darkness. 'Clarissa, have you got your torch? I don't want to go any further in case I fall.'

'No, dammit, it's on the kitchen table. Move against the wall and I'll go past you; I'm pretty sure I can find the matches and light a candle.'

'That's going to be tricky. I'm the size of a barrage balloon and this is a very narrow space.' The situation was ludicrous and an unexpected bubble of laughter escaped. 'There's a very rude song about old ladies locked in the lavatory — for some reason I have a sudden urge to sing it.' She flattened herself against the wall and Clarissa's hands reached to feel her bulk.

'This is going to be harder than I thought. Perhaps it would be easier if you sat down and then I can step round you.'

'Good idea. Hang on a minute, I'll slide down the wall.' By the time her bottom touched the concrete step they were both giggling. 'Okay, I'm down. I'll squash myself on the left — you try and squeeze past on the other side.'

Clarissa bent down and gripped Barbara's right shoulder and then carefully eased past. 'Good show! I'll have a light on in a minute. Don't try and move until we can see.' A few moments later the flicker of a match glowed in the suffocating darkness. 'Almost done — just got to find the bloody candles.'

Soon the interior was lit by a flickering flame in an upturned flowerpot. Barbara pushed herself upright and edged down the final steps. 'It's a good thing we're not down here in the middle of winter. It would be freezing, especially as we now know we can't use the paraffin stove because of the fumes.'

'Take a pew, Barbara. I'll find the Tilly lamp and get it going and then we can get ourselves organised.' Clarissa had to shout because of the noise of the plane outside. As she turned to walk to the far end of the shelter there was a hideous whistling sound. A deafening explosion shook the walls and the candle went out.

Barbara instinctively crouched down, putting her head between her knees in the hope she might protect her precious burden. She couldn't breathe, couldn't see, the noise so loud it hurt her ears. What was happening?

What was that terrifying noise? She closed her eyes and prayed to a God she wasn't sure existed that her baby would survive.

The appalling din could only be falling masonry — Radcliffe Hall must have taken a direct hit, and the building was collapsing on top of the shelter. The air was thick with the dust that fell from the ceiling and walls. It was difficult to breathe. The clattering continued, but Barbara was sure the noise was less than before. She didn't dare get up, didn't want to move at all until everything was quiet.

An eternity later the noise had all but stopped — just the occasional bump of falling masonry accompanied by the groans and creaks of a building breathing its last. Thank God there were no gas or sewage pipes to flood the shelter with poisonous fumes.

Slowly Barbara pushed herself upright, shaking off the debris from her lap before calling out to her friend. Her first attempt failed; her voice was too weak to be heard. She tried again. 'Clarissa, are you all right? I'm okay, but I'm surrounded by God knows what and don't dare to move.'

There was a faint groan and then an equally feeble voice replied, 'I'm fine, I think, but it's difficult for me to breathe in all this dust.'

'I think it will settle onto the floor if we leave it a bit longer. Try covering your mouth with your skirt — that's what I'm going to do. Don't try and talk for a bit.'

'We're trapped down here, Barbara. It sounded as if the house fell on top of the shelter.' Clarissa coughed and wheezed before continuing. 'It's going to be ages before anyone can dig us out.'

'It doesn't matter how long it takes. Once things settle we'll get organised. Thank goodness your father put water and food down here.' Talking was painful. 'Try and sleep; let's keep quiet until the air's clearer.'

She dragged the front of her smock over her head and leant against the wall. The baby shifted inside her and some of her tension released. He was fine; he wouldn't be affected by the choking air.

The minutes dragged by. The air was marginally better and there were no more sounds from above. Barbara tore the cloth from her face. Before the bomb dropped they'd been able to hear the outside world; now there was an ominous silence. It could mean only one thing. They were buried under the rubble — completely cut off. They wouldn't hear when their rescuers arrived — but far worse, those who were coming to save them wouldn't know they were alive.

Would they abandon the search after a couple of days, leaving them trapped?

Clarissa's heavy breathing must mean her friend had taken her advice and gone to sleep. Barbara squeezed her eyes shut and opened them again several times, hoping this might improve her vision — but it remained inky black. She needed to pee. If she used the wall to balance she might be able to inch her way to the steps; once there it should be relatively simple to find the curtain concealing the portable lavatory.

Standing up was nerve-wracking. She was unsure if the roof had caved in, and she might crack her head open. She was reluctant to lift her arms above her head to check, as Mrs Hughes had told her doing this might put the cord around the baby's neck and strangle him.

The atmosphere was cleaner at head height and the dust was beginning to settle, which was a good thing. Barbara took several deep breaths and sneezed a couple of times, but otherwise suffered no ill effects. Keeping her right hand touching the wall, she slowly moved forwards. Twice she cracked her knees on fallen objects, but she was fairly sure these were just bits of furniture and not bits from the ceiling.

Eventually her fingers touched material.

She was there. She was bursting and prayed the Elsan hadn't toppled over in the blast — if it had, she was going to use the alcove anyway. She edged around the corner, behind the curtain, and kicked forward. Her toe clanked against a metal container. She lifted the wooden lid, unpinned her knickers and sat with a sigh of relief. At least they could maintain their dignity until they were rescued, which was something to be grateful for. Having emptied her bladder, she felt much better and was ready to grope her way to the rear of the shelter and try and find the dropped matches and candle.

How long had they been trapped down here? She wasn't hungry, so didn't think it could be more than an hour or so — perhaps around midday. She waited at the steps to get her bearings. Joe and Grandpa would be above ground somewhere; they'd been due to arrive about then. Would there be ARP wardens, policemen and fire officers on the scene already?

She kept her eyes closed and tried to visualise the interior of the shelter. She'd only been down here briefly, but was almost certain it would be about eight or nine steps to the end where the larder and other bits and pieces were stored. If she was quiet she might be able to find the Tilley lamp and get it going before Clarissa woke up.

They couldn't have a hot drink, but there was plenty of water and more than enough to eat for several days. Cold sweat trickled between Barbara's shoulder blades and a wave of panic almost overwhelmed her. The walls began to close in and she wanted to scream, to kick and hammer on the walls, begging for someone to let her out.

She pushed her fear aside. She wouldn't give in to her claustrophobia. If they were to get through this, then she needed to remain calm. Her breathing slowed and she was ready to move forward again. She wasn't sure where Clarissa was sitting, but was moving so slowly that even if she did bump into her, it wouldn't be a problem.

Counting the steps in her head helped her to keep focused. With the fingers of her left hand trailing against the wall, and her right hand extended in front of her, she headed for the far end of the shelter. She reached it more quickly than she'd anticipated and the shock of her hand meeting a solid object made her squeal.

'Is that you, Barbara? What have you done? Are you hurt?'

'Sorry, didn't mean to wake you. I bumped into the dresser. I'm going to find some matches and a candle or two. You'll be pleased to know the loo is fully functional, thank goodness.'

'I need to go, but I'll wait and see if you can find me a candle first. You'll never find the one I lit, or the matches, not in the darkness. I'm certain there's a spare box in the right-hand drawer. The candles are in the left-hand one.'

After a great deal of rummaging and muttering, Barbara located both. Looking after Silver had given her plenty of practice at doing things in the dark and soon the shelter was bathed in a flickering golden light. Clarissa didn't react to this triumph and Barbara turned to speak to her. She almost plunged the shelter back into darkness. Her friend had slumped against the wall, her face ashen, and her breathing suddenly sounded laboured.

'Do you have your tablets? You need to take your medicine immediately, Clarissa.' Her friend was unable to speak but indicated she wanted to be helped upright. Barbara braced one knee against the edge of the narrow bed and grabbed Clarissa's hands. Pulling an almost dead weight upright was difficult — she was sure someone as huge as her shouldn't be doing it, but she had no choice.

'Put your arm round my shoulder and I'll get you to the steps where you can lean on the wall.' The dreadful sound of Clarissa breathing into her ear gave her the strength to stagger the necessary few feet and gently prop the girl against the wall. 'I'm going to let you go, but hold on to my arms until you're sure you can stand on your own.'

Was Clarissa breathing more easily or was that wishful thinking? She hardly dared to look at her friend's face, terrified she would see the tell-tale blueness around her lips which would indicate her heart was giving up.

'Pills, on floor.' That was all Clarissa could manage but this was enough to show she was a little better.

'I'll find them, don't worry. Everything will be fine in a minute.' Barbara stepped away from the stairs and as she did so she experienced a sharp spasm in her back and for a few moments she couldn't move. Then it faded and she began the search for the missing medication.

The floor was thick with dust and bits of plaster. There were piles of cushions, books and a miscellany of other things she couldn't identify under the debris. How was she going to find a small box of pills in all this mess? Slowly she lowered herself to her knees and began a fingertip search of the floor. Each time she encountered a larger object she carefully brushed it off and put it on one of the beds that lined the space.

This was taking too long. 'I'm sorry, I'm sure I'll find them soon.' She couldn't twist in the confined space to see if her friend was any better.

'Under the bed — where you are now. I need a pee.'

'Right, I think I can get my arm underneath — I'll have to lie on my side and just hope I can get up again afterwards. Keep your knees crossed; I'll help you to the loo in a minute.'

By rolling onto her back, Barbara was able to push her arm into the narrow space and after a few seconds her fingers brushed the missing box. She hooked one finger round it and carefully dragged it forwards until she could pick it up properly. Her back hurt and she'd cut her arm on a protruding nail, but she didn't care; she had what she needed to save Clarissa.

Standing up again was as difficult as she'd anticipated and she was gasping for breath when she finally managed it. She had to sit down for a moment until she felt well enough to move. Scrabbling about in the dust had not been good for her lungs. She didn't want Clarissa to know how poorly she felt; her friend was relying on her help to get through this.

She injected a jolly note into her voice as she carefully regained her feet. 'I hope you haven't wet yourself. I almost did. Can you take these without water, or shall I get you some?'

'As they are, thanks. And it's going to be a close-run thing — I can't hold on much longer.'

Barbara tipped three tablets into Clarissa's hand and waited while she swallowed them. Then she helped her into the alcove. 'Can you manage? Do you need me to help you with your knickers?'

'If you don't mind, I'm still feeling absolutely vile.'

There was no room behind the curtain for both of them but, by draping the curtain across her back, she was able to lift Clarissa's skirt and petticoat and ease down her pants. She checked the wooden lid was up and then carefully lowered her friend onto the container. She straightened and dropped the curtain back.

'I'll wait here and then I can help you. I'll need to go again myself when you've finished.'

Clarissa was able to sort herself out and emerged from behind the curtain looking a lot better. 'The pills are beginning to work, thank God. I think I can get to the bed on my own. I'm sorry — '

'Don't worry about it. We're both alive, which is a miracle. We've got plenty to eat and drink and although the air is pretty nasty, I doubt we'll run out before we're rescued. I seem to remember reading about a mining disaster — the men trapped underground survived because they didn't move about too much. We will use less air if we're asleep.'

'I could do with a drink, if you can find one. There are several flasks of water in the dresser. I don't want anything to eat, but you go ahead if you're hungry.'

'I'll see what I can do. I'm going to find the Tilley lamp and get it going. We don't want to go to sleep and wake up in the darkness because the candles have burnt out.' She dusted off several of the pillows and arranged them behind Clarissa's back so she could sleep sitting up if she wanted to. 'Is there anything else I can do? Do you need a blanket? You feel rather cold.'

'I'm freezing. I'd love a couple of blankets if you can find them in all this mess.'

Barbara tucked her friend in and then began a search for the lamp. She'd pulled a muscle in her back heaving Clarissa to her feet, but that couldn't be helped. When she got everything sorted out she would stretch out on the other bed and have a rest.

The lamp made a comforting hiss when she eventually got it going. She left it on the dresser and prayed it would keep burning until the rescue team broke through. They had both gulped down the water and Clarissa now appeared to be sleeping, although her breathing was shallow and erratic. What was the time? The bomb had dropped at eleven o'clock and she was fairly sure more than two hours had passed.

Her back still ached, but the pain was less acute than before and she didn't think she'd done herself any serious harm. She made her way to the steps and used the facilities again before carefully climbing the stairs and pressing her ear against the door. Were they so deeply buried they wouldn't be able to hear the rescue operation until they arrived? Was there any point in shouting to attract attention, or would this just disturb Clarissa and use up precious oxygen?

She might as well try and sleep. Although there were books and cards, she wasn't interested in either at the moment. The upper bunk, which cleverly folded against the wall, must have spare blankets — the shelter was unpleasantly cold and she'd used all she could find for Clarissa. She unhooked the catches and the bed dropped down with such force she tumbled backwards onto the floor.

A pillow and two blankets landed on top of her — so that was one problem solved. The next was turning onto her knees so she could use the edge of the bed as leverage to regain her feet.

Clarissa hadn't stirred. Barbara wasn't sure if that was a good sign or a bad one. She'd learned to check a pulse during her first-aid course and carefully rested two fingers against her patient's throat. She must be trying the wrong place, as she couldn't detect a heartbeat at all. No, she was wrong — there was a faint but perceptible pulse. She adjusted the cocoon of blankets around her friend and then picked up those she was going to use herself.

She found it impossible to get comfortable; her back was sore and her arm hurt where she'd cut it earlier. She hadn't liked to use too much water to clean it as she wasn't sure how long they would be buried in the shelter.

She must have dozed off, because something woke her. She looked across at Clarissa and her chest squeezed. 'I'm coming. Do you need to take more tablets?'

The girl shook her head slightly and one finger moved. Immediately Barbara scrambled up and knelt beside her, taking the icy hand between hers. 'Clarissa, isn't there anything I can do? Please, hang on. I'm sure they'll dig us out soon and get you to hospital.'

'Too late. Hold me — I'm frightened.' The words were barely audible but Barbara understood the implication. Gently she lifted Clarissa and slipped in beside her so her friend was cradled in her arms. There was nothing she could do but hold her until . . . until she . . . She couldn't complete the thought. Tears trickled unheeded down her cheeks as she murmured words of comfort and encouragement — talked about a better life in heaven, one without pain and illness. But she didn't believe a word of it herself.

She wasn't sure exactly when Clarissa died. There was no hideous rattling, no sudden twitching and jerking; the girl just slipped away. One moment she was alive the next she wasn't. Barbara was paralysed by grief, unable to move or think coherently for some time. Then she pulled herself together and wriggled out from under the body. She removed the pillows carefully before stretching her friend out on the bed, folding her arms across her chest and then covering her with the blanket.

She was numb and couldn't take it in — how could Clarissa have died so easily? A wave of nausea rocked her and she barely made the alcove before being horribly sick. The dull ache in her back became a second spasm which doubled her up. She waited until it passed and then backed out from behind the curtain, not sure what to do.

After drinking a glass of water she felt a little better; her mind was less woolly and she was ready to consider her options. She collapsed on the bed and flopped against the wall. There was nothing she could do for Clarissa; she had to keep herself and her baby safe until rescue came. Therefore she'd better think about making herself something to eat, even though that was the last thing she wanted.

As she stood, a band of pain encircled her stomach and she collapsed on the bed a second time. She closed her eyes and attempted to breathe through the contraction — for she was in no doubt that was what it was. Her baby was coming and there was nothing she could do to prevent it.

The pain subsided. She must time the contractions. As long as they were ten minutes apart there was nothing to worry about, but when they got closer she would be in trouble. The baby was premature, wasn't due for another five weeks. How could he survive such a delivery?

She mustn't sit here; she had to get things ready. She would need something clean and soft to wrap the baby in. There were no sheets provided for the beds, nor slips on the pillows, and the blankets would be too rough and dirty. Her smock would have been ideal if she hadn't bled all over it and then rolled on the floor, covering it with dirt. She would use some of the water to wash her hands and save some to wash the baby if necessary. She'd seen calves and lambs born, so had some idea what was involved, but if the baby had been full-term she would have been less worried.

The shrouded shape no more than a yard from her kept drawing her attention. Clarissa was wearing a cotton petticoat — that would be ideal to wrap the baby in, but Barbara wasn't sure she had the courage to remove it from her body.

A second vicious contraction made her squirm in agony. They were barely three minutes apart — she must prepare for his arrival. First babies were supposed to take ages, but for some reason this one was determined to arrive in a hurry.

She had no choice. She shuffled across and rolled the blanket back from Clarissa's legs. Her skin was cold, the front of her legs unpleasantly white. Barbara couldn't do this; it was indecent. She closed her eyes and took several steadying breaths, then reached under the dead girl's skirt and rolled the petticoat up so it was bunched at her waist. The blankets were replaced and now she had to uncover the top half of the body, but she didn't think she could do it. Legs were somehow anonymous, but she just couldn't look at the dead face of someone she'd become very fond of.

There was another contraction building. She straightened and braced herself against the opposite bed, waiting for it to peak and fade. There must be a knife or scissors in one of the drawers of the dresser; she could cut the petticoat from the bodice. The contractions were so close together there wasn't much time to do anything between them.

From somewhere she found the energy to stagger to the dresser, and her frantic search came up with a pair of sharp kitchen scissors. She gripped the edge of the dresser and breathed through her mouth. Her eyes were screwed up and it was all she could do not to howl with pain. She wasn't going to give in; she owed Clarissa a dignified departure. It would be sacrilegious to scream in front of a recently deceased person.

She hurried back to her gruesome task and very quickly snipped the petticoat in half. She opened the centre seam and was satisfied she had what she needed to wrap her baby in when he was born.

What next? She couldn't give birth on the

floor; that was too dirty. It would have to be the bed, even though there was barely enough room to lie down, let alone push a baby into the world. She folded the blanket and put a pillow against the wall. It would be more comfortable with Clarissa's pillows as well, but she couldn't bring herself to use them.

As she straightened, a gush of liquid soaked her knickers and feet. For a horrified moment she thought she'd wet herself, and then realised her waters had broken. Valerie, in one of her detailed conversations about birth, had told her that once this happened the baby usually came quite quickly. She wriggled out of her knickers and kicked them under the bed.

The contractions were now almost continuous, and getting herself on the bed was almost beyond her. Her insides were falling out; the pressure was unbearable. Did this mean she should push? She felt as if a football was trying to escape from inside her. She gritted her teeth and pushed as hard as she could and the baby crowned. She groped between her legs and touched a downy head. As she bore down the shelter seemed to move and she became aware of a rhythmic thumping in the region of the stairs.

No time to think about that — she had to deliver her baby. The head burst through and

366

the slippery shoulders followed. A final push and the rest of her son appeared. She had to clear his mouth and nose, make sure he could breathe. He'd come so easily — did this mean he was too small to survive? Why wasn't he crying? What should she do now?

Instinct made her reach down and pick up her son. As she lifted him he coughed and the unmistakable sound of a healthy newborn baby filled the shelter. Clouds of filthy dust began to fill the space and she wrapped her son in the petticoat skirt and cradled him against her shoulder, praying the dust-filled air wouldn't get into his lungs.

★ ★ ★

Alex snatched the phone from the orderly. 'Flight Commander Everton here. What's the emergency, sir?'

'Radcliffe Hall took a direct hit, old chap. Your wife and the Williams girl are somewhere under the rubble.'

For a moment he couldn't speak; shock and horror held him immobile. 'I need to get over there, sir. She's pregnant . . . '

How could this have happened? His kite had been all but destroyed, and yet he'd returned unscathed. His darling girl could be dead and his baby with her. His knees all but buckled and someone shoved a mug of oversweet tea into his hand. He swallowed it automatically but still he couldn't speak. He had to get to Radcliffe Hall and help with the rescue.

'There's a lorry leaving for the base, sir. It's waiting for you,' the orderly said.

Alex left the tent at a run and threw himself on the back of the vehicle. It roared off across the field and bumped onto the tarmac. He was racing towards his MG before the vehicle was stationary. He covered the two miles in minutes and skidded to a halt in front of the ruins of Radcliffe Hall. Thank God there were no flames belching from the bombed building. There was already an ambulance, with a fire engine and various other vehicles standing by.

Someone had organised two human chains to pass back rubble. He scrabbled over the bricks, ignoring the protest from the other rescuers as he barged past, until he was at the head of one queue. He almost didn't recognise the person he replaced because he was so filthy.

'She'll be all right, Alex. It's not as bad as it looks.' Doctor Sinclair stepped aside, allowing him to start digging.

'Christ, I can't believe she's under all this. Is she on her own down there?'

'We're not sure, but we think Clarissa is down there too.'

Alex was still wearing his flying gear and this gave him extra protection against the debris, although he was bloody hot. He removed another bucket of rubble and saw steps.

'We're almost there. Come on, men, another few feet and we can break through.'

He was pretty sure his stitches had burst, but nothing was going to stop him until he reached his wife. He was working shoulder to shoulder with an ARP warden and together they reached the door to the shelter.

'We need to smash it down. We're never going to open it,' the warden said.

Somebody handed Alex a sledgehammer and he swung at the timber like a madman. On his third blow it shattered and willing hands tore away the splintered wood, making a hole big enough for him to crawl through. He dived in and someone shoved him from behind so he fell headfirst into the shelter. For a moment he couldn't see, then the dust settled a bit and he saw the shrouded shape on the right-hand bed and his heart almost stopped. Then on the other side he saw his darling girl huddled on the bed.

'Babs, are you hurt?' He reached her side and she raised her face. He'd never seen anything more beautiful.

'Alex, Clarissa died.'

Her face contorted and he pulled her into his arms. Something small and warm rested between them. He stared in astonishment at the tiny head of a baby. 'My God, is our baby okay?' He didn't wait for her to answer but carefully pulled down the white material.

'I think he's absolutely fine. My darling, meet your son, Charles Edward Sinclair Everton.'

THE DUKE'S RELUCTANT BRIDE
HANNAH'S WAR
THE DUKE'S REFORM
THE DUKE & THE VICAR'S DAUGHTER

We do hope that you have enjoyed reading this large print book.

Did you know that all of our titles are available for purchase?

We publish a wide range of high quality large print books including:
Romances, Mysteries, Classics
General Fiction
Non Fiction and Westerns

Special interest titles available in large print are:
The Little Oxford Dictionary
Music Book
Song Book
Hymn Book
Service Book

Also available from us courtesy of Oxford University Press:
Young Readers' Dictionary
(large print edition)
Young Readers' Thesaurus
(large print edition)

For further information or a free brochure, please contact us at:
Ulverscroft Large Print Books Ltd.,
The Green, Bradgate Road, Anstey,
Leicester, LE7 7FU, England.
Tel: (00 44) 0116 236 4325
Fax: (00 44) 0116 234 0205

Other titles published by Ulverscroft:

BARBARA'S WAR

Fenella J. Miller

As war rages over Europe, Barbara Sinclair is desperate to escape from her unhappy home, which is a target of the German Luftwaffe. Caught up by the emotion of the moment, she agrees to marry John, her childhood friend, who is leaving to join the RAF — but a meeting with Simon Farley, the son of a local industrialist, and an encounter with Alex Everton, a Spitfire pilot, complicate matters. With rationing, bombing and the constant threat of death all around her, Barbara must unravel the complexities of her home life and the difficulties of her emotional relationships in this gripping coming-of-age wartime drama.

THE DUKE'S REFORM

Fenella J. Miller

Devastated by the deaths of his wife and daughters, Alexander, the Duke of Rochester, vows never to love again. Drinking and gambling numb the pain while he searches for a woman to enter a marriage of convenience and produce an heir. The beautiful Lady Isobel Drummond seems ideal for the task, and the union saves her family from financial ruin. But Alexander's high-handed and dissolute ways soon drive Isobel away, just as he acknowledges his growing feelings for her. Can he convince his beloved that he is a changed man? And can Isobel ever regain trust in the man she once loved?

HANNAH'S WAR

Fenella J. Miller

World War II brings divided loyalties and tough decisions for Hannah Austen-Bagshaw. Her privileged background can't stop her falling in love with working-class pilot Jack — but Hannah has a secret. Torn between her duty and her humanity, she is sheltering a young German pilot, all the while knowing she risks being arrested as a traitor. Hannah's worst fears are realised when Jack finds out what she has done and their love begins to unravel. Will her betrayal be too much for Jack to forgive?